...dressed all in black from boot toe to gauntlet to the tip of the plume on his hat. Under the hat, a piece of cloth tied pirate-style covered his hair. The upper half of his face hid behind a half mask trailing a swath of inky satin over the rest of his features. Through the holes in the mask, the eyes shone preternaturally blue. Across his broad chest, a golden bugle hung. The wind lifted the rider's cape, and the lining furled back over his wide shoulders like wings of red flame. He scattered the gang of chicken catchers as easily as a hurricane wind hurls clouds and rode straight for Suzanne. He reached down and heaved her across the saddle.

She shrieked in the spirit of the moment and asked breathlessly, "Are we going behind the barn for a kiss?"

The lips pressing against the black cloth did not smile. The dark rider wheeled the horse, cantered down the hill, and raced along the soft edge of the bayou. At first, Suzanne thought what a great story she'd have to tell Dr. Dumont and her friends back home, but when Magnolia Hill vanished behind its trees, and the saddle horn began to dig into her ribs, she suggested, "Don't you think we should go back now?"

He did not reply. Silently, he rode on.

"Okay. Enough is enough. Take off the mask, and let's go home."

No answer.

She began to struggle a little to see if she could slide off the saddle without killing herself. The rider stopped abruptly, pulled her up and around and tight against his hard chest. He kissed her so suddenly and thoroughly her lips bled slightly when she bit herself. Later, she would notice the bruises the bugle made on her breasts.

Courir
de Mardi Gras

by

Lynn Shurr

The Mardi Gras Series

Courir de Mardi Gras

Cover Art by *RJ Morris*

The Wild Rose Press, Inc.
PO Box 708
Adams Basin, NY 14410-0708
Visit us at www.thewildrosepress.com

Publishing History
First Mainstream Edition, 2014
Print ISBN 978-1-62830-513-5
Digital ISBN 978-1-62830-514-2

The Mardi Gras Series
Published in the United States of America

Dedication

For my quiet sister, Celeste, because of all she does.

FOREWORD

The Courir de Mardi Gras or Mardi Gras Ride is a country custom of the Cajun prairies and takes the place of fancy parades, floats, and balls found in the cities of Louisiana. Lately, I have seen the event referred to as the Courir du Mardi Gras as being more proper French, but Cajun French has never been proper French, so I will stick to the way I first heard of it.

On Fat Tuesday, the day before Lent begins, costumed riders gallop from house to house begging for the ingredients to make a communal gumbo: a bag of rice, a pound of sausage, a sack of onions or flour, and best of all, a live chicken that is tossed into the air to be chased down by the members of the ride. This form of celebrating Mardi Gras harkens back to the Middle Ages when revelers went from door to door seeking coins or small gifts of food and entertained with songs and stunts. Needless to say, much of the revelry is of the drunken variety, though in today's world this has been toned down as entire busloads of tourists follow the riders on their course.

Courir de Mardi Gras is my third book with a Mardi Gras theme. This theme and the locale of Cajun Country is all that loosely connects them. Sometimes characters from one story will make a brief appearance in another tale, but mostly, the stories stand alone. *Queen of the Mardi Gras Ball* explored the meaning of the formal Mardi Gras celebrations of the past. *Mardi Gras Madness* portrayed a small town Mardi Gras. Now, we come to a country party with *Courir de Mardi Gras*.

Whatever the location, the masks and mystique of Mardi Gras lead to a turning of the plot—a brief affair, a hasty marriage, an abduction of a pretty woman. Anything can happen on Mardi Gras day, and often does. Enjoy the celebration!

Chapter One

Suzanne's story

On the morning of Suzanne Hudson's farewell to Philadelphia, she sat on the very edge of Paul's bed and attempted to apply a pair of pantyhose to her legs with a minimum of mattress shakage. If Paul had remembered to shut the mini-blinds the previous evening, she might have completed the chancy maneuver in the living room of the apartment without giving a free peep show to street level traffic. The bathroom was still too humid from a hurried shower to allow nylon to glide easily over flesh. Coiffured, dressed, and ready to be on her way, she had only this small logistical problem to solve. Suzanne reasoned if the hollow thunder of hot water drumming in a fiberglass tub had not awakened the one who slept like the dead, then neither would a small jiggle of the mattress.

Paul's king-sized bed filled all the available space in the small bedroom. She simply had nowhere else to lean. There, a successful completion of the challenge. Lying on his back, arms splayed, mouth open, blond stubble so light as to be barely noticeable, Paul resembled a well-fed, untroubled child. He slept on with the wintery morning sunshine throwing bars of light across his body through slits in the bedroom blinds.

She slipped into her sensible traveling shoes and, glancing into the still-misty bathroom mirror, straightened the red silk scarf that stood in for a tie on the white oxford cloth blouse. "Suzanne Hudson is dressed for success, dressed for success," she chanted mentally. "Navy blue is a positive color for a suit, a good travel color, and an attractive foil to honey-brown hair"—though to be completely honest, her hair was more brown than honey. Today, very little of it showed since she'd attempted to duplicate Dr. Dumont's chic twist, subduing the thick, curly strands with combs that matched her hair color. Small wisps already escaped around her ears and forehead, but that could not be helped now.

Her suitcases stood by the front door. The purse containing the plane ticket beckoned from Paul's glass-topped coffee table. Tiptoeing out of the bedroom, Suzanne continued to make her escape. After removing her heavy, red wool coat from Paul's closet and wrapping her head carefully in the matching muffler withdrawn from the sleeve, she pulled on her fleece-lined leather gloves and let herself quietly out into the hall. From the doorway of 3-C, she nodded goodbye to 3-B, her old apartment, now stripped of all belongings, the bed and dresser returned to her adolescent bedroom in Villanova, the secondhand couch and the dining room set from the unpainted furniture store now in the hands of new owners. Everything else was boxed and stored in the attic on Pine Street to await her return. The elevator came quickly. The taxi summoned by cell phone arrived in five minutes. Sigh of relief.

As the cabbie stood in the steam of the exhaust and stowed her bags, Suzanne settled back into the taxi's musty cushions smelling of cigarette smoke and sub sandwiches, and reveled in her flight away from safety and security, from predictability and routine, from Paul Alvin Smith, Jr. What a close call. She'd almost convinced herself she wanted and needed a man like Paul.

After the Barry Cashman affair, she had been very cautious, feeling her way emotionally through her senior year at the university and into graduate school like a leper with numbed fingertips. She tried to recall Barry's exact parting words. Once vivid red scars in her mind, they had faded to a pale pink.

Oh yes, he said, "I wanted to experience someone artistic and uninhibited before I settled down in Middletown with Beth Ann. You must admit she'll make a better attorney's wife, especially if I go into politics. But she'll never equal your enthusiasm in bed, Suzanne—so hot, so ready to try anything. When I'm with her, I'll be thinking of you." At least, she'd had the presence of mind to knee him sharply where he would remember it just as long.

Her pain, equally sharp, manifested itself in a shoulder-length haircut, the donation of all her handcrafted, natural fiber clothes to the thrift shop, and an abrupt veer from a fine arts career of painting ethereal pictures of castles in the mist. She took up a more sensible course of art history studies with some business management thrown in to guarantee a real job running a gallery or curating in a small museum sometime in the future. Abandoning her interest in Renaissance Italy, she immersed herself pragmatically into Victorian America. She wanted to be someone's beloved, not someone's experience. Since that didn't seem possible, time to get practical both in love life and career. Her parents, perplexed but inwardly relieved, approved of her lifestyle changes. Although things had not worked out with Barry of the suits and matching vests, they concluded he had been a positive influence.

No wonder Paul Smith had such instant appeal. When her parents amiably agreed they would provide support for two years of graduate school in museum management because they put Blake through law school, Suzanne upped the ante to include a modest apartment. After all, they paid Blake's fees at the fraternity house all those years while their daughter commuted to the university. So, she moved into 3-B and met Paul Smith, 3-C.

Paul, as solid, dependable, and dull as a cement block wall, worked as a computer analyst. His habits were so regular she could to intercept him at 7:45 a.m. on the stairs or at 6:45 p.m. by the mailbox. A date with Paul inevitably consisted of dinner at a nice restaurant, a show, and a kiss at the door. After rough seas and cold plunges with Barry Cashman, Paul Smith relaxed her like a tepid bath. Honestly, she believed him to be exactly what she wanted until the proposal came as predictably as the red velvet box with the satin lining containing the diamond solitaire engagement ring. While the waiter poured the champagne, she felt the sudden need to plead for more time and his understanding. She answered not "yes" but "maybe."

She slept with Paul that night. He might have thought of this as a consolation prize or a promise for the future or a way of binding her to him. It could have been any of those things to him, but not for Suzanne. She wanted to discover in Paul the passion and stimulation she'd had with Barry. No one, absolutely no one, could be as bland in bed as Paul in everyday life.

Wrong. The man she considered marrying made love as methodically as he rotated the tires on his Chevrolet sedan when the required mileage came around. Foreplay consisted of warm breath blown in the ear, two kisses with slightly parted lips, five minutes of stroking beginning just above the breasts and moving downward at the speed of four inches per minute, and then penetration and rhythmic pounding for another five minutes.

He kept his eyes tightly closed and breathed like a Lamaze mother through his mouth. His beat never varied until the final stroke after which he rolled aside, said "thank you," and passed into a deep, death-like sleep. Looking up at the wall above the bed, she thought he must have a flow chart posted outlining each step of the carnal act, but evidently he had the procedure memorized. In the fifteen minutes elapsing from start to finish, her answer changed from "Maybe" to a "Hell, no."

Paul did not believe her. Doggedly, he continued courting with dinners and shows and occasional references to the "consummation of our love," which had not been consummated again. On her last night in Philadelphia, he offered the two-carat ring again.

"Not now, Paul," she answered, distracted by the waiter who waited to open the champagne. "Let me sleep on it."

Thinking she might have wronged the man—first times are always awkward and tense—except for the first time with Barry, she tried Paul's brand of lovemaking again. Afterwards, she looked in the drawer of his night table for the manual he must have been following, but the drawer stood empty. This wasn't pity sex, more like trying to talk herself into a safe, secure marriage sex. By morning, certain they would have made each other miserable for the rest of their lives, she made her escape.

She would call Paul and tell him so when she landed in Atlanta for her transfer flight. He'd be up and awake, showered and shaved, and drinking his morning coffee. Not at all like her to be a coward—she'd told off Barry easily enough—but Paul was such a nice guy. Why roust him out of a sound sleep to tell him she did not love him?

"Where to, miss?"

The cabbie must have asked the question before, but since the meter was running, he showed extraordinary patience with his passenger. Suzanne thought she saw a small movement at the blinds of 3-C.

"The airport. Hurry, please!"

"What time's the flight?"

"Not until nine."

"Mind if I take it a little easy, then? The roads are slick."

"Yes. Okay."

As the mainstream of traffic absorbed the taxi, she felt easier than she had all during the weeks of Paul's persistent courtship. Even rocks will wear away beneath a steady drip, drip, drip of water, and she was not made of stone. Somewhere, a man must exist who combined stability and passion. The future held interesting prospects. And, somewhere else, a perfect woman waited for Paul's brand of love, but not Suzanne Hudson.

"So where you off to?" Great, a chatty driver who spoke English—just what she needed.

"New Orleans."

Actually, she was bound for Port Jefferson, Louisiana, a town so small she used a magnifying glass to find its name on the map. But somehow, she wanted even the cabbie to think a grand adventure in an exciting locale awaited her.

"The Big Easy. Naw Orlins', is how they say it down there. My buddy and me, when we were in the Navy, spent a weekend pass there. Some city! They got all these topless bars on Bourbon Street. Topless and bottomless. One place even had guys who looked as good as women. We thought they *was* women until this one fella comes up to my buddy, gives him a kiss, and flips up his skirt to show his package. Should have seen my pal's face! I hear Bourbon Street is up and running again, same as ever since that hurricane hit." The cabbie har-harred and continued on with a lurid description of weekend pass exploits that drowned out the clicking of the taxi meter.

Suzanne blocked out the one-sided conversation. She had high hopes for Louisiana. After all, Dr. Dumont uttered the name of Jacques St. Julien in exactly the same tones she reserved for Versailles. "Ah, Versailles!" she would say with longing, her favorite time period being Louis Quatorze. If Suzanne believed in reincarnation she would have sworn Dr. Dumont had once been a mistress to the Sun King in seventeenth-century France. Evidently, no man measured up to the great King Louis because Dr. Dumont never married. She was hardly celibate though. She packed her conversation full of tantalizing references to "the time

Jean-Claude and I had our little flat on the Left Bank" and "when Philippe and I went motoring through the wine country."

Suzanne admitted that what remained of her romantic notions attracted her to Dr. Helen Dumont as advisor and mentor. The professor tried persuasively to lure her back to the study of Renaissance Italy, even dangling the possibility of a fellowship in Florence. She resisted and remained solidly entrenched in the uptight, stuffy Victorian era, no female poisoners or randy popes who commissioned great art for her. After all, the curators at the Victoria and Albert Museum kept a handy plaster fig leaf around to hang on their copy of the statue of David if their nineteenth-century queen happened to visit. Nope, Suzanne Hudson would never be carried away by romance again!

"Your attitude is enough to make me tear my hair," Dr. Dumont exclaimed. The doctor's hair now dyed blonde, slicked back smoothly, and knotted elegantly into chignons. No one would ever call her hairstyle a bun. With age, Dumont's figure became spare and straight. She still wore clothing with a flair that rounded youth could not duplicate. Suzanne admired Dr. Dumont and knew she would never be like her, not even if she studied in Florence and went motoring with someone named Aldo.

She introduced Dr. Dumont to Paul Smith one evening when they happened to be dining in the same French restaurant. The doctor, escorted by a young associate professor from the English Department, paused at Paul's reserved table to exchange courtesies.

"Paul Smith, Jr., computer analyst. And this, I hope, is my soon-to-be fianceé, Suzanne Hudson." Paul barged into the conversation, pumping the hand of the young professor. "Your son, Dr. Dumont?"

"But no, Mr. Smith, my lover."

Paul dropped the associate professor's hand as if pandering to older women might be contagious. Dr. Dumont looked at Suzanne with pity and issued a reminder of an appointment to discuss her master's project in the morning. The next day, she gave her a ticket to escape Paul.

"You know, my dear, it is time to choose a suitable project to complete your degree requirements. Since you seem devoted to the Victorians and determined to have a career as a curator, I have something which just might do." Dr. Dumont removed a letter from under a glass paperweight with a medallion of Louis XIV impressed in gold on its base.

"The son of an old friend has written to me. He is the possessor of an antebellum home in Port Jefferson, Louisiana. I have never been there. Jacques, his father—ah, Jacques!—Jacques and I came to know each other in New Orleans when I taught at Newcomb College. We met during Mardi Gras of course. With all the masking and the gaiety, we began a little flirtation. We danced all night and breakfasted on warm beignets and café-au-lait at dawn. Ah, Jacques!" Dr. Dumont stroked the facets of the paperweight in her hand.

"But about the letter. The son is a businessman, and evidently, the house is crammed with antiques acquired by his mother. He is willing to pay a qualified person to catalog the contents of the house and write a brief history of Magnolia Hill in preparation for opening the home to public tours as a moneymaking venture. He requested me, naturally, but I shall be spending the summer in the south of France assisting Professor Jung with original research for his doctoral thesis on the poets of Provence and their influence on English literature. Are you interested?"

"Yes, very." Suzanne held back the smile brought on by the mental image of Dr. Dumont "doing research" with Associate Professor Jung, but her grin burst out at the prospect of getting away from Paul.

"Mr. St. Julien will pay your transportation costs, provide room and board at Magnolia Hill, and give you a small salary for your efforts. I spoke with him on the phone yesterday and suggested you might be available in mid-January as soon as the semester ended here. Will that interfere with any personal plans?"

"No, not at all."

"Good, then. I rather feared you were so engaged with Mr. Smith that you would be unavailable."

"We are not engaged. The man I thought I would marry has settled down with Beth Ann in Middletown."

"Let us hope there is a Beth Ann for Mr. Smith. As for Georges St. Julien, for your sake, I hope there is some of his father in him." Dr. Dumont pronounced the forename lingeringly in the French manner, though the "George" of the letter's signature had no "s" on the end.

"I have never met the son. I did see his picture once, a very solemn boy with Harry Potter glasses, rather gangling and horsey like his mother, a very cold woman, much opposed to divorce, Jacques told me."

Probably over coffee and hot beignets the first day of Lent, Suzanne thought. The professor sighed again. "If only Jacques were still alive, I could be sure I am delivering you into good hands, but he died as he lived, flamboyantly—taking a fence on his white horse during the Courir de Mardi Gras. Killed instantly with a broken neck. So fitting he went while still full of vigor and virility. I would hate to think of Jacques growing too old to ride. He served as the Capitaine of the Courir, you know."

Suzanne braced for another "Ah, Jacques" but forestalled it with a question of her own. "Is his wife living?"

"No. She died fairly recently of some lingering disease. There will be only you and Georges at Magnolia Hill. You must give me progress reports."

Suzanne startled.

"On your project, of course, sample pages so I can review your format and research." Dr. Dumont smiled, thoroughly enjoying her small joke.

Dumont's little, bowed smile remained behind like that of the Cheshire cat in her mind, and Suzanne found herself duplicating it as the taxi pulled up in front of the airport terminal. The driver took this as a show of appreciation for his inside information on New Orleans, but he probably placed more value on the lavish tip his passenger pressed on him in the first full flush of her freedom from Paul. She allowed a porter to seize her bags since one contained a layer of reference books that might be difficult to find in Port Jefferson. The man gave her a questioning look when he heaved the suitcase onto his hand truck and trundled it to the appropriate counter. "There be an extra charge for that one," he said, but he also received an exceptionally good gratuity. Suzanne hardly grimaced when forking over the money for the number and weight of her bags.

Early for her flight, she spent the spare time having hot tea and a day-old cheese Danish freshened for fifteen seconds in a microwave at the airport lunch counter. The man next to her on the row of stools glanced at his watch, deserted the newspaper he'd been reading, and rushed down the concourse. She picked up the paper full of bad news headlines—stabbings on the ell, rapes in the park, serial killings suspected in the murders of half a dozen young women. Snow expected over the weekend. The 76ers had lost another game.

Glad to be leaving the city with its dirty slush and winter cold for an exotic, warmer clime, she experienced the return of the jitters of excitement in her stomach, previously calmed by the tea and stale Danish. Suzanne set off down the concourse toward the gauntlet of metal detectors and got into the slowly moving line. As she stripped off her watch and placed her carry-on bag on the conveyor belt, she heard her name being shouted.

Paul came charging down the concourse. As meticulously dressed as ever, he had taken time to put on a blue tie before setting off in pursuit. His face burned red, an infuriated shade she had never seen in the six months of dating the man. He caught up, leaning over dividing ropes to grab her arm just as she tried to pass through the metal detector. "You can't go, Suzanne! We're going to be married."

"I never told you that. Now let me go. This trip is important to my career."

"Is that what you want? A career and young lovers like that Dr. Dumont? Or do you expect some Superman in a cape to come down out of the sky and fly away with you, some knight on a white horse to carry you off to his castle?"

"All that would be very exciting, Paul, but let's

face it, we simply aren't right for each other. Now let me go!"

Passengers began to change lines to avoid the delay and the strident voices. Two men in trim blue uniforms moved toward arguing pair.

"I'll be coming for you! Do you hear me?"

The uniformed men took places on either side of Paul and requested politely that he come with them. Dropping the grip he had on her arm, he stalked off with the guards. The woman running the detector asked her please to move on so other passengers would not be inconvenienced. The last sight of Paul—not pretty. He stood spread-eagled against a wall while one guard patted him down and ran a wand over his body. The other held a tazer ready to fire.

Suzanne jogged down the concourse and got into the line for the already-boarding flight. She hurried into the tunnel connecting the terminal with the plane, and in her haste, tripped over the floor seam and ended up in the arms of the steward. He escorted her to a seat in the economy section under the eyes of the first class passengers who probably believed she had begun the trip with a few strong drinks at the airport bar. Sinking into place, she stowed her hand baggage beneath the seat in front of her, buckled up, and pretended to heed the flight attendant as she demonstrated the emergency breathing apparatus while the plane taxied out onto the runway. Her fingers trembled on the armrests.

Her seatmate, a concave-chested little man of about sixty, patted her hand in a fatherly way. As he nodded reassurance, the cabin lights reflected in little glimmers off his bald head.

"Your first flight, honey? Nothing to be scared of.

I'm in sales. I travel nearly every day of my life, would you believe? And nothing bad ever happens."

"Actually, I have flown before. It's just that I had a quarrel with a man I've been dating before getting on the plane. It shook me up a little."

"Girls, girls, girls! They always have boy trouble. I raised three of my own. 'Margery,' I said to my wife, 'When I'm out of town, you make sure those girls are in by midnight, and check out their dates, find out about their families.' Look at this, would you?" Mr. Salesman flexed his folded newspaper in her face. "*Serial Killer Stalks Young Women.* They met him in a bar, I bet, or at one of those rock concerts. Nice girls have to be careful."

"Oh, I've known Paul for a while. We lived in the same building and dated for six months. The most excessive thing about him is his fondness for musk cologne."

"But do you know his family?"

"Well, his father travels a lot on business, and his mother left when Paul was small and married some real estate agent in California. The grandmother who raised him died when he was thirteen, and he spent his teens in a military academy."

"No brothers, no sisters?"

"No."

Suddenly, pity and guilt wedged themselves into her anger over the scene Paul had caused and splintered it apart. Paul tended to drone on about his job: his great salary, most of which he saved, his stock portfolio, his negotiations over a new car or television to get the best possible price. Only through direct questioning had she learned this much about him. Now, he must feel

Suzanne was abandoning him just as his mother did.

True, she hadn't accepted his proposal or even taken him home to meet Mom and Dad, but she could have broken with him more cleanly. Never should have slept with him hoping some raging volcano of passion lay beneath his pile-of-ashes personality. Really, this outburst of temper was the first interesting facet of Paul Alvin Smith, Jr. she'd seen, and it wasn't a good one. Well, she had four months ahead to mull it over, but sincerely doubted if his tirade would change her mind about the relationship.

"No family is bad news, young lady. How can you tell anything about a man with no family? Let me treat you to a Bloody Mary." He peeled off the dollars for the drinks the stewardess vended from her hospitality cart. They parted company in Atlanta at the gate where men with walkie-talkies glanced at their tickets and pointed left for her and right for him.

"Can I buy you lunch, dear? Your mother would feel better knowing you aren't traveling alone."

"No. I only have an hour to find my Delta connection, and in this place, it won't be easy."

Mr. Salesman nodded, patted her hand once more, wished her luck, and warned her away from strangers. "Any one of them could be this Philly Slasher, you know."

Suzanne found the stairs to the monorail, waited for the next car to her concourse, and easily made her flight. No need to call Paul. Surely, airport security had released him by now. It wasn't as if he was armed, and definitely, Paul wasn't dangerous.

Her new traveling companions, an exhausted couple who had been on the road since 5:00 a.m., dozed for most of the flight. She regretted being unable to draw some information about Port Jefferson from her fellow travelers since they were Louisiana natives, but spent her time in solitude dismissing Paul Smith from her mind and conjuring up images of what the son of a man who danced all night would be like. She favored a flashing smile, a graceful stance, and a witty repartee.

In preparation for meeting this dream man, Suzanne retired to the restroom, hunched over the tiny lavatory mirror, shook out her twist and fluffed her hair around her shoulders. She applied a lighter shade of lipstick and a little more blusher. Suzanne Hudson was now totally prepared to meet the possibly dashing Georges St. Julien. To hell with businesslike—though she would have described all their correspondence typed by his secretary on letterhead and signed "Georges W. St. Julien" as very, very businesslike.

She spent a two-hour layover in New Orleans browsing through gift shops selling voodoo dolls, Mardi Gras masks, and pralines until Bayou Aviation called her flight. A handful of people clustered in the waiting area. They filed down a flight of stairs and out on to the tarmac where the small commuter plane sat. The unexpected warmth and humidity of the air made the arm carrying her wool coat sweat. On the horizon, thunderheads welled up from the Gulf. She considered the idea of lightning storms in middle of January. Oh well, Suzanne, you're not in Philly anymore.

The passengers negotiated a narrow set of stairs and crowded aboard, a half dozen businessmen with briefcases claiming the front cabin seats. She sat with a gangling serviceman, PFC Boudreaux, in the tail section. Private Boudreaux had a great deal of trouble arranging his limbs to fit the small seat. Mercifully, the flight lasted less than an hour.

Private Boudreaux, speaking with a strange accent not exactly French and certainly not a twang or a drawl, told her he was glad to be going home where he could get some well-seasoned food. For sure, his mama would have a nice, hot court-bouillon or gumbo on the stove. She questioned him about Port Jefferson and learned it lay "nort" of Lafayette, a tee-tiny town on Bayou Brun.

"Dey have one helluva basketball team for such a hick place, but dey got dis coach was once in da pros," the private confided. His high school team lost to them every season. He remembered this one game, the retelling of which took up the rest of the flight.

She envied Private Boudreaux a little when they debarked across the tarmac toward the smallest terminal of the day's travel. The businessmen dispersed throughout the building, some heading for the car rental counter, others shaking hands with acquaintances, some picking up bags and departing by taxi. Private Boudreaux, however, waded into a pool of loving relatives.

Suzanne got out of the way of the family reunion at the baggage pickup and looked for her escort. Nope, not a single handsome, dashing man worthy of Dr. Dumont's attention waited for her. She heaved her heavy suitcases from the carousel and, pulling one and dragging the other full of books, moved toward the exit doors.

"Miss Hudson?" An extremely tall man she'd struggled past without a second glance approached. He wore a gray suit with a subdued striped tie and leaned over like a person who had practiced poor posture all his life—or perhaps because of his height, had spent a decade bending to look people in the eye. His own eyes were a pallid gray overwhelmed by the dark frames of his glasses, no longer Harry Potter in style, but more ultimate nerd lacking only a strip of adhesive tape on the bridge. An application of greasy cream kept his dark hair from falling into his face as he bent over. He had nice full lips, but no flashing smile, no smile at all.

Swallowing her romantic illusions, she answered, "Mr. St. Julien?"

"George, please call me George."

No foreign French "s" on the end of his name. He was simply a plain old George.

"Suzanne." She offered her hand. He took it clumsily in his large, long-fingered, and loose grip, gave one shake, and dropped it.

"Suzanne, then." He pronounced it "Suz-ahn", giving the name she'd never cared for a much more sexy and sophisticated quality. At home, her family called her Suz-anne or Suzy. She looked at him more closely for other hopeful signs and found none.

George hefted her bags very easily for a man who had much more height than breadth and started off toward his car. A steel gray Honda Accord waited in a no-parking zone. An overweight security guard was writing down the license plate number prior to issuing the announcement that the car would be towed if not moved. George reached the vehicle three paces before her on those long legs, even though he didn't hurry.

"Leaving right now," he told the guard. "Didn't want to waste money on airport parking," he explained. Obviously not a big spender.

Being of average height, she never felt short before

this instance and had difficulty keeping up with him. The man stood at least six five, probably taller. After holding the door for her, he bumped his head climbing into the driver's seat. He had the front seat pushed back as far as possible to make room for his legs. Even so, he occasionally shifted uncomfortably throughout the drive of over an hour. Suzanne did wonder why he hadn't invested in a car with more leg room for the ridiculously tall.

Mr. St. Julien, George, hardly said a word unless she posed a question. He steered competently through the small city traffic and took the highway running with dart-like straightness across the flat terrain bisecting farmland into neat halves containing trailers and cattle and uniform stretches of plowed ground that he said, when asked, would later be planted in soybeans. Clouds continued to move in from the Gulf, covering the landscape like a woolly Quaker blanket about the same color as George's eyes and the interior of his car. Like the couple from New Orleans, travel time caught up with her on the long drive. Her head bobbed against the window. Suzanne dozed.

George turned off the highway. Potholes galore pitted the rural road and jolted her awake as the car took the turns in the hill country. George slowed from his consistent fifty-five mph to a creeping thirty-five as she blotted a tiny drop of drool from the corner of her lips with a tissue.

"Sorry, jet lag, I guess," she apologized.

"No problem. I'm not much of a conversationalist."

To say the least, she thought. The land had lost its openness. Trees hung over the road, their branches low enough to testify to a total lack of heavy truck traffic.

They swung around a bend and came to a stop before a red light. She had ample time to read the historical marker planted at the crossroads.

"Port Jefferson, Incorporated in 1840. Once a ferry crossing and later a center of the steamboat trade, the town is now known for its cotton and yam industries."

Thus far, she had probably made the same impression on George St. Julien as he made on her—dull and indifferent. Time for some brilliant repartee.

"Thomas Jefferson or Jefferson Davis?" she asked.

"What?"

"The man they named the town after."

"Neither. Eli Jefferson, a steamboat captain and cotton broker, founded the place, though my great aunts will debate that. They had the marker erected and omitted old Captain Eli. Up until ten years ago, they tried to have the town renamed St. Julien since our family settled here first when the place was just a ferry crossing."

"What stopped them?"

"My mother. She said she was tired of being humiliated by crazy old women and would put them in Pineville if they kept it up."

"Pineville?"

"The state mental hospital."

"Oh."

They took a sharp left turn when the light changed and by-passed most of Port Jefferson cluttering the road between the stoplight and the bayou in the distance. At the top of a fairly steep hill, they turned again onto a shell road bordered at regular intervals by young evergreen magnolias with neatly pruned, whitewashed trunks and dark, drooping leaves waiting patiently for the arrival of spring. George drove even more slowly and winced when a shell pinged against the side of the sedan.

"I plan to hardtop this road if we can get enough tourists out here to see the house."

They pulled into a parking area. Magnolia Hill presented a blank white stucco face pierced here and there by windows like large, dark eyes. A small ell with a screen door stuck out of one end of the rectangular building. From this angle, she couldn't imagine what a tourist would pay to see. The screen door burst open, and the doorway filled with a rotund woman the color of milk chocolate.

"Ya'll come in now. Coffee's on."

"My housekeeper, Birdie Jones. Birdie, this is our guest, Miss Suzanne Hudson."

"Pleased to meet you, Miss Suzanne." Birdie smiled broadly, nodded, and wrapped her hands in her white apron.

"I want to take her around the front first. Please serve coffee in the parlor today."

"Sure thing, Mr. George." Birdie, chuckling and shaking her head at the change in routine, went back into the kitchen.

The front of the house on its bluff overlooked Bayou Brun. Now, this was a vista tourists would pay to photograph. Ancient magnolias stretched their tips toward the clouds and brushed the earth with their lower leaves. They formed irregular clumps on a neatly mowed lawn. Obviously, these trees had been singled out when someone cleared the woody ridge in 1842. No one path led down to the river. No matter which way a visitor went, a tree blocked the course and caused a veering to the left or right. Some of the small groves, dense enough to hide behind or in, must have provided spots for delicious lover's games once upon a time.

"On late spring nights, the whole yard smells of lemon from the blooms."

Caught up in a vision of uniformed cavaliers and crinolined ladies playing hide-and-seek in the fragrant, moonlit arbors, Suzanne glanced expectantly up at George and waited for his next words.

"Makes me sneeze," he said. Turning toward the façade of Magnolia Hill, he continued, "This column has some Yankee bullet holes. There's half a cannon ball lodged in another. That should interest the guests. How they managed a gunboat barrage from the bayou with all the trees in the way, I don't know, but the Jeffersons surrendered fairly quickly, moved into town, and let the Yankees take over."

"I thought Magnolia Hill had been in your family for over a hundred years."

"It has, but old Captain Jefferson built the place exactly where the bayou becomes too shallow to navigate a steamboat. That way he had the convenience of not having to cart his goods up the hill from town, and he avoided the heat and mosquitoes down in the bottoms. The St. Juliens weren't much until after the war, only French farmers with a hoard of kids and six or seven slaves. Eli Jefferson built most of the town except for the Roadhouse and the St. Julien place."

"He must have been a remarkable man."

"My mother thought so."

She examined the eight rounded brick pillars, carefully stuccoed, smoothed, and whitewashed to resemble marble. The brickwork showed through where the minié balls and cannon shot lodged. The columns had been left unpatched for posterity as if to say, "Look what the Damn Yankees did to our home."

She'd studied enough in advance on the area to realize with most of the traffic coming by river, the house put its best face toward the water and turned its back on the muddy roads to the rear. Unfortunately, the university library contained about three sentences on Port Jefferson, and it had been too late to borrow any material. Having no intelligent comment to make on the Battle of Magnolia Hill, she felt as if her ignorance about the project showed as lavishly as a petticoat when they crossed the flagstone terrace.

She grew more comfortable in the front hall. The mansion had the typical two rooms deep, three rooms wide with a central hall pattern. Being more English than French in style, the important rooms for entertaining sat on the first level, not the second, and tall ceiling to floor windows took the place of French doors.

Birdie had placed the coffee service in the parlor to the right. A settee of rosewood and red velvet and a pair of matching, tufted petticoat chairs that appeared to be real John Belter faced each other across a square of Brussels carpet. Blocking the way to the seating, a massive round table reared up on legs snaking out from the central pedestal like the paws of an angry dragon. A single crystal bowl full of wax fruit ornamented its center.

Between the tall windows with their view of the magnolias sat that Victorian curiosity, a tête-à-tête, with its joined seats facing in opposite directions so that courting couples could share intimacies and strain their necks at the same time without snuggling too close. On the mantel, a gilt clock chimed four under its glass case. To one side of the fireplace stood a fire screen that appeared to be made of eighteenth century needlework. Charmed by its miniscule scene of women in panniered dresses strolling in a formal garden, Suzanne went to it immediately.

"That was Mother's favorite piece."

George nodded toward a portrait reigning over the room. Not an oil painting but a nicely executed, hand-tinted photograph of a woman who had height and grandeur, even on film. She wore her light blonde hair pulled back from her face. Her steely gray eyes had a piercing quality that her son's eyes lacked. She did not smile. She did not lean against the rococo chair on which one hand rested with its red, polished nails pointing downward. The lady wore a strapless ball gown ornamented with pearls around her neck, but Suzanne had the feeling Mrs. Jacques St. Julien could have posed naked with the same icy and elegant repose. She wouldn't have called the mistress of Magnolia Hill gangling or horsey at all, more like imposing and imperial. Suzanne chose to sit down for coffee with her back to the disturbing portrait.

Birdie bustled in to pour and offer around a silver plate full of lemon squares dusted with powdered sugar. George sat huddled over the delicate porcelain cup lost in his large hands and said not a word.

"So, tell me about your mother. I understood from Dr. Dumont that she collected many of the antiques in the house."

"Yes. She was Virginia Lee of Richmond before she came here. She liked to say she descended directly from both George Washington and Robert E. Lee."

"George Washington was childless. You must mean the Custis family."

Having just put both of her socially graceless feet in her mouth by correcting the boss, she took a gulp of the rich and very strong coffee. Coughing, she casually added milk and hoped Mr. St. Julien would let her comment and the fact that she couldn't handle her coffee slide.

"Of course Washington had no offspring. She meant the Custis family, but it was one of Mother's little jokes on people who didn't know American history as she did. Supposedly, Martha Washington did the fire screen."

"Don't tell me the W in your name stands for Washington?" Suzanne quipped lightly.

"It does." George neither smiled nor cringed. He simply seemed fatigued by remarks about his name. "Mother kept a card file on each piece in her room. You will need to verify her information, write a brief history of the house, and organize her material into printable book format. The sooner I start making money off this place, the better."

"I see."

"Birdie has your room ready if you want to rest before dinner. I can have her bring a tray if you would rather relax this evening."

"I think that would be very nice. It's been a long day."

She would get a good rest and be more on her game tomorrow. No worries that George St. Julien might ask her out to dance all night.

The guest room had a canopied bed with a rising

sun headboard, a small writing desk, and a French armoire that opened to reveal a television set on the shelf above the drawers. A chaise on which a lady could languish sat at the foot of the bed.

Birdie brought up a homey meal of heavily-seasoned fried catfish, double cornbread, greens, and a square of freshly baked bread pudding dotted with raisins for dessert. The maid apologized, saying she was not a fancy cook, that the fancy cook had gone when Miss Virginia got sick. Suzanne assured her all the food looked delicious, and it was, damn the fat and cholesterol count. The only portion she didn't care for was the mess of greens, spinach-like and larded with bacon grease, but as the only vegetable on the tray, she sucked it down.

Settling in for the evening, Suzanne figured with any luck she could complete the project in three months, stay in her room at night, and never have to drink coffee with boring George Washington St. Julien again. Wasn't it just her luck to travel all this way to find another man even stiffer and stuffier than Paul?

Chapter Two

Suzanne's story

As it turned out, Suzanne did not have to avoid awkward conversations with George Washington St. Julien. The man, slightly absurd like his name, always left for his office on the main street of Port Jefferson before 8:00 a.m., lunched downtown in the home of his great-aunts or at the Roadhouse—Port Jefferson remaining undiscovered by Burger King or Kentucky Fried Chicken—and seldom returned home before 7:00 p.m., if at all. An accountant, a licensed CPA, the small stack of business cards he left on the hall table proclaimed to visitors who never arrived. He handled the books for all the businesses in Port Jefferson large enough to need the service, but had to travel frequently into Lafayette to audit the larger accounts that paid the bills at Magnolia Hill. Often, he stayed overnight.

She learned all of this and more within two days of her arrival from Birdie, whose only birdlike qualities were her tendencies to sing and nibble all day long. She wore the headset of the old Sony Walkman stowed in her apron pocket like a headband as she cleaned her way around Magnolia Hill. Birdie had a strong voice and an amazing repertoire. Best at doing the blues, she could handle Diana Ross, Michael Jackson, and old spirituals equally well. Rap, in her opinion, was trash music. On days when her batteries ran low and she could not get the all black R & B music station out of Baton Rouge, Birdie sang a cappella.

On her first morning at the Hill, Suzanne woke to a powerful and sultry version of "Stormy Weather," instead of to her little, plastic travel alarm sitting incongruously on a massive marble and mahogany nightstand. Birdie sang as she made up "Mr. Georgie's" room across the hall. The song was apt. Outside, a warm, heavy rain fell, churning the bayou a deeper shade of coffee brown. A baritone rumble of thunder accompanied her song.

Ashamed to be sleeping late on the first day on the job, Suzanne put on a robe and stumbled toward the bathroom where Virginia Lee's hands had recreated turn-of-the-nineteenth-century luxury. The walls wainscoted in cherry wood matched the tank and seat of the commode. A crystal pull chain on the water closet made it a pleasure to flush, and the marble pedestal sink was almost too lovely for toothpaste spit. With the deep ceramic tub encased in more cherry, clearly no showers were intended to be taken to wet the cabbage rose-patterned wallpaper. A concession to practicality had been made in the tile floor, mostly hidden by a bath mat resembling a small oriental rug. As impressive in its own way as the parlor, this bathroom was not place where one would want to be ill for fear of spoiling all the pretty things.

Suzanne hesitantly used a crystal tumbler from the nickel-plated rack by the sink to rinse her mouth after brushing her teeth and winced at the white ring left on the expensive glass. Birdie knocked politely.

"Sorry to wake you, Miss Suzanne."

"It's okay. I overslept."

"Here's clean towels. Mr. Georgie just has coffee and biscuits most mornings, but I'm about to do a little cooking for myself. Can I make you some grits and eggs, maybe a little sausage?"

"No, thanks. Coffee and biscuits are enough for me. I'll be right down."

She did come down fairly quickly as there wasn't much reason to primp over hair and make-up and clothes. Doing the minimum to be presentable, Suzanne passed down the mahogany staircase and enjoyed the silky feel of the waxed, wooden handrail from first step to last. A place had been set at one of the twelve chairs around the immense table in the formal dining room. Beneath the chandelier with its tiers of electrified candles, her plate with two large baking soda biscuits, a pat of butter, a jam caddy set to one side, and a single steaming cup of coffee sat seeming slightly ridiculous in the grand setting.

Suzanne took a seat between two empty chairs and looked across three empty chairs toward a massive mirrored and crested Renaissance revival sideboard with a pink marble top. Even though she loathed watching herself chew in the mirror, she did appreciate the fact that the twelve crested and leather-seated chairs and the matching glass cabinet were a rare find, probably original to the house. She would certainly find out when she tackled Mrs. St. Julien's files. Ignoring the wonderful sounds and scents of frying coming from the kitchen, she wiped her lips on a real linen napkin and started for the room belonging to the Mistress of Magnolia Hill. George had neglected to show her its location, and she hated to interrupt Birdie's breakfast, but finding the place would not be hard.

Designed on simple neo-classical principles, Magnolia Hill was capacious but not ostentatious. Unlike the multi-roomed piles constructed by wealthy late Victorians, Eli Jefferson deemed five bedrooms upstairs, two parlors and a large dining room to be enough. Of course, the place once had a detached kitchen, rooms for servants under the eaves, and outbuildings aplenty, most of them now gone except for an old stable visible from her side window. The upstairs room that had possibly been a nursery housed the elegant bath. Her room and George's room faced the gallery and the bayou beyond. Mrs. St. Julien's sleeping quarters had to be either to the left or the right of the bath. On the left, she guessed, by George's room.

As soon as Suzanne turned the brass doorknob and walked into a place of classical revival elegance, she knew she'd found the place. Virginia St. Julien favored the style of Louis XVI, one-hundred-fifty-year-old imitations of a two-hundred-fifty-year-old style. The upholstery on the gilded chairs matched the yellow brocade covering the walls. A fanciful brass bedstead bedecked with curlicues and cherubs sat between the two windows overlooking the parking area and the long row of young magnolias.

Suzanne went directly to the spindly-legged secretary near a corner étagère holding an extensive collection of porcelain figurines. Virginia Lee kept her notes in very functional metal index card boxes, one for each room including the kitchen. Each item in the house had a card of its own with a brief description, a possible date, and the provenance of the piece. She found a small key in the back of the first box clearly labeled

"Safety Deposit—Docs."

With records so disappointingly complete, Suzanne believed she would find nothing much new to discover about the collection. Mrs. St. Julien had attempted to create a room for each one of the rapidly changing Victorian styles. Personally, she objected to the concept. A better plan would have been to take the house back to a definite date in its history and furnish the place accordingly if she intended to give tours. As for making Magnolia Hill a home to live in and raise a family, Suzanne would have furnished it with a few heirlooms, comfortable favorite furniture, and some contemporary additions. But if George wanted a Victorian showcase to lure the public, he was nearly there.

Taking the appropriate file along, she inspected the master bedroom of the late Jacques St. Julien. His wife had decorated his personal space in that rare and currently unpopular style of furnishings known as Gothic revival. Virginia Lee must have gone to some trouble to assemble the half-tester bed with enough pointed arches in its makeup to satisfy a cardinal. A rather ghastly carved bureau retained a set of silver-backed men's brushes. Several rigid side chairs capped with crosses sat against the walls like worshippers in the cathedral-like gloom of the dark and heavily draped room. A pope might have lain down here to die and felt perfectly at rest. Given Jacques' romantic reputation, Suzanne appreciated the irony.

Examining George's room gave her a different feeling. She opened the door with hesitation. It was one thing to enter the museum quality room of a deceased man and another to barge into the space where a living man sleeps. Unlike the dead rooms in the rest of the house, this area held bits and pieces of George St. Julien's life.

The simple cottage style bed with its spooled maple head and footboard looked too short for the length of the man who slept under its quilts. A faded university sweatshirt drooped over the golden pattern on a Hitchcock chair. Stenciled linoleum covered the floor as if this were the one place Virginia Lee despaired of keeping clean. Instead of the period prints or sconces holding knick-knacks adorning the walls in other rooms, George had tacked a few school and sports pennants to the paneling. They'd faded with age.

In one corner, a baby's crib in the style now called Jenny Lind overflowed with dusty basketballs and dirty sneakers. The plain pine dresser held mementoes: a few old sports trophies surmounted by leaping men balancing balls; a formal wedding photo of a tall, slim bride with a wreath of orange blossoms crowning her veil and her groom, a short, broad-chested naval officer with his hat worn at the same jaunty angle as his crooked smile; a small snapshot of a little boy wearing thick, round glasses and balancing precariously on one of the rococo petticoat chairs in the parlor. The child's forehead wrinkled with anxiety. Was this the picture of the solemn son Dr. Dumont had seen? She left the room quickly to rid herself of the feeling of invading her employer's privacy, as if she had been looking into his personal records without consent.

Bringing the boxes to the rococo parlor, Suzanne began her inventory there. In the evening, she'd enter the confirmed information on her laptop computer for easier reference and indexing. The settee and side chairs proved to be absolutely real John Belter, see documentation folder #1, and score one for the art history major.

Around noon, Birdie called her guest to lunch. Suzanne found a ham po-boy sandwich large enough for two and a glass of iced tea occupying the lonely space on the dining room table. She took her meal into the parlor and continued to crawl under and squeeze behind furniture looking for identifying marks. Toward six while she worked on the dining room, Birdie came to set a place for dinner.

"I swear ya'll as bad as Mr. Georgie when it comes to eating. Most nights I have to wrap his meal in foil and put it in the oven. Now you just leave off working and sit down a minute."

"Honestly, I hate to eat alone."

"Well, Mr. Georgie won't be back 'til late." She hesitated a moment. "Come on in the kitchen, then. I was having a little something before I go home to my own."

Suzanne followed Birdie through the connecting door and down two steps into the kitchen, somehow not raised to the same level when attached to the house after cooking became a less smoky and hazardous duty. A steaming bowl that looked like a chipped serving piece already occupied one of the places at a small oak table, its leaves folded down to make it fit under the square of window where the last light of a gloomy day faded.

Birdie opened a glass-fronted cabinet and selected a porcelain soup dish from one of the four sets of china. She scooped into a red-enameled rice cooker and filled the dish with a mound of white rice, then turned to a stockpot bubbling on a huge professional gas range. A few spatters of brown roux dripped off her ladle as she fished out a piece of chicken. She carefully removed the spatters from the stainless steel before serving. A loaf of French bread lay on the wooden counter. She sliced off enough pieces for the two of them and brought the basket to the table, along with the butter dish straight from a refrigerator paneled to look like an antique icebox. While Birdie fetched two small plates of potato salad and left a third covered with plastic wrap on the counter, Suzanne studied the old pieces of cookware mounted on the walls above the china cabinets.

Birdie sat down, jiggling the table a little as she landed. "Good gumbo night," she said, staring out at the weather.

Suzanne took a sip of the thin brown broth and gasped on the pepper, took a quick swallow of water, followed that up with a bite of potato salad, and ate more cautiously. Her piece of chicken, boiled nearly off the bone, had absorbed the spiciness of the gravy and the smoky taste of the bits of sausage. Eaten slowly, the gumbo warmed the insides on a dismal evening. The drizzle outside thickened into rain again.

"I'm sorry if I'm keeping you," she apologized, not knowing how far Birdie had to drive in the mess outside.

"No bother. Now that Mister Jacques is dead, Lionel, that's my husband, he ain't so likely to fuss. My boys are grown. I got two in the service, three married, and just two grandbabies. Those boys of mine is mighty slow on starting families. My youngest is going to business school." Her large chest puffed up, and she smiled, showing one gold tooth.

"When Mr. Jacques lived, he was a devil with the ladies. Lionel said, 'I want you home every night 'fore dark, woman!' even after having babies took my figure. Lionel says now there's just more to love. Oh, he's a devil, too. But Miss Virginia wouldn't have none of that under her roof, so I never had no trouble with her husband."

"So it's okay to be here alone after dark now?"

Birdie missed the intended humor. "Oh, Mr. Georgie won't bother you none. It's only me who saved him from being one of those sissy boys, but he don't have much of his daddy in him neither. I used to bring my sons up to play with him out on the lawn. They'd roughhouse and get good and dirty. Then, I'd scrub him all clean before his mama got home from one of her club meetings. It was one of our secrets."

Birdie sucked the meat off a chicken bone and rattled on. "For awhile there, they thought Georgie was slow, but I knew that wasn't so. He sat up and crawled around just when little ones are supposed to and, having three boys of my own by that time, I knew when. Mr. Jacques wanted him to be doing everything early, and Miss Virginia feared Georgie had gone wrong because he was a hard birth. Mr. Jacques insisted she deliver up in the four-poster instead of a hospital. Doc Sonny was kind of young then, inexperienced. We all thought Miss Virginia was gonna die the way she screamed all night. Mr. Jacques didn't want no drugs used. Natural was best for his child, he said. Georgie came at dawn, a skinny thing with these red marks on his head where the doctor pulled him out with forceps. By night time, Miss Virginia took her dinner on a tray, and her breasts filled with as much milk as a baby could use, but she didn't nurse. Put her foot down there."

"She had no other children?"

"No, ma'am! Doc Sonny said there was something wrong with her female parts that made the birth so hard, and he took 'em out a year later."

"What a shame!" Suzanne made sympathetic noises as a contribution to the conversation.

"No, no, it weren't. I wouldn't call Miss Virginia a natural born mother. Raising a child came hard to her, but she fussed over Georgie like a hen with one chick. You should have heard the screaming when Mr. Jacques decided to send the boy off to St. Mark's Academy. As much howling and carrying on as the night he was born, but the boy went. By that time they had figured out only his eyes was bad, and what's why he bumped into things and didn't read so good. After he got glasses, he turned out to be right quick. Then, the other boys began calling him Four-eyes instead of Dumb George. The first time he licked 'em, I said, 'Good for you, Georgie!' His daddy took him for ice cream, but we had to keep that a secret, too, and get the glasses fixed on the sly. We told Miss Virginia he fell down since he did that often enough. Just after, Mr. Jacques sent him away to school. A good thing, I guess."

"He was all right after that?"

"Sure. He grew up. But he was such a loving child before, always wanting hugs. Afterwards, he came back as this tall, skinny kid who barely spoke to anyone. He got on the St. Mark's basketball team because of his height, but he was no good the first year, so Mr. Jacques stopped going to the games. Then his senior year, there's Georgie on the front page of the sports

section of the *Port Jefferson Sentinel* along with Linc
St. Julien, them's the black St. Juliens. '*Local Sons
Lead Leagues*', it says. And we never knew 'til then
how good he could play. 'Course, Linc played in a
tougher league, all big public high schools, but they
was both good. Went to the university together, played
together. The coach over there made Georgie a guard,
said he wasn't skilled enough for forward. Linc was the
star, but they got along…still get along."

Suzanne stifled a yawn. Gloomy weather and
basketball talk, not her kind of things. She changed the
subject. "So, George has no family."

"'Course he got family. All Cajuns have family.
There's the old ladies in town, Aunt Esme and Aunt
Letty, great-aunts really, which is like having
grandparents. His own passed on young before Mr.
Jacques got done sowing his wild oats. Well, maybe he
never got done, but they was plain folks and wouldn't
have got on with Miss Virginia, so just as well. And
then there's the uncles, Claude, Jean, and René. Vincent
died fighting overseas. Only Claude came around much
after Mr. Jacques bought out their shares in the house
with Miss Virginia's money. The brothers have kids all
over the parish, but Georgie keeps to himself."

Birdie dumped some of her potato salad into the
remains of her gumbo and went on talking. "Don't you
listen if they tells you Georgie is one of them gay guys.
He's just shy. If his mama hadn't broken up an
engagement to Miss Cherry, he'd have a family right
now. I didn't think that girl was good enough for him
either, but when my Earl wanted to marry up with
Lucerne Narcisse, I kept my mouth shut. It's all worked
out. She give me my only grandson so far, and I see

him all I want."

By now, they were down to the part of the gumbo you can't get at without tilting the dish. Birdie mopped hers up with the last of the bread.

"I have to get on now. Just leave the dishes." She stocked a straw carryall with a quart jar of the gumbo and a plastic container of rice. After tying a plastic rain bonnet over her head, she motioned toward the refrigerator. "There's a banana cream pie for dessert. Store bought, but good. We got a nice bakery here in town, and it's their specialty."

"Later, maybe."

"Good evenin', then."

Suddenly, Suzanne sat alone in a large, dark, and strange house, so not the same as being on her own in an apartment or the house where she grew up and knew what each odd noise meant—more like being locked in a museum after hours. She stayed in the coziness of the kitchen, had a slice of the banana cream pie, made a cup of tea, did the dishes, and still lingered until she saw the headlights of George's car peering down the lane. When he came in by way of the screen door, he seemed surprised to see her. Not wanting to be banished into the darker regions of the Hill, she offered to heat his dinner.

He said, "No, thanks. You probably have important work to do."

Suzanne took the hint she should get back to work and felt her way from light switch to light switch, first turning on the brilliant dining room chandelier, then an electrified wall sconce in the hall, and next the gasolier with its ornamental grapevines illuminating the upstairs hall. In her room, a fake kerosene lamp by the bed chased away the boogeyman. She watched a little television, tried to read one of her reference books on southern antiques, and finally decided on another piece of banana cream pie. Nothing like sugar overload to make a person groggy enough for sleep.

The hall lights still burned and more brightness flooded onto the stairs from the open door of the second parlor. Since it would be rude to pass by without speaking, she poked her head in the doorway. The room overflowed with large Eastlake pieces in light woods. George sat stretched out in a deep leather chair with his feet on an ottoman. He had a little rolling bar full of decanters with silver tags designating "Bourbon" and "Scotch" and "Brandy" drawn up next to him and was indulging in one of the brown liquors over ice and reading the *Times-Picayune*. In stocking feet, without a coat and tie, a little rumpled, George appeared younger than she first thought, around thirty, instead of pushing forty.

He didn't notice her presence until she exclaimed, "A Wooten desk!" just spotted across the room. She was pawing at the latches of the bullet-shaped antique by the time George got to his feet and wiped at the whiskey he'd spilled on his white shirt when he jumped at the sound of her voice.

"The desk was my father's, but it's empty now. Mother cleaned it out after he died."

The desk was truly empty, every little drawer and cubby in this organizer's dream bare, and not even locked by the brass key that held its two halves together.

"I've seen only one other. This might be your most valuable piece, and you do have some great ones."

George took off his glasses and rubbed the red ridge on the bridge of his nose. Glasses that strong had to be irritating. She wondered if he could see her now, so she spoke to give him an idea of where she stood.

"I'm sorry to barge in. I craved another piece of pie. Would you like some?"

"No, thank you." He held up what was left of his drink. "You go ahead. Birdie will eat it in the morning, and she is supposed to be on a diet because of her blood pressure."

Suzanne moved for the doorway and then gave into another impulse. "Is that your ancestor?" She pointed at the portrait over the mantel. Its dark eyes seemed to be following her.

"I guess so. My father."

"Oh, I thought he might be some Civil War hero."

The man in the portrait sat astride a white horse that looked much more patient than its rider. Jacques St. Julien wore a deep purple cape with a golden lining thrown back over his shoulders and a Jeb Stuart hat with a black plume in the band. What appeared to be a powder horn hung from a strap across his chest. The likeness was poor if it portrayed the man in the wedding picture, but the artist did capture the essence of his personality. A crooked smile dominated the face, and the black eyes seemed to rove the room in search of the prettiest girl.

"He's wearing his captain's costume for the Courir de Mardi Gras. You'll be here when they come to get a chicken in a few weeks. For the gumbo. For the last party before Lent."

"I see." Really, she did not.

"A local artist painted this right before my father

died and then moved on to better things."

Looking closely, she noticed a little gray in the subject's curly, black sideburns. A vague Magnolia Hill partly obscured by dark trees, filled the background along with some minuscule clowns cavorting with a rooster on the lawn, way too strange for her taste.

"I should move on to better things, too. Your mother's notes are in such good order I think I will concentrate on the history of the house. Could I go into town with you in the morning, check out some of the documentation at the bank, and spend the rest of the day in the library?"

"Fine."

"See you then." Committed to early rising, Suzanne decided to skip the pie and go to bed. After all, George St. Julien stood guard in the second parlor against any boogeymen.

Chapter Three

Suzanne's story

Full of honey, biscuits, and hot coffee, they waded across the flooded gravel to George's gray sedan. The ground had reached a degree of saturation possible only in Louisiana. At least the rain had stopped pouring down for the moment. She'd shared breakfast with her boss across the small oak table in the kitchen. George read the sports section of the *Port Sentinel* that Birdie brought in with her. Suzanne skimmed a stack of his mother's note cards. Then, they went on their way to town in a companionable silence associated with long-married couples like her parents. What an unsettling thought. If she wanted this kind of dull man, she could have married Paul. Suzanne began to babble to fill the void by the time they reached the traffic light at the foot of the hill.

"Is the library open this early? Could you call the bank and make sure I can get into the safety deposit box?"

"The library is always open. Knock on Miss Clara's door, and she'll let you in. I called the bank yesterday."

"Good. Then I can start on the history and check over the documentation on the parlor furnishings."

"You won't find much in the library. If you want

history, I'll take you to meet my aunts. They know all there is to know about Port Jefferson. Come by my office at noon."

"The same aunts who put up the historical marker?"

"The same."

"Fine. A little oral history would make the paper more lively." And probably inaccurate, her inner curator thought.

George dropped her off in front of the library, a little frame building appearing to be a converted garage. Up close, she saw that it was. A hand-lettered sign read "Knock next door if you need to use the library." She rapped on the indicated door and explained her visit to a lean woman, still in a robe and curlers, but cordial nonetheless.

"So pleased to meet you. I'm Clara Huval, the branch assistant here in Port Jefferson. We're only a little branch, but I can get you anything you need from the parish library or even the university." After making sure the street was clear of people, she scuttled over to the door of the branch and unlocked it.

"Make yourself at home. I'll be over directly," she trilled.

Inside sat a desk with one chair and a computer monitor, a library table with four chairs, a rental book collection of best sellers on its own cart, enough paperback racks filled with romances and mystery novels to supply a Walmart, a few sets of encyclopedias, and an outdated atlas. A disconnected public terminal occupied a small table shoved up against the wall and hemmed in by the spinner racks.

Suzanne discovered the very small non-fiction

section in the back corner. There, marked with a prominent "LA" on the spine, she found a parish history in a sturdy red binding. As the introduction noted, the book had been compiled by a retired schoolteacher, who'd dedicated it to her former students. The table of contents promised a whole chapter on Port Jefferson. She settled down at the library table and read until Miss Clara, fully groomed with a slash of red lipstick adorning her face, and completely dressed in a dark green jumper and crisp white blouse, came in bearing coffee on a tray.

"I was just about to have to have my second cup. Won't you join me?"

Suzanne did, full of guilt, feeling that at any time a university guard would ask her to take the beverage outside the library. Miss Clara finished her coffee, dusted the shelves, checked in a small stack of paperbacks that had been slipped though the slot in the door overnight, then settled down to a novel off the rental shelf. About mid-morning, she made more coffee, watered the plants, and rearranged the picture books very quietly and with great respect for her only patron's studies.

The parish history, though blandly written, said a great deal, especially if one read between the lines. It contained a nice map of the early land grants stretching in narrow sections back from Bayou Brun. Each family had an access to the lifeline of the river. The St. Julien holdings extended more broadly than most, reaching 250 arpents into the raw land. Other sections were held by Huvals, Sonniers, and Patouts, and for the Badeaux and Dugas families. The Jeffersons had not yet arrived. Huval's Ferry possessed the only notable buildings in town.

All this changed around 1840 when Eli Jefferson came to town and bought out the Huvals, all but the square containing the ferry station and roadhouse. He subdivided the section into lots along the only road to the ferry. Down by the river, warehouses sprang up along with a cotton gin. The Sonniers traded their section for a lot to build a general merchandise emporium. Plots were set aside for a public school and the Methodist church. The Patouts sold off their land and opened a smithy. The Dugas family went into the feed and seed business. Eli Jefferson grew cotton on his own land, ginned cotton in his own mill, and shipped cotton on his own steamboats. Magnolia Hill raised its white pillars above Bayou Brun on the acreage that had been Huval's wood lot. Meanwhile, the St. Julien strip remained blank except for a small X denoting a house a half-mile from the bayou.

Then the War—the one still being talked about and studied in the South—came to Port Jefferson. Yankees "ravaged" the town according to the author, Miss Juliette Mouton, and took "all that was of value", using Magnolia Hill as their headquarters. During Reconstruction, the town endured the disgrace of having a black mayor, but prosperity returned when the cotton bloomed again and the steamboats ran.

Changes appeared on the St. Julien property. A Catholic church and parochial school, a city hall and infirmary rose on donated land. Valorous Confederate veteran, Victoir St. Julien, succeeded the Reconstruction mayor. He went on to the state senate while his brother, Felix, ran the town. He invested in land to the south and in railroad stocks. He became rich when the tracks fortuitously cut across his distant property. Steamboats went out of style; the boll weevil arrived causing as much damage to the economy as the Union Army. Magnolia Hill was sold intact as a virgin to Victoir St. Julien, who gave it to his son as a wedding gift. That son went on to the state senate, and his grandson became a personal friend of Huey Long.

The chapter ended with a disappointing segment on the development of the yam industry, which restored Port Jefferson to some of its former glory. Even Miss Mouton could not rave about the yam.

Around eleven, a mother and child entered the library to get some picture books. The small boy filled every inch of the building with his noise, and the mother, briefly introduced as a second cousin to Miss Clara, began a long conversation about Aunt Tillie's surgery. Suzanne asked for permission to check out the history book. Miss Clara allowed this after a short call to George confirming her identity. She gave her address as "Magnolia Hill," and that was sufficient.

Concluding a morning spent hunched over Miss Mouton's book, Suzanne welcomed the mile walk down Main Street to the bayou. She stayed on the right side where most of the public buildings with the exception of the school had sprouted on St. Julien property. On her side of the right-of-way, she sauntered past St. Joseph's Catholic Church and its appendage, the parochial school, where idle swings and dejected seesaws sat unmoving under the gray skies like sinners doing penance until recess. Stepping off of the high, broken cement sidewalk, she crossed a grassy patch fronting a private home set back among its live oaks and veiled by Spanish moss. An old-fashioned shingle on the gate of the white picket fence read, "Jefferson Sonnier, M.D.—Office in Rear."

Suzanne clambered up and across the boardwalk of a destitute dress shop with "Gone Out Of Business" soaped on its window. The buildings across the street shared the same erratic paving and just slightly more prosperity. A single car sat before a store and faced in the wrong direction along the railing where mules once munched corn on Saturday afternoons. Protruding bricks on the façade spelled out "Sonnier's—1854", but a metal sign screwed into the wall informed the public the building was now the Purvis Pharmacy.

She paused for a moment to watch an old black man sitting in the window of the last and only occupied store along her side of the boardwalk. He leaned toward the grimy glass to get more of the day's watery light on his work. In and out, he wove white oak splints into a basket of immense size, choosing a cane now and again from a heap at his side. Behind him like a wicker mountain a pile of finished products rose—cotton baskets, egg baskets, flower baskets, and lidded hampers, a wide selection for a small clientele. The shop had no name. It lacked a doorknob and latch as if no one would come here to steal, and if they did, they would leave in disappointment. The weaver never looked up though Suzanne stood close enough to the window to see the spaces amid the tight, white knots of his hair.

Thinking those baskets would add a nice touch to Magnolia Hill's kitchen collection, she crossed Main at St. Julien Street to get to the First National Bank of Port Jefferson. The old building, solidly supported by six stumpy columns, still gave off an affluent Victorian air, though no other person stood in line before the teller's wrought iron cage. Just inside the door, an anxious manager sprang from his desk behind a railing and seized her hand.

"Welcome to Port Jefferson. Ernest Prevost, branch director. How may we serve your banking needs?"

"I believe Mr. St. Julien called yesterday. I'm Suzanne Hudson. I came to check the records in his safety deposit box."

"Oh. Yes." The small mouth under the thin moustache quivered with disappointment. "I'll get my keys. Perhaps you would care to open a checking account while you're working in town," he suggested as they walked toward the vault over chipped but highly polished marble floors. Mr. Prevost paused and nodded at the view from one barred window.

"We've never closed, not even during the Depression. Only a few incompetent farmers lost their land. Port Jefferson really had no need for that." He pointed across the street.

The window framed another bank, the Farmer's Savings and Loan Association. The competition housed itself in an Acadian-style cottage with a shake roof and deep porch under the overhang. A few unoccupied rockers painted the same gray as the railings and uprights gave the building a comfortable rural atmosphere. An incongruous electronic sign on a thick pole flashed the time, then the temperature, then the message, "Farmers—we understand your business."

"I'll only be staying a short time, and I do have a checking account in Philadelphia. Will I have any trouble cashing checks locally?"

"No, oh, no. Glad to serve you in any way we can."

Mr. Prevost unlocked the gates separating the safety deposit boxes from the rest of the room and seated her in a cubicle for privacy. He placed a rather large box in front of Suzanne and backed away with a salaam-like bow. "Happy to help. Glad to help. Call when you want to leave." The gate clicked behind him.

Within the box lay a treasury of documentation. The first pieces, yellowed with age, were bills of lading from the Jefferson Steamboat Line. A marvelous brown-inked script described the contents of each crate brought up the river over several years to furnish Magnolia Hill. As she suspected, the Renaissance dining room set and the Belter settee and side chairs were original to the house along with most of the imported goods designed for the public rooms of the mansion. No mention of bedroom furnishings, which had most likely been in the family or produced locally. Several tester beds, trundles, armoires, miscellaneous washstands, and chamber pots were mentioned in the inventory at the time of the sale to Victoir St. Julien.

Suzanne believed her transitional bedroom harbored what remained of the oldest furnishings. The St. Juliens in a burst of redecorating and bad taste had purchased the ornate gothic half-tester. Yes, a bill of sale confirmed that. The rest of the papers were contemporary, copies of purchases, some Xeroxed, made by Virginia Lee St. Julien over twenty years as she built her collection. She'd bought the Jenny Lind crib as one of her first acquisitions. In the bottom of the box, Suzanne found a curiosity—a sales receipt for the gilt clock on the parlor mantel. That object had been sold ten years ago to Dr. J. Sonnier for the sum of $10,000 and repurchased for $1.00 five years ago. Both amounts seemed extreme, one inflated and one gratuitous. The story of that clock might be a piece of local history to be had from the great-aunts.

She summoned Mr. Prevost and asked his permission to use the office copier to photograph the oldest and most interesting documents. He refused any offer to pay for the service, despite a longing look thrown at the few dollars she held out. The bank manager assisted with the copying personally and gave directions to George's office, as if any were needed. All that mattered in Port Jefferson lay along Main Street.

The clock on Farmers Savings and Loan read 12:10. Suzanne jaywalked across the road where a few cars and a pickup truck had come to life at the noon hour. George stood locking the door of a prim little dwelling with a lace of gingerbread trim hung across its eaves and a once red tin roof, its paint fading off into a gentle pink. The office sat on its own patch of lawn, brown from a late frost at this time of year, but showing promise around the roots of a naked althea bush where the first tips of narcissus pushed out of the soil. Charmed by the idea that the flowers would bloom in February, she remarked on the buds, but George passed if off as "nothing special about that." She thought he might be angry about her tardiness and apologized.

"Doesn't matter. The aunts are happy to have the company. It's not too far to walk."

She had to concentrate on keeping up with those long legs and got only an impressionistic look at the other end of Main Street. They passed one exceptionally old house with whitewash flaking off the mud and moss bousillage between the crossed timbers of the walls. A sign designated it as the Port Jefferson

Museum, but George, looking back over his shoulder, called it the old St. Julien place. Just when it seemed as if he would stride at top speed into the bayou, her guide took an abrupt right turn on Front Street. To the left, she could see the Roadhouse Restaurant with its curiously Dutch-looking stepped façade and beyond that, a row of red brick warehouses. The drawbridge on the bayou rose upward for the passing a pleasure craft, and delighted, Suzanne paused to watch. George strode on, ignoring another "nothing special" in his life. She scurried to catch up.

He arrived ten paces before her on the porch of another of the white gingerbread houses abounding in varying states of repair all over the town. This one, freshly painted, had a broad-bosomed verandah and a congenial lap in the form of a porch swing. It held the hem of its skirt above the mud on brick pilings discreetly hidden behind latticework. The dry brown stalks of hydrangeas promised more camouflage of the bricks by summer. George knocked while Suzanne seated herself, panting, on the swing. The shade covering the etched glass panel in the front door fluttered upward, and the two aunts flew outward grabbing George's collar and pulling him down to peck at his cheeks like tiny sparrows attacking a hawk. Then, they turned on Suzanne.

"Oh, Georgie, you've winded her. Poor child!"

"It's all right," Suzanne puffed. "Aerobic exercise, good for the heart." A summer as a tour guide and a winter as a student had left her in worse condition than during her earlier lifeguarding days.

"Come in, come in. Dinner is ready. Sally will serve as soon as you've caught your breath."

Lynn Shurr

Though one had aged thin and bowlegged and the other obese and humpbacked, each aunt grasped an elbow to raise her from the swing. As an afterthought, George, who was erasing little smears of pink and orange lipstick from his face with a white handkerchief, introduced the ladies.

"My great-aunts, Miss Esme St. Julien, Mrs. Letty Dugas. Aunt Esme, Aunt Letty, this is Suzanne Hudson, the student who is doing a history of Magnolia Hill."

He pushed his enormous glasses back up the bridge of his nose, raked his creamed, disheveled hair into place, and opened the door for the women to totter through. They went directly past the parlor and into the dining room where four places were set at a mahogany table, not as old, but every bit as massive as the one at the Hill.

"Shall we talk while we eat? I do love good dinner conversation," said the spare, spritely aunt in the pink polyester pants suit. "Ring the bell, Letty."

Plump Letty in her blue polyester pants suit clinked a small silver bell by her place at one end of the table. The louvered door to the kitchen opened slowly as a black maid with limbs as thin and twisted as licorice whips backed in holding a serving tray. She appeared to be as ancient as the great-aunts.

Suzanne jumped up. "Let me help you!"

"When I can't do my job no more, I'll up and quit, go home and die, you hear?"

The aged servant pushed out her flabby lips over toothless gums. Her yellowed eyes glared from red-rimmed sockets. Suzanne sat and allowed Sally to serve her.

Fortunately, a brisk dinner conversation covered

her faux pas and gave her an excuse to pick at the food and take large gulps of instant iced tea between mouthfuls. Pieces of the dry pot roast stuck in her throat, and she could not bring herself to do more than push the grayish canned peas with their flecks of salt pork around on her plate. The best of the dinner, a mass of sticky candied yams, made the sweet tea seem sour. Each time she finished her beverage ancient Sally reappeared with a pitcher to fill the glass. She figured the elderly servant must spy through the kitchen louvers. Asking questions helped to cover her lack of appetite for the meal.

"I noticed this morning that most of the commercial development is on the old Jefferson property, while the St. Julien side is mainly public and residential property."

"The St. Julien side. Oh, that describes it perfectly, doesn't it, Letty?" Miss Esme said.

Letty nodded her large head into her double chin. "That's just how it was. You see the outsider, Eli Jefferson, came here around 1840 looking for a place to grow and ship cotton. He went to Pierre Huval who owned the inn and the ferry and said, 'Let me buy your land, and you'll get rich off the steamboat trade when my gin starts operating and shipping.' Then he went to the Sonniers who had a nice, well-run place and said, 'Sell me your land, and I'll set you up to run a store since I can see you've got the talent for it.' And he went to the Patouts and said, 'Your mules are the best shod in the parish. Sell me your land, and I'll help you get a smithy started. A lot of trade will come with the wagons bringing cotton, the women coming to shop, and so on.'"

Miss Letty paused to shovel up some yams, and Miss Esme stepped into the narrative like a scrawny tag-team wrestler. "Well, Josephe St. Julien saw what was happening, and when Eli Jefferson came to him, he said, 'I got six living children and six healthy slaves to work my land. I don't need your help. And one more thing, my Phillippe is to marry Babette Huval. Where are they going to farm with you buying up all the land?' 'They can farm in hell for all I care,' said Jefferson. That started the feud. Phillippe and Babette had to share the St. Julien land and house until they could build one of their own. The two wives arguing made Josephe's life a misery. They say he sent two daughters off to the convent just to prevent their marrying into any of the families who had sold out. The other two he drove to dances in Opelousas to be sure they would find a husband elsewhere. The younger son drowned in the bayou, and that let Josephe pass his property on intact to Phillippe, but he made his son swear never to sell to a Jefferson. Phillippe let his hogs and chickens dust on Main Street and never whitewashed his house to spite all the merchants that Jefferson controlled, but his son, Victoir, got the revenge."

"Yes," agreed Miss Letty, "but it was not revenge, just a sharp head for business, I say. Victoir studied Eli Jefferson's methods all his life, and when the time came he knew what to do. Both his brothers died in the War of the Rebellion, his sister was carted into Opelousas and married off. He had land in the center of town. First, he donated some to the Catholic Church, and all the priests told the people how devout he was. Then, he gave his former slaves small holdings on the edge of his property and asked the priest to marry them to his

Negresses exactly like white people. At the wedding, he said, 'You are free men and women now. Go and be thankful.' They were so thankful all four families took the name St. Julien."

"Not because they shared our blood, you understand. They were merely being grateful," interrupted Miss Esme.

"Yes, well. So Victoir St. Julien built a political base?" Suzanne prodded.

"Exactly." Miss Letty took over. "When he ran for mayor at the very end of Reconstruction, he had the black vote and the Catholic vote. The only folks left to vote for Jefferson's grandson were a few Americans, the non-French, you see, and a handful of Methodists."

"Do you know anything about the big railroad deal?"

"Victoir St. Julien worked his way up to state senator. He had power, but not the kind of money Eli Jefferson had in the bank. Victoir ran the town, but Eli Jefferson owned it, and at nearly eighty years of age, showed no sign of giving it up. Then, through his political connections, Victoir got wind of the new railroad. He knew the lay of the land, knew the tracks would pass on flat country to the south not up here in hill country. Rail is faster, rail is cheaper than the steamboat, you see. He bought the right land and made a fortune when the tracks crossed it."

"He put Eli Jefferson out of business?"

"Oh, yes! And out of his house, too." Miss Esme clapped her frail hands with joy. "And then, he gave Magnolia Hill to his own son, the second Josephe, for a wedding gift. Wasn't that marvelous?"

"But didn't he ruin the town as well?" Suzanne

questioned. Feeling on shaky ground, she looked across to George for support, but he seemed absorbed in chewing a bite of the leathery pot roast into a digestible mass and stirring his peas and yams together with a fork. An old story heard many times held no interest for him.

"Oh, no! The railroads and the boll weevil ruined Port Jefferson," Miss Esme asserted.

"Now that we've got yams, times are better," Miss Letty added, forking more of the orange potatoes between her jowls.

"We were both born at the Hill. Granddaddy Josephe would not have it any other way," Miss Esme chimed in, shooing the subject away from yams and back to happier times. "I do believe we spent more time there growing up than we did in this house. Granddaddy gave elegant weekend parties, all those politicians and their ladies, fancy dress in the evenings, rowing on the bayou in the afternoons, picnics, riding, all so fine."

"If Daddy had lived, we would have gone to stay on the Hill permanently, but he passed on of pneumonia when he was still only the mayor. Brother, that's Georgie's grandfather, got to the senate. He got the big house, too." Miss Letty savagely sawed at a piece of the pot roast.

"He was a personal friend of Huey Long, you know," offered Miss Esme.

"He dragged the family down to Huey's level, Esme. The St. Juliens 'just plain folks', indeed! Those dreadful dresses Beatrice bought at Sonnier's and having themselves photographed eating in the kitchen, horrible, just horrible! All the money in the world, and they let the Hill go to pieces."

"Now Letty, you're still sore because Fred cut you off when you insisted on marrying Henry Dugas." Appealing to Suzanne, Esme said, "He called it a traitorous act to marry into one of those families who sold out to Eli Jefferson."

"At least I had the spine to do it! I didn't let Fred or Granddaddy turn me into a nun or a spinster school teacher." Miss Letty's round face turned a dangerous shade of purple.

"That's just not true! My beau died in the World War." Miss Esme paled. She tugged on the zipper at the throat of her pink tunic, but it seemed to be caught in the fabric.

Again, Suzanne looked to George for help. He'd cleaned his plate. He rose and bent over Aunt Esme, brushing her sunken cheek with his lips. He did the same to Aunt Letty, pressing his lips to her fleshy jowls.

"I have to get back to the office. Ya'll have a nice visit with Suzanne." Nodding to his hired historian, he said without expression, "Stop by the office if you want a ride home."

Then, he deserted her in the midst of the battle. "Coward!" she wanted to shout after him. An unexpected ally appeared in the form of Sally. "Ya'll want coffee now?"

"In the parlor, Sally," Miss Letty indicated.

"Yes, in the parlor," Miss Esme echoed, entirely recovered from her brief fit.

Evidently, the two old women adhered to the old code of not arguing in front of the servants. With a silent truce called, they retired to the parlor. Sally appeared with her tray and stood holding it while

Suzanne took a demitasse and added sugar. Still, the servant continued standing right in front of her.

"Take a cookie," she said in disgust, as if a Yankee didn't know a thing about fine manners. Suzanne selected a gingersnap with a burnt bottom. Sally moved on to serve Miss Esme.

Miss Esme took her cup and cookie. "Sally has been with our family since she was fourteen. She still does all the cooking. Isn't she a marvel?"

"Definitely," Suzanne quickly agreed.

"Why, when Letty and I attended St. Joseph's, she would bring our lunch to the school yard on hot days so we needn't walk home in the heat and dust. It always came on a covered silver tray, cooling things like cucumber on bread and butter and a bucket of cold lemonade. She'd wait under the trees while we ate, then take the bucket and things back home." Esme sighed over the good old days and nibbled at her charred cookie.

"Sally does the cooking because Esme never learned how. She was too genteel." Miss Letty raised her cocktail sausage-sized pinkie in the air.

"You did learn to cook and look at you now!" Miss Esme counterattacked.

"Tell me about the historical marker," Suzanne intervened. "I understand you are responsible for it."

"Oh my, yes!" Miss Esme's face filled with delight again. "We thought up the words, and Brother put up the money. Bronze casting is very costly, you know."

"She left off Eli Jefferson and put in the yams," Letty responded.

"It was too expensive to have both, and 'yam' is a shorter word than 'Jefferson', that's all," Miss Esme explained.

"Brother wouldn't pay for 'Jefferson', you mean. Now I say when a feud is over one hundred fifty years old, it has got to stop. Why, Henry and I were just like Romeo and Juliet."

"Big, fat Juliet, little, skinny Romeo," Esme taunted like a schoolgirl. "Traitor to the family!"

"Now look here, Esme, I tried just as hard as you to get the name of this town changed to St. Julien."

"But Georgie's mother stopped us. What a terrible woman!" Miss Esme leaned confidentially toward Suzanne. The cuff of her pink polyester tunic took a dip in the coffee cup she held in trembling hands. "A disappointed woman."

"Well, we were all disappointed in Jacques. We thought Nephew would come back from Vietnam covered with medals and follow in Victoir St. Julien's footsteps. He looked so handsome in his naval officer's uniform. All his brothers who hadn't gone to college were just plain foot soldiers who got drafted. Jacques enlisted, but he went and brought home that woman from Virginia. The only thing she liked about this place was Magnolia Hill," Miss Letty continued.

"Oh no!" cried Miss Esme. "She liked one other thing." The sisters cackled like co-conspirators, both of them turning pink.

"Jacques was surely a womanizer. He seemed happy to spend his days living off the rents and investments and chasing skirts. Then, he'd go to Joe's Lounge and drink and tell all about his conquests."

"A trial to his family, a trial to his wife. Maybe that's why she turned so mean," Letty continued.

Suzanne wondered if Dr. Dumont knew about

Jacques St. Julien's reputation on his own turf.

"That's just family talk. Women loved Jacques, and the men liked him, too. Wasn't he elected Capitaine of the Courir de Mardi Gras when old Alonzo Guidry died? You say you and Henry wanted to end the feud. Jacques was the one who did it, I say. He drank with the Huvals and the Patouts and the Badeaux boys every night at the Lounge. They got along fine. I think Virginia turned ugly when they took out her female organs. That causes early change of life, you know," Esme whispered. Suzanne did not contradict her.

Esme continued working on her theory. "Virginia Lee came here and found out she had married a 'coonass.' Forgive me, Letty. I hate that word, too. Cajun was bad enough, then people like the Jeffersons brought back 'coonass' from overseas after the war. We should be called Acadians as in that lovely poem, *Evangeline* by Longfellow," she instructed Suzanne. "I always had my students read it and memorize the prologue. Are you familiar with the poem, my dear?"

"Eighth grade English. '*List to a tale of love in Acadie, home of the happy.*' Yes, I am." Suzanne suppressed a wince brought on by middle school memories of Miss Farrell cramming epic poetry into adolescent brains. Secretly, she loved the poem and doted on *Romeo and Juliet*, but who wanted to be teased? She could see Miss Esme gave her a gold star smile for her knowledge.

The former teacher went on talking. "Do you know, I never use the word nigger because I know how ugly words hurt?"

"That's not what soured Virginia Lee. It was discovering when her money ran out she had to stop buying those fancy antiques because Jacques wouldn't raise the colored folks' rent or put anybody out of business. He just let things keep rolling downhill. And he slept with every woman he laid hands on except his wife." Letty made her comment more graphic by snatching at her own large breasts straining the stretchy blue fabric of her top.

"Oh, Letty. You can be so crude. We have a guest here."

"No one thinks anything of it now! Look at this young woman sleeping up at the Hill with Georgie, not a chaperone on the premises."

"Well, they aren't sleeping together. Georgie is such a good boy. He painted our house last fall."

"How would you know? They could have met on one of his business trips. Maybe, this history thing is a hoax. He might be his father's son in disguise."

Suzanne finished her coffee in one gulp and rose. "Excuse me, but I have a lot of work to do at the house."

"There, now you have embarrassed our guest, Letty."

"Forgive me, my dear. Georgie is a nice boy, but let's face it. All men are animals underneath. You just forget I said anything and do your job at the Hill."

Suzanne accepted the apology gracefully, but still insisted she had to leave. Esme trailed her out on to the porch. "Do, do come again. For coffee. Please. Next week."

"If I can," she promised and started off along Front Street.

At a safe distance from the storm center, she slowed down and began to take in the scenery she'd missed on her headlong walk two hours before. Below the drawbridge on the opposite side of the river, a large hollow live oak stood, green in winter, but with a gap in its trunk large enough to hide a man. A stout knotted rope hung from its lowest branch out over the water. The rain-swollen bayou reached to within a foot of the rope, but she suspected in summer when children swung out over the river and played in the hollow, the water ran much lower. Beyond the tree, a house with a screened porch sat safely raised on its brick pilings. She took in the serenity of the scene and a deep breath of the mild January air. *Acadie, home of the happy*, indeed. The sun came out, brightening the bayou from a sullen gray to a pale, sparkling brown.

She continued down Front Street past Main and the Roadhouse still serving a few late diners. The warehouses beyond decayed by the bayou, the edges of their soft red bricks sloughing away into dust, their high, small-paned windows milky like cataracts or black and blind where young boys practiced rock throwing. Tucked among them, the infamous Joe's Lounge flourished under a yellow neon sign hanging out over the street where the road turned to gravel. Tempted, Suzanne opened its red metal door. Dark and abandoned at midday, midweek, a fat bartender washed glasses by the light of the beer signs.

She made her way to the bar through a maze of small tables with four upturned chairs crowning each one.

"Could I have a Coke, please? With plenty of ice."

"Don't you see dat sign, *cher*?"

Among the display of bottles fronting the mirror behind the bar, a taped message read, "No Ladies without Gents."

"It keeps down da fights, you see. We ain't one of dem city singles bars, no. If a guy brings a lady, well, we don't ask do she come from a good home. But, no mother's son ever come in here and got rolled if it wasn't his own damn fault. On Fridays and Saturdays, we got da best Cajun music in da state. You get yourself a man, honey, and come back den. Be glad to serve you."

"But no one else is in here, and I really need something to wash down my lunch. Please!"

He started moving his bulk around the bar as if he were going to bodily remove this annoying Yankee girl. Rolls of fat undulated softly beneath his Lite Beer T-shirt as he made headway. She tried another tack.

"You see, I'm doing research on Port Jefferson, and everyone said you have to go to Joe's Lounge. They have the best bands in Louisiana. Are you Joe?"

"Me? No! Dere ain't no Joe, no more." The bartender's big belly quivered with laughter as if she had tickled him in the stomach, but he stopped advancing. "Me, I'm Hypolite Huval. 'Hippo' people call me. Guess you can see why. I own dis place now. Used to have da Roadhouse, but one of da young Sonniers bought me out to fix it up fancy. Old Joe, he was ready to retire down by Grand Coteau wit' his daughter, and I had to have me a place, so I bought him out. *Bon*, no? Old Joe's been dead, I t'ink, since some time last year. You gonna put Joe's Place in da city papers, *cher*?"

His pudgy fingers pulled on the soft drink tap and extracted an extra-large Coke onto half a glass of crushed ice. "On da house," he said, pushing it toward

Suzanne.

"Actually, I'm not with a newspaper. I'm staying up at Magnolia Hill while I prepare a booklet on the house and town." She half expected the friendly Hippo to repossess the drink. "I understand Mr. Jacques St. Julien came here often."

"Near every night. You be sure to mention dat. Here's where da men meet to plan da Courir de Mardi Gras, and Jacques, he was da Capitaine."

"Tell me about the Courir."

"Well, I can't. It's a secret society like da Masons, you see. Womens ain't supposed to know not'ing about it."

"I understand." She thought "male chauvinist pigs," but didn't say it.

"But you come back wit' a date on Saturday night and dance. I always say, me, free drinks to anyone from da Hill, but George ain't sociable like his daddy. He don't even ride wit' da Mardi Gras."

"Then tell me about Jacques." It would take a while to swill the Coke she'd begged. To leave after her victory seemed out of character for a journalist who was going to put Joe's Lounge on the map.

"Oh, Jacques, he was da best of all da Capitaines in all my years. When he blew dat horn, all dose riders had better saddle up or he'd fight 'em, and he stayed sober so he could do dat. *Mais cher*, he let you have some fun, too. Sometime, he ride off wit' one of da pretty girls on his horse. Da mamas would cry and pray 'til he brung her back, but dey was only gone jus' a minute. Maybe he kiss her out around da barn, dat's all. Rest of us do da Mardi Gras song and dance for da old and ugly ones to make 'em feel good. We have a little beer, chase da chicken for gumbo, and move on when Jacques tell us. He gallop us into town, stirring up dust and scaring dose old roosters, and we dance and eat and drink 'til midnight. Den, he make us all go to Mass."

Hypolite sighed deeply. "Now dey want to let the womens ride. Man, dat's da end of a real good time. I mean you could piss off da side of your horse, and everyone laughed. Can't do dat wit' womens along."

Wondering why any female would want to ride, drink beer, and chase chickens all day, Suzanne almost sympathized, but her mother's feminist upbringing held her back. How much more appealing to be carried off on a white horse for a kiss behind the barn than to be one of the boys, but to each her own. She finished enough of the enormous drink to be polite and said good-bye and thanks to Mr. Hippo who shouted after her, "Y'all come back Saturday." Between coffee with the St. Julien sisters and Saturday night at Joe's Lounge, her social calendar was certainly filling up.

She rounded off the afternoon by exploring another of the side streets, appropriately named St. Julien, running alongside the old basket maker's shop. Behind the row of shops lay a pleasant residential strip of small white, blue, and pale yellow cottages. The road sloped gradually downward, the housing having less paint and more peeling the lower the street went. Trailers sat in the yards behind gray wooden shanties. She passed the Pilgrim Baptist Church with its one pane of stained glass shining like a ruby in the forehead of a Buddha over the narthex.

Suzanne experienced the same feeling of anxiety she might have if she'd wandered innocently into the black ghetto of Philadelphia, but no one threatened her.

The elderly sat on porch steps or tended the remnants of their winter gardens. Tiny, dark children stared as she passed, but the elderly nodded pleasantly enough.

The sky clouded over again and grew as black as her surroundings. She had no desire to bring attention to herself by returning the same way she'd come, but St. Julien Street appeared to have no crossroads. The street transformed into a rural route where a few shabby lounges hugged a curve in the road.

Resigned, she crossed the street, and marched purposefully up the other side as if she were late for a very important engagement. Most of the children had gone inside when the weather threatened. She approached the Pilgrim Baptist Church when the deluge let loose. In moments, water cascading down the decline lapped over the low curbs. She shoved the parish history book under her top to protect it, but her shoes grew soggy. Her hair plastered to her skull in wet ringlets. She kept walking directly into the rain, back toward the security of Main Street. A woman, middle-aged and medium brown, hailed her from a screened porch where she sat watching the storm.

"Come on in, come on in! Get yourself out of that rain."

Suzanne hesitated and then made her way up the walk and the three cinder block steps leading to the porch. Her hostess wore a brightly striped caftan over her ample body and covered her gray hair with a stiffly styled black wig.

"I saw you pass and wondered what would happen to you when the storm broke. It wasn't likely you were visiting anyone on this end of town. Why, you looked as out of place as a crawfish in an oak tree. I saw that once back in the big flood. Come in and dry yourself. I'm Odette St. Julien."

"Suzanne Hudson. Thank you for inviting me."

"Just being Christian. Let me make you some hot mint tea. Take off those wet shoes and get a towel out of the bathroom to dry that hair." She hesitated a moment, then suggested cautiously, "You could put on my robe hanging there on the peg. It's clean. I have an electric dryer, and we could get the wet out of your clothes."

Suzanne put on the warm, red flannel robe even though it wrapped twice around her and padded barefooted into the living room where she exchanged her dripping clothes for the cup of mint tea and a seat on the sofa. Despite the sagging porch and flaking paint that made Mrs. St. Julien's home blend with the rest of the neighborhood, the interior was clean and cozy on this dreary day. A burnt orange area rug covered the gray linoleum of the floor, and a hand-knit afghan of umber, green, and yellow yarns fanned across the divan. A large single room air conditioner, not operating this moist January day, filled one window. An immense television took up most of the wall opposite the sofa.

The air conditioner served as a stand for potted plants: begonia slips wintering over in small clay pots; an avocado grown from seed in a Mexican jar; broad-leaved house plants set in baskets like the ones the old man wove. The television had its own burden of framed photos: large and small snapshots of children and grandchildren; a very tall young man in cap and gown; a couple with the bride in white lace, the groom in a tuxedo; and one that looked like a black and white publicity still of a sports figure kneeling by a basketball. She got caught examining them more closely when Mrs. St. Julien returned with her own cup of tea.

"There now. Let's have our tea and talk while your things dry."

She could hear the whir of the dryer and the clanking of the zipper of her jeans against the drum coming from the kitchen. The air smelled pleasantly of perfumed dryer sheets. She and her hostess settled comfortably on the sofa.

"You have a handsome family." Suzanne nodded toward the framed pictures. She'd seen her activist mother do this countless times to set people at ease when she went out soliciting for her favorite charities. In this case, her daughter was the object of charity.

"My daughter, Harriet. My son, Lincoln." Her hostess rose, gathered an armful of the photos and brought them to the coffee table where the teacups sat.

"They're both school teachers. I'm a retired teacher myself. Harriet has two sons, and Linc, he got a boy on the fourth try. This is Linc and Doris on their wedding day. And these are my grandchildren."

She handed Suzanne a multiple portrait frame stuffed with school and baby pictures. "Harriet's boys, Ohin and Salim. Those names mean 'chief' and 'peace' in some African language. They laughed at me for naming them after Harriet Tubman and Abraham Lincoln. At least those people were Americans. And here's Linc's girls, Tiffany, Crystal, and Misty, and the baby, George Lincoln, Little Linc we call him. Here's my boy when he played basketball for the NBA." She showed the glossy still with obvious pride.

"Your son was *the* Lincoln St. Julien," Suzanne said, mentally thanking Birdie for the information and trying to remember what NBA stood for, not that it mattered. The word basketball gave her the clue.

Mrs. St. Julien's brown face brightened with pride. "That's my son. He played with the NBA five years before his injury. He coaches at the high school now. When he was making all that big money, he wanted me to have a new house and a big car, but I said to save for the future because you never know what plans God has for a person. Besides, I like it just where I am. He got me that big TV and the air conditioner even though my old set still worked fine, and I've been used to the heat all these years. Well, truth to tell, I'm glad I have them and gladder still he saved his money so he and Doris could build a nice place for their family in the country. I'm too old for change."

Mrs. St. Julien paused a moment as if she were aware she monopolized the conversation in a typical proud parent way. "Rain's quitting," she said almost regretfully. "You want me to call you a taxi? There's just the one in Port Jefferson, and Willie sometimes takes a while to get here, especially if the streets are flooded. Are you visiting family, honey?"

Suzanne hesitated. She had no idea how staying in a big white mansion would be taken by a person like Mrs. St. Julien—politely no doubt. Oh well, the words "Magnolia Hill" had opened the library, the bank, and Joe's Lounge to her. She tried the magic words once more. "I'm staying at Magnolia Hill." And received an instantaneous reaction.

"Then you're George's special visitor. I'm so happy he finally brought a nice woman to stay at the

Hill. You're a sweet girl, and he's such a fine young man. I'm sure you two will hit it off. I can't understand why he hasn't brought you to see me sooner. When he and Linc were playing ball together, George spent more time down here than up at the Hill. And when Linc went away to play for the big leagues, George would bring me flowers on my birthday from the both of them. Look here."

She went to stand by a large ficus tree in a wooden tub filling one corner of the room. "George gave me this one Mother's Day when Linc was away. It's almost as tall as he is now. I remember…"

Mrs. St. Julien sat on the sofa to do her remembering. "I recall the weekends those boys would come home from college when they weren't playing ball. That wasn't often, not often enough for a mother. When they *were* here, I thought I'd have to go on food stamps to feed the both of them. George's favorite was yam pie. He would eat the whole thing and wash it down with a quart of milk right out of the carton. I'd say didn't his mama teach him better manners, and he'd just grin at me and say I'd have to teach him. Yam pie! I have one in the refrigerator. You take it to George and tell him he's been a stranger. Now let me check your clothes and call that cab."

"No cab! Really, I'd rather walk," Suzanne intercepted. How would she explain showing up at George's office with a yam pie in hand? "You do know I'm simply doing research at the house? I only met George, Mr. St. Julien, a few days ago."

"Oh, that's a shame. I hoped he was going to settle down when Birdie mentioned he had a girl staying up there. I guess I would have heard from Linc if George had found someone special," she called from the kitchen.

Mrs. St. Julien returned, smoothing the wrinkles out of the still-warm clothes with her hands. Suzanne went to change. When she returned, Odette St. Julien had the pie covered with aluminum foil and ready to go, but she held it back a moment.

"It's a pity for George, always getting mixed up with the wrong women. Between us, I thought he was going to marry Linc's cousin, LaDonna Williams. No big thing in the city, but that would have set the kettle to boiling in Port Jefferson. They were seeing each other in college. I wasn't supposed to know, but Harriet told. LaDonna ran a little wild back then. I was just getting ready to say something about how that relationship was bad for both of them and all of us," she gave a general nod to the vicinity of St. Julien Street, "when they broke it off. Then, LaDonna married that boy from Metairie and took a weight off her folks' mind. He's a dentist, and their twins have settled her down a bit. That's just between us, you understand."

Suzanne gave her promise. Really, who did she have to tell except Birdie, and Birdie probably knew already. Mrs. St. Julien walked her out to the porch steps and gave her the pie. "Tell George to return the plate in person. You are welcome any time, too, dear."

She waved and started up St. Julien Street. Yellow school buses dropped batches of children along the way. They flowed past her, some shucking shoes and wading barefoot in the puddles, brown feet in brown water, none pausing to stare because they were at the busy age and had homework or odd jobs to do, a television program to catch, a basketball game to get started. With the library book tucked under one arm, Suzanne moved against the dark tide back to Main Street.

She loitered on Main long enough to arrive at 4:45 on the steps of George's office. All too aware her clothes looked as if she'd spent the afternoon curled up in the trunk of a car and her hair had puffed out around her face like a giant dandelion going to seed, she balanced the pie on one hand and knocked with the other. A white woman well past forty answered the door.

"Yes?" She eyed Suzanne as if she might be an itinerant pie salesman whose goods were suspect.

"I'm Suzanne Hudson. I'm supposed to meet Mr. St. Julien for a ride back to Magnolia Hill."

"Yes. I'm sorry to keep you standing on the porch. We do have a policy about solicitors coming to the door." She stood aside to let Suzanne pass. "You aren't exactly as Mr. St. Julien described. He said you had a very businesslike demeanor."

As hard as she tried not to, Suzanne blushed with embarrassment.

"I'm Lonnie Breaux, Mr. St. Julien's secretary."

"Pleased to make your acquaintance, I'm sure," Suzanne said in her toniest up-east accent. Miss Breaux took a turn blushing as she shook hands formally. Still holding the pie in one hand, Suzanne thought she'd brought the whole situation off rather well.

A dark walnut desk dominated the outer office. Straight-backed chairs with needlepoint cushions waited for clients and blended nicely with the old pine flooring and wavy glass in the small panes of the windows. An old upright typewriter would not have looked out of the place on Miss Breaux's desk, but she had a sleek, black computer, this being a business and not a museum.

The door to the inner office was closed, but George must have heard the conversation. He looked out, said Miss Breaux could leave a little early, he would lock up, and ducked back as if a secret society met inside. Lonnie Breaux pulled on the white cardigan sweater hanging on the back of her chair, told Suzanne what a pleasure it was to have met her, and departed.

George emerged from his inner sanctum a few minutes later. Before she could present him with the pie, he said, "Did you do something to your hair this afternoon? It looks all fluffy."

Her mother always said it was a high compliment and a minor miracle when a man noticed a change in a woman's appearance. At the moment, Suzanne disagreed. The pie was *so* handy, but the impulse to lob it in his face passed. Really, he seemed clueless and completely sincere.

"I got caught in the rain this afternoon. My hair does this when it's wet—without conditioner—instant frizz. But, I did meet the nicest woman who took me in and dried me off, Mrs. Odette St. Julien. She sent you this pie and said you were to return the plate in person."

Since she held his favorite treat, she expected some expression of delight or gratitude. Instead, she received a minor explosion. "You went walking in Coon Hollow alone!" He stared at her rumpled clothes as if they were evidence of an assault.

"I was trying to get the feel of the town, and I thought St. Julien Street might have a family connection."

"It does. That's where Victoir St. Julien's settled his former slaves. Don't do that again."

"You go there," she retorted.

"I'm a man."

She looked him up and down as if she doubted his statement. Hmmm, his eyes turned a darker, stormy gray when angry, and George's shoulders filled out his suit very well when he pulled himself up to his full height instead of slumping forward.

"This is incredibly Old South of you, George, ah— Mr. St. Julien. Look, nothing happened. I met a lovely woman. We had tea. I came here. Okay?"

"Listen to me. Those dives at the bottom of the hill are hangouts for dopers, crackheads, and petty thieves. People like that would snatch the purse of a stranger in a minute, do worse if they were high on something. Heaven knows, they prey on their own, Suzanne—Miss Hudson. Being a Yankee you wouldn't understand," he said as if this constituted an apology.

"Mr. St. Julien, I've spent the last several years living in Philadelphia where, I can assure you, we have crackheads and purse snatchers in abundance. Racial relations there are probably a thousand times worse than in Port Jefferson. We even have a serial killer of young women on the loose, and see—" She had craned her neck back to stare him in the eyes and started to feel the strain. Lowering her gaze, Suzanne twirled around with her arms spread wide. The pie, forgotten her moment of anger, nearly slid to the floor. She caught it in both hands.

"See, I'm still in one piece."

"More than I can say for that pie."

"Here. Enjoy!" She thrust the pie at him.

George seized it in his large hands. He raised the aluminum foil covering. The filling had split and slumped to one side of the crust. He took a deep breath that strained the buttons of his jacket.

"I asked you to call me George. Suzanne, if you want to visit Mrs. St. Julien again, it would be my pleasure to take you. If you need to do research in the Hollow, I would like come along. I would be happy to escort you anywhere in Port Jefferson."

She suspected this speech to be some kind of southern bullshit meant to undermine the autonomy of women, but she seized the opportunity anyhow.

"There is a place you could take me—Joe's Lounge on Saturday night. The music is supposed to be great." Suzanne definitely did not want him to think she had designs on his body, though he was broader through the chest than she'd first thought. His height disguised its breadth.

"I guess it is if you like Cajun and country. I can't take you. I won't be around much this weekend."

"Some other time, then," she answered curtly. She'd find someone else to take her.

"Shall we go?" He held the door to the office open for her despite juggling the pie and his briefcase.

The silence deafened all the way back to the Hill. She noticed for the first time the road leading to Magnolia Hill was named Jefferson Street. A few premature, paper white narcissus bloomed in a sheltered spot, but she did not bother to point out any of these observations to George. One minute he was a geek accountant, the next, a MCP, male chauvinist pig. Her mother taught her that term. Still plenty of them in the world, Mom said. Then, he put on the Southern gentleman act. She really did not care much for George St. Julien—even if Birdie and Odette thought he'd hung the moon over this tiny town.

She took her dinner in her room that night, despite the fact that Birdie set two places in the formal dining room. Best to put her relationship with George back on the professional track and establish some distance. Now that she'd cooled off, she gave him points for forbearance and manners. As her employer, he could have told her to catch the next plane north.

When Suzanne came downstairs in the morning, all of the yam pie had vanished. She'd wanted to try a piece never having any since in Philly cheesecake ruled. Birdie, a little miffed, too, said Mr. Georgie had passed over her nice, hot dinner in favor of the pie and a whole quart of milk. He could have saved pieces for her and his houseguest. Suzanne added greed to the side of the list of things she did not like about George St. Julien.

Chapter Four

Suzanne's story

What a totally boring weekend. George was gone as much he had said he would be. Suzanne saw him briefly Saturday morning when she stood in the kitchen scrambling some eggs. Trying to mend fences, she offered to do the same for him. Looking surprisingly scruffy and masculine in old jeans and a stained, gray university sweatshirt, he turned her down and left the house. He came back after midnight. Hoping he noticed she was still up and working, she clacked away on her computer, entering his mother's inventory.

She swore she could smell beer fumes emanating from his room when she went down the hall the next morning. Sunday, George slept in until eleven, and then took off again more neatly dressed. He said he had been invited for Sunday dinner at a friend's house. Suzanne thought this a strange lack of the southern hospitality that she hadn't been invited, too. So, she ate Birdie's leftovers, not too shabby, out of the refrigerator and sent messages home to pass the time.

She gave Dr. Dumont a dry, academic overview of what the house contained. Since her mentor would want to know, she added that George St. Julien bore very little resemblance to his fiery father and mostly took after his mother, except for his dark hair. Unfair of course with George being more quiet than cold. If he wasn't the master of Magnolia Hill she had envisioned, not his fault. Mentioning George's affair ten or more years ago with a black girl, now a married mother of twins, would have been entirely out of line.

For her mother, she gushed over the Belter settee and the Wooten desk. Converting her interest to the Victorian era had brought them closer. Instead of lurking in galleries displaying art beyond her mother's comprehension and definitely not to her taste, they'd begun spending weekends haunting antique shops together. If she did not experience the same thrill as Mom over finding a mother-of-pearl handled fish fork in a New Hope tourist trap, she did begin to develop an eye for the flawed and the fake as she compared the goods on sale to the real items she'd been allowed to touch at Winterthur or tout during her duties as a guide.

She told Mom about the "lovely" magnolias that had given the house its name and about the "charming" basket maker in his shop on Main Street, hardly believing she used those words. At the moment, the trees seemed like black growths on a dead lawn sweeping down to the brown bayou, and the basket maker a prime example of rural poverty. Before her mood could infect the upbeat tone of the letter, she signed it off with a "Love, Suzanne."

She'd considered adding a note about George, his quaint manners and protectiveness, the temper he had so quickly subdued, but didn't want to get Mom started on another man. Mom still asked about Paul, the steady fellow with the good job. Right now, her mother was probably online selling some of her antique finds on eBay, her mailbox open. No, Mom would get too inquisitive about her boss if they started to chat. She didn't feel like talking about George at the moment. After all, Suzanne Hudson was a twenty-first century woman who does not need a man on a white horse to rescue her, a castle to live in, or even someone to open doors for her—but the last was sort of nice along with Magnolia Hill.

Instead, she scribbled off a few picture postcards of the Hill she'd found at the pharmacy to friends so they could see where she'd landed. She debated whether to send Paul a conciliatory e-mail note saying something like "you are a nice guy; it just wasn't meant to be," but doubted if the note would do any more than make him angry again in that red-faced, snarling way.

The cards written, she turned back to the computer and contacted her brother, asking Blake if he had ever heard of a basketball star named Linc St. Julien or an old college player called George St. Julien, because she was living right in their hometown where nearly everything except the town itself seemed to carry their name. In the short time she'd been offline, a message from Mom had popped up beneath the half dozen from Paul she hadn't opened or answered. Suzanne did not open any of them now, either.

The afternoon wore on. Somehow, she rebelled against working on her project. Sunday, a day of rest, a day off even for non-churchgoers—she loathed Sundays featuring the stuffiness of a church service followed by a big meal and a boring afternoon when most of the more interesting non-mall shops and galleries stayed closed. Wondering what the people of Port Jefferson did on a Sunday afternoon, she found the telephone book and called Willie's Taxi Service. Willie knew how to get to Magnolia Hill, good because she doubted if he could have heard directions over the background noise of the television set and the clamor of dogs and children in his house. Willie said he would be right over, and forty-five minutes later, he arrived.

"Had a little trouble gettin' up the hill, ma'am," he explained, "but we can coast back down. I never been up here befo', but I sure know where it at."

She studied Willie's vehicle, a '56 Chevy Bel Air spray-painted a bright yellow to resemble city cabs. The upholstery appeared to be the original blue plaid, she discovered when he opened the back door. By sliding to the center of the seat, she avoided snagging her slacks on any protruding springs. Willie gunned his engine. It responded with a series of pops.

"Where to?" he said in the best tradition of cabbies.

"What's open on Sunday?"

"Here in Port Jefferson, you mean?"

"Yes."

"Dairy Queen out by the highway and the museum about all. I could take you into the city to see a show for forty bucks."

"Let's try the museum."

The cab stalled on the way downhill, but Willie popped the clutch and had it going again by the time they got to the traffic light where, fortunately, they did not have to stop. Main Street sat deserted except for a few cars at the Methodist Church. Willie swung up in front of the Port Jefferson Museum without mishap.

"How much?" Suzanne asked. The cab had no meter.

"Six dollar," said Willie sizing her up, a smile on his shining black face.

She paid and threw in a dollar tip even though she suspected just having paid the out-of-town stranger rate. Coming from a city where simply turning on the cab came to more than a dollar, she wasn't appalled. Maybe, Willie could save up for new brakes.

"Thank you, ma'am. You jus' call when you ready to go back, now."

"Sure," she answered and went through the gate in the rickety sticks of *pieux* fencing. The hollow sound of her steps on the broad boards of the porch must have awakened the guide.

The woman suddenly straightened from a position of nodding over the table containing the guestbook and a Plexiglas box with "donations" stenciled on the side. She wore a red volunteer button stuck on the chest of her yellow gingham costume. The sunbonnet shoved back from her badly dyed or unfortunately natural orange hair slid off of the guide's head and dangled by the strings. The volunteer wrung her hands in her white apron and began. "My name is Evelyn Patout, and I am your guide," she announced, coming to attention but avoiding her visitor's eyes.

"Hello," Suzanne said. As if this were a magic word that set off a chain reaction, Evelyn Patout began her tour by rote. "We are standing in the living quarters of the Jean-Baptiste St. Julien home built, we think, about 1794. The home is constructed of cypress timbers and bousillage. That is mud, moss, and animal fibers packed into the walls."

Marching to the fireplace, Evelyn pointed to a glass plate covering a hole in the wall. "This here is a section which has been cut way to show the thickness of the wall. Bousillage made excellent insulation in this hot climate."

Past the opening sentences, Evelyn's voice continued on in a very un-French twang. "The chimney and fireplace are also made of mud because we got so much of it 'round here. Now the family of ten slept in these here two rooms mostly. Not all at onct. Some of 'em died young. People did that then."

Beads of sweat began to form between the freckles stretched across the guide's cheekbones. "Now the mama and the papa slept here with the babies. See the cradle hand hewn from cypress. This was the girls' room. There ain't no other door but through the parents' bedroom. The boys slept up in the loft called a garconierre entered by the stairs on the porch. Tells you something about those times, don't it?"

"All the furniture in those days was handmade and very simple. Here is where the family ate. See the cowhide, hair and all, stretched over a frame to make a seat. And what did they eat? Corn ground up in this here stump and lots of rice." Evelyn raised a large wooden pestle and let it fall with a thump into the hollowed log. Chips of cracked corn scattered through the air, pelting Suzanne like rice at a wedding.

"Lots of wild game and fish, naturally. Chickens, too. They raised chickens." Her guide began to look tearful. "Oh, and I forgot. This was the birthplace of one of our state senators, Victoir St. Julien. From these humble origins sprang a long line of prominent politicians. Any questions?"

Without pausing, Evelyn raced on. "Please stop to look in the glass case which contains pictures of Port Jefferson one hundred fifty years ago. The Port Jefferson Museum is operated entirely on your donations. Please feel free to browse in the rooms and stop at the other points of interest in our town." Evelyn exhaled. "How did I do? This was my first tour."

Suzanne understood. Four years of college and several public speaking courses had not made her first tour of the historic home where she worked in Philadelphia last summer any more relaxed. "Fine," she said, smiling. "What are the other points of interest?"

"Uh, they didn't tell me. I mean the Historical Society ladies. See, I'm from north Louisiana, up by the Arkansas border. I come here when I married Billy Patout last year. He's real good with my boys. Billy said get out, join some clubs, do something. So I volunteered for here. I had to get this costume made, and this ole bonnet here is just driving me crazy." Evelyn pulled the bonnet up on her orange hair where it cast a sallow pall over her freckles and pushed it back again.

"I'm a stranger here myself." Suzanne walked over to the glass case and viewed the pictures of very unglamorous steamboats laden with mountains of cotton bales and a Main Street of dirt and board sidewalks, but full of mule and wagon traffic. "There's not much to do here on a Sunday."

"You're telling me!" Evelyn sympathized. "But you should have been at Joe's Lounge last night. As they say around here, you can pass a good time at Joe's. Say, if you're still here next week, Billy can fix you up with a date. He got a slew of brothers and cousins, all good dancers, these Cajun boys."

"I might take you up on that."

Suzanne put a couple of dollars in the donation box where a handful of change rested. Evelyn wrote her number on the back of a Port Jefferson Museum brochure and handed it to her as she escorted Suzanne to the door of the cabin. Even the cars at the Methodist church had gone by now. She decided to walk up the hill. Not only would it be faster, cheaper, and safer, but the walk would consume the remains of Sunday afternoon.

While Suzanne toiled along the narrow gravel strip between the deep drainage ditch and the macadam at the crest of the hill, George pulled over in his gray Honda. She would have liked to refuse the ride and assert her independence again, but the early winter dusk began to settle over the landscape, and she had out-walked any lingering issues she had with her boss.

"I brought you some fried chicken and a piece of yam pie for dinner." He nodded in a shame-faced way toward a bag on the front seat.

"Thanks. Were you at Mrs. St. Julien's?" she asked, trying not to show any curiosity about where he had been all day.

"No, not at Odette St. Julien's place."

End of conversation. At the Hill, George went directly to the Eastlake parlor for a nightcap. Suzanne ate her chicken and pie cold in the kitchen and pondered deep thoughts: how similar yam pie was to pumpkin, one of her favorites; how even the fried chicken batter had the bite of red pepper in it; whether or not to go to Joe's Lounge next Saturday night with a blind date. She liked the pie, disliked the chicken, and could not make up her mind about Evelyn Patout's offer.

Chapter Five

Suzanne's story

On Monday morning, Suzanne woke to Birdie singing a hearty version of *I'm gonna wash that man right out of my hair*. She could not agree with the housekeeper more. George had gone for the day. The sunshine sparkled through the window and robins, their red breasts so bright against the foliage they resembled living Christmas ornaments, festooned the dark trees and dreary lawn. Feeling fine with a week of work ahead, Suzanne bounded down the stairs and shouted to Birdie in the kitchen. "Spring is here!"

She did not find Birdie in the kitchen. Instead, she intercepted the maid in the dining room where the immense table lay covered with an old blue oilcloth. The doors of the massive Renaissance sideboard stood unlocked and open as Birdie hauled out treasure like a fat caliph about to get his weight in gold. But this was silver—ornate, invaluable, Victorian silver. Her polishing cloths and jars of silver cream stood ready for the task. Abruptly, Suzanne changed her plans for the day from beginning on the inventory of the upper rooms to surveying the silver.

"You'll have to eat in the kitchen, honey. This takes me most of the day." Birdie grunted as she hauled a huge punchbowl from a low shelf. Suzanne went to help her.

"Feel the weight of this stuff. There must be a hundred ounces of silver here," she marveled. "Worth a fortune."

"I always keeps it locked up and out of sight." Birdie flourished a rag and settled down to a day of polishing. "Go on and eat your breakfast."

Suzanne brought her orange juice and sweet roll back to an unused corner of the dining room table, then ran upstairs for the card file. Virginia Lee kept a special section set aside for her silver, and the files had been heavily used. Obviously, she'd lavished her time on this area of her collection. Some yellowed cards held notations made in a firm, elegant hand with a blue-inked fountain pen, but most were on crisp, clean sheets scrawled in shaky black ballpoint. The newer cards seemed out of character for the mistress of Magnolia Hill, but then, Virginia's last years had been spent dying slowly and painfully. Maybe, the fast scrawl represented her sense of time running out.

Suzanne fingered the first card, an old one for a sterling teething rattle, mother-of-pearl handle, Tiffany, circa 1895, valued at $50. Not wanting to bother Birdie who was warming up her hands and her voice with a little humming, she started with the small pieces in the long shallow drawer in the top of the sideboard. Once used for storing table linens, a modern cabinetmaker had inset the space with small cubicles lined in gray flannel. Each niche held an object of Victorian tableware that would have sent her mother into raving fits of ecstasy.

Virginia Lee had owned all the oddities of the era: grape shears with handles like twisted vines, asparagus tongs in Tiffany's Chrysanthemum pattern, bacon forks, oyster ladles, berry spoons, a chipped-beef server, a set of ice cream forks, even an Unger Brothers food pusher used by children to pursue elusive peas around the plate. Item by item, they were worth no more than twenty to two hundred dollars each, but cumulatively several thousand in melt value, and much, much more to a collector because of the breadth of the collection. As dreary as Suzanne found some aspects of Victoriana, these absurd utensils delighted her.

Chortling over cheese scoops and lettuce forks, she pawed among them most of the morning while Birdie polished and sang under her breath to keep from disturbing her studies. Every item checked out against the cards, with the exception of the baby rattle. She asked Birdie about it.

"Oh, that ole thing was the first bit of silver Miss Virginia brought home for Georgie who hadn't even been born yet. She was four months along and so slim you couldn't tell. I said, 'Now don't you be tempting things to go wrong by buying all sorts of stuff for your baby, better to wait for the last month,' but she just laughed and had me boil it, shine it up, and wrap it in flannel. When Georgie come, she give it to him and let him chew all over it. You could see his little tooth marks on it. That rattle is long gone down a crack or lost in the yard. Imagine giving a baby something fine to play with. They can teeth just as well on a frozen carrot."

With her head bent over her work, Birdie scrubbed diligently at a bit of repousse work on the punchbowl.

"But I guess that was all right for her if it give her some pleasure. By nine months, Miss Virginia got no bigger than a muskmelon down there, not big and sloppy like some women get. She had all these clothes made up special to look nice, while most everybody else just stayed home and wore them big T-shirts or their own man's shirts when they was breeding. It made no difference to Mr. Jacques. He went out tomcatting around before their first anniversary. Once he took off that uniform, turned out he was just a low-life person. I hate to say it of the dead, but a low-life person. Him too low and her too high with me stuck in the middle. Those were some bad years early on, but things took care of themselves later. Yes, they did."

Suzanne did not press her to go on, being more interested in the silver than in George's mismatched parents. She put a question mark on the card for the rattle, stretched, and suggested a lunch break. Birdie agreed, though she had just snacked on coffee and the last of the buns an hour ago.

The day turned strange when George's car came up the drive. Birdie shrugged and raised her eyebrows to show she had not expected his company for lunch either. He plunged in the door with two long loaves in white paper bags under his arm, smiled without looking at Birdie or Suzanne, and said, "Savoy's had hot French bread. I thought you ladies would like some for lunch."

"Nice of you, Mr. George." Birdie took the loaves and began opening another can of soup to put in the saucepan. "We just having a little chicken noodle today."

"Great. My favorite." George smiled inanely again, and stretching his long legs out into the kitchen, took a seat. Birdie eyed him as if he had gone insane.

"I thought my gumbo was your favorite."

"My favorite of the canned kind, I mean. Look, I brought the mail. Two for Miss Hudson, one for occupant, and three bills for George St. Julien."

When he looked at his utility bill, the flood of pleasant conversation stopped. Suzanne tried to renew the flow by remarking she'd seen robins, a sure sign of spring. George glanced at her blankly through those heavy glasses, then informed her otherwise.

"No. We only see robins around here in December or January, sometimes February. Then, they all fly north. Robins winter around here."

She sighed. He had spoiled her joy in the flock, hopping and worming across the lawn. Ignoring George, Suzanne rudely opened and read her letters in front of him while Birdie served the soup. Of necessity, Birdie took hers out to the dining room to eat among the polishing rags since George had taken her chair. She would have offered to eat in the other room, but Birdie, quick to see the situation, moved out. Her speed came from years of practice in coping with the whims of white folks, Suzanne assumed.

Her mother's letter, long and chatty, began by asking why a week had gone by without so much as a quick e-mail or a phone call. Since she had taken care of that complaint, Suzanne ignored the paragraph, just as she continued to ignore George who kept fidgeting with his soup spoon and knocking his fingers against the kitchen window to startle the robins. The letter ended with a postscript saying that Paul Smith had called to get her new address because he wanted to write and had lost the one Suzanne had given him.

Suzanne had told Paul that she would send him her address when she got to Port Jefferson, but hadn't done so. No sense in prolonging the relationship since she was one hundred percent sure Paul didn't want to "be friends."

Naturally, the second letter came from Paul. After reading it, she allowed her soup to get cold and carried the bowl half-finished toward the sink. No longer ignoring George but simply forgetting he existed, she tripped over his big feet. The yellow broth sloshed on the sleeve of his white shirt as he reached out to catch her. With a strong grip, he steadied her with one hand. For a second, she wondered if George could or would protect her from Paul if the threat in the letter came to pass.

Printed very neatly in heavy lead pencil across a single sheet of computer graph paper, Paul wrote:

Dearest Suzanne,

If you do not return, I am coming to get you.

Your Loving Fiancé,

Paul

The words chilled with their directness. Mentally, she felt frozen, and physically, her arm numbed where George gripped her elbow.

"Is something wrong?" he asked with genuine concern.

She should have told him then, but George was only her employer, a quiet and sometimes bumbling one, not a man whom she could expect to take on her problems or do anything about them. In fact, having a threatening ex-boyfriend might jeopardize her job.

"No. It's just that I seem to keep ruining your shirts. First brandy, now soup."

"I drink Jack Daniels and have plenty of shirts." George dropped her arm when Birdie pushed into the kitchen.

"Go on doing whatever you was doing. Old Birdie has to wash those shirts. Don't think about me none."

"I'll take it off right now and put it in some cold water." George fled the scene.

"Now, I didn't mean to do that. I was only joking with him, but Miss Virginia made him jumpy like that. Just when he was starting to warm up to you, too. Why, he hasn't come home to lunch in months, and this time it wasn't to see old Birdie."

Great, Suzanne thought, returning to the silver spread on the dining room table. Now, she had two men she did not want, and one of them happened to be her boss. The afternoon rolled downhill from there. She started to check the larger pieces: the punchbowl; a pair of candelabra; a tea set with an amazing number of pieces from a waste bowl to sugar tongs. Each item seemed to have some little niggling thing wrong with it. The manufacturer's mark and the sterling symbol were obscured and illegible on the punch bowl, though Virginia Lee listed it as Tiffany. The candlesticks had the proper weight for sterling, but something about their patina bothered her. She questioned Birdie, too heavily, perhaps.

"So you've been here thirty years," Suzanne began subtly.

"More like forty. Mr. Fred and Miss Beatrice took me on right out of school to help old Effie. Then they died within a year of each other, Mr. Fred of a stroke and Miss Beatrice from missing him, I think. She got the pneumonia and wouldn't call in a doctor 'til it was too late. Effie and me kept the house up until the boys got home from the war and settled everything. Then,

Effie retired. Said she was too old to learn new tricks from the likes of Miss Virginia."

"How often have you polished all this silver over the years?"

"Oh Lawd, least once a month, more when Miss Virginia entertained, maybe not so often after she got sick. I mean Mr. Georgie never has folks over, and it takes all my time to keep the place clean by myself. 'Fore, we had other maids and a cook. I does my best."

"Of course you do, but look at these candelabra. When a piece has been polished often, it develops this sort of deep glow called a patina. This article seems almost new, but Mrs. St. Julien's note dates it as 1853 and values the pair at nearly $4,000."

"Well, I don't know nothing 'bout that. That's one of her new candlesticks she got the last five years, traded it for her old set with her antique dealer, trading up she said. So maybe I didn't shine it so much. It's hardly been out the bag since she got it. Liked the old ones better myself. They was all covered with curlicues and had these little cups to catch the wax."

"Bobeches."

"What say?"

"Bobeches, the little cups that catch the wax."

"Yeah. They were the devil to clean, but I liked them sticks better. They did sort of glow."

"Did Mrs. St. Julien trade any of the other pieces?"

"Nearly all the big ones. Trading up, she told me, every time."

"It's just that some of the pieces don't quite match their descriptions."

"I don't know about that neither. When Miss Virginia died, the estate people took the inventory, one punch bowl, one tea set. They was all here. They still is." Birdie's lower lip protruded belligerently.

"She might have made some mistakes," Suzanne suggested, trying to calm her down.

"Miss Virginia collected that silver for thirty years. You just a kid. What you know about it?"

Suzanne decided not to argue the point. She needed Birdie's goodwill, and even more, her friendship in this lonely house.

"I think her dealer may have tried to cheat her."

"Not old Mr. Mort. She dealt with him twenty years or more. Why he'd go off to New Orleans or New York, even London, England, and Paris, France, and bring back things only for her. They would sit right here at this table, and I'd bring tea in the special service. Mr. Mort would be showing her something nice from one of his drawstring bags. Each and every time, he'd admire the tea set, and Miss Virginia would say what a pleasure it gave her just to use it."

"I'd like to talk to Mr. Mort myself."

"You'd have to go on up to heaven. Mr. Mort's been dead about twelve years."

"Then, who traded for Mrs. St. Julien's candlesticks?"

"Mr. Mort's son, Randolph, took over the business. He's nothing like Mr. Mort. He'd come and go with his little bags while Miss Virginia lay sick. He'd see her in her bedroom and lock the door behind him like I'd steal his ole silver. They never called for tea or coffee, and he never stopped to pass the time of day. No wonder Miss Virginia didn't buy from him. They'd trade or they wouldn't, and that was that. And every time he come, she'd say, 'Don't tell Mr. Georgie that Randolph has been here because he don't like Mr. Royal.' Royal, that's the family name. Sounds made up, don't it?"

"Why didn't Georgie, I mean Mr. St. Julien, like Mr. Royal?"

"Because Georgie ain't one of those sissy boys, I told you, and Mr. Royal is. Oh, young Mr. Royal was married, all right. He has a son, too, but we all knew why that marriage didn't take. Yes, we do. He moved the shop to Opelousas after Miss Virginia died, said he needed more 'custom' to survive, but he wasn't fooling anybody about why he got out of town. He married to one of the Patout girls under false pretenses, and her brother, Billy, was fixing to fix him forever."

"By 'sissy boy', you mean gay? Randolph Royal preferred men to Mr. Patout's sister?"

"You got that right!"

Birdie warmed up again, now that the conversation turned to local gossip and away from the silver. Unfortunately, Suzanne needed to know the whereabouts of Randolph, not his sexual preferences.

"I think I'd like to meet Mr. Royal."

"No, you wouldn't."

"I think I must because something is definitely wrong here." She picked up the sugar tongs that did not quite match the rest of the tea service and told Birdie that she wanted to borrow it for a while.

"You got to ask Mr. Georgie."

"Naturally." Suzanne had a few favors to ask George. Maybe it was just as well he had warmed to her lately.

****

Suzanne approached George that evening while he imbibed his solitary drink. He had not come home for dinner following his appearance at noon. She knocked on the door of his den loud enough to announce her presence, but not loud enough to make him slop his drink on another white shirt.

"Would you like something?" he asked every cordially, removing his stocking feet from the ottoman and trying to slip them back into his size thirteen shoes. Suzanne took another of the big leather chairs and accepted a gin and tonic that tasted a little oily without the twist of lime. Some liquor might move the conversation along, but she wanted him to know immediately this was a business call, not a social visit.

"Actually, I've run into a few problems with the inventory. I'd like to do a simple test on some of the silver with your permission."

"What for?"

"Well, to be honest, I want to see if it is all sterling or just plate."

"My mother was an infallible woman. If she said it was sterling, it is."

He looked more stubborn than angry with those vertical lines forming behind the bridge of his glasses and his rather nice full lips turned down in a frown. She tried again. "It's a routine verification. If you won't let me do a test, then I must assume it is all plate. That's the rule when it comes to silver."

"Okay, do the test. My mother was never wrong." He paused to take a big gulp of his drink and looked over at her. "I thought we might go to the Roadhouse for dinner on Saturday night. Maybe, we could discuss your results then."

She almost said she planned to be at Joe's Lounge on Saturday night, but changed her mind. She had more favors to ask, and one favor deserves another. "Fine," Suzanne answered. "What time?"

"Seven?"

"Good. Oh, could I borrow your car tomorrow? I have to drive into the city to get some supplies for my test, and I'd like to take along one of the small pieces to get a second opinion from a dealer."

"You'll have to get up early and drive me to work. I'm always in the office by eight."

"I don't mind."

"See you tomorrow early then." He seemed pleased to be giving her his car keys, and she felt a trifle guilty as she went off to bed jingling them in the palm of her hand.

****

They had another of those old married couple, companionable mornings. George slung a leather garment bag and his briefcase into the backseat. Suzanne did not ask about the baggage and drove him to work saying very little on the way. She half expected him to give her a peck on the cheek and say, "Have a nice day, honey," but he simply waved on his way to the office door.

Suzanne had no trouble getting to the larger town—only one road went there—and little problem finding Royal Antiques in the yellow pages. The ad stood out as the most artistic block in the antiques section. While waiting for Randolph Royal to open his shop, she killed some time drinking coffee in a diner across the street. When he arrived about ten, she gave him fifteen minutes or so to get comfortable, then wandered over. First, she peered at the playful display of antique toys in the window set up to look as if a child had just left the room and would be back at any moment to pile the blocks, feed pennies into the mechanical bank, and ride the rocking horse. A little brass bell rang as she entered and brought Randolph Royal hurrying to her side.

"Is there something special I could show you, or would you like to browse?"

She did not find Randolph Royal to be flamingly gay, not compared to some of the activists she'd known in college. Slim of build and balding, he wore a tidily-trimmed moustache to make up for his hair loss. His well-manicured fingers hosted several large gold rings. He was, perhaps, a tad too graceful for Port Jefferson tastes, and she suspected that town had a very low tolerance for the different. Though admiring his neat little shop with its clever displays, she recalled how her mother always said the best buys came out of dingy, cobweb-afflicted places. Almost without intending it, she adopted her mother's persona.

"I found these lovely tongs in a shop in New Orleans, and I've just fallen in love with the pattern. Beautiful, isn't it?" Suzanne thrust her possession at Randolph for his perusal and praise.

"I've been looking for matching pieces ever since. I have the creamer and the teapot, but I'm really looking for the sugar bowl. I saw your charming little shop while I had coffee at the café and thought I'd inquire before going on my way to Alexandria."

As Randolph Royal handled the small treasure, his palms became sweaty. "A set like this passed through my hands a few years ago, but a wealthy client purchased it. I haven't seen anything similar since then."

"Do you think your client would be interested in selling?" she pressed. "If you would give me his name and address, I could…"

"Oh no! Certainly not. He is a private collector and sensitive about his dealings. It would be a breach of trust on my part to divulge his name."

"Rotten luck for me. Oh well, I'll be passing through Port Jefferson on my way north. It's such an old town. Perhaps, I'll have some luck there."

"Believe me, there is nothing but nothing in Port Jefferson. I used to have the only antique shop in town and could barely make a go of it. With only a very few exceptions, the people are impossibly ignorant and crude with no appreciation of art or beauty. I tell you, it's a hell hole. I had to get away from that place."

Randolph clutched her arm and stared into her eyes in his attempt to convince her of the wickedness of somnolent Port Jefferson. "And to think my son is being raised there among the barbarians."

Now, he captured both of her arms and dropped the tongs. "The laws of this state are as backwards as that town, I tell you. I'm not allowed to see my son unless his mother or his Uncle Billy or his grandfather is present, and I cannot endure that family. Louise was so sweet and innocent when we married, but she turned out to be a true Patout just like the rest of the clan." He released her arms and sighed as he picked up the tongs. He plucked a polishing cloth from his coat pocket and wiped them off.

"I'm so sorry. I hope I haven't scratched it. Forgive my little outburst. Port Jefferson is a sore point with me."

More like a raw nerve, Suzanne thought, but

replied soothingly, "Oh, I do understand. My gay brother had similar problems after his divorce, but he was able to get permission to see his children as often as he wanted." She wondered how Blake would take her portraying him as a homosexual, divorced father when he was none of the above, a little payback for introducing her to Barry Cashman.

"What enlightened country are you from? It must be paradise!"

"Actually, it's near Philadelphia. I have only a limited time to spend here and had better be moving along. It's been a pleasure to see your shop." She extricated herself from a conversation becoming far too intimate for her tastes. She'd come to uncover a crooked antiques dealer and gotten his life story instead.

"Just a thought. I might be seeing my client in a few weeks. I could ask if he would be interested in selling the tea service, but more likely, he might want to buy your pieces. Please leave your name and address and telephone number. I will contact you if he wants to get in touch." Randolph produced two "Royal Antiques" business cards, beautifully embossed, white on white, with a golden crown above the name.

Thinking that the best lies are the ones closest to the truth, Suzanne wrote "Mrs. Patricia Hudson" boldly across the back of one card and gave her parents' address. Her mother would not mind being on one more antique store mailing list. She pocketed Mr. Royal's card and went on her way to the nearest drug store.

When she asked the druggist for dichromatic acid, he snapped that he did not run a chemical supply house. Suzanne wondered if he knew what the substance was.

Instead of arguing with him, she tried a placating technique and bought a bottle of aspirin, asked his advice about which vitamins he recommended, and finally came away with a small glass bottle of nitric acid. She could have tried a specific gravity test, but frankly had done that only once in one of her seminars and doubted the outcome. The hardware store down the street provided a set of small, fine-toothed files. Mission completed and suspicions inflamed, she made her way back to Port Jefferson by lunchtime.

Birdie, having prepared a luscious chicken salad full of chopped pecans and green grape halves, got a little put out when Suzanne barely touched her meal in a desire to get at the silver immediately. Birdie absolutely refused to give up the key to the cabinet and took exactly sixty minutes to finish her salad, crackers, iced tea, and a dish of ice cream. Slowly, Birdie swayed through the kitchen and dining room. Painfully, she knelt by the latch and fiddled with the lock for several minutes, then parted the doors of the sideboard with a slow motion gesture.

Suzanne snatched up the punch bowl and lugged it into the kitchen. Her set of metal files and the acid sat ready by the sink. Birdie gasped when she began to saw a very small notch into the base of the bowl. With her best chemistry class technique, Suzanne pulled the stopper on the acid bottle between two fingers and placed a drop on the scratch. The acid turned a sickly green. Most of the large pieces in Virginia St. Julien's collection tested the same way. Except for the candlesticks, George's infallible mother had amassed the largest assortment of forged silver-plated replicas she had ever seen.

The candlesticks still puzzled her. They tested as sterling silver. Then, she applied her file to the fine crack around the base and prayed she wasn't destroying a $5,000 antique. She hadn't. The base popped off like the lid of a paint can. Beneath the silver shell lay pure cement. A few of the large bowls had been similarly packed in the base. As for the tea set, only the overlooked sugar tongs were sterling. The rest of the pieces tested as silver plate adhering to a poor casting of the original set.

Birdie disappeared during the first act of desecration and pounded down the hall to the telephone. Suzanne could hear the maid reporting her crimes to George. Birdie returned and found her standing over the dismembered candlesticks, file in hand like a murder weapon.

The housekeeper crossed her arms over her big bosom and said, "Mr. George says not to worry, just to help you out. He's going down to Lafayette to work with a client for the rest of the week and check out a new business. Says he see you Saturday night."

Birdie stared fixedly at the candlesticks as she gave her report. "Just 'cause I said I didn't like those as good as the old ones don't mean you should of done that to 'em."

"Look." Suzanne tapped the silver base into place. "Now only the experts will know this is a fake, but I dread telling George his infallible mother was duped."

"Honey," said Birdie, "I'm glad I don't work weekends."

Chapter Six

Suzanne's story

No matter what Suzanne did, the days marched relentlessly on toward Saturday. Relieved, she found no discrepancies between the cards and the furniture downstairs at the Hill. She thought of all the nice things she could say about the Renaissance sideboard and the Wooten desk to temper what must be said about the silver collection.

She'd moved her cataloging upstairs and was working on the Jacques St. Julien gothic bedroom when the dreaded day arrived. With her nerves jangling by the time George returned at 6:00 p.m. sharp, she did not have enough courage to ask for an immediate interview. Saying "hello," Suzanne watched him pass with his bulging garment bag over one shoulder like a cape.

"I'm going to clean up and change. You might want to put on a dress to go to the Roadhouse," he directed, looking at the dusty jeans and T-shirt she wore, grubby from crawling around his father's bedroom.

Too hell with this weird and awkward date. She wanted to tell him about his mother's fraudulent silver collection right this very minute and simply get it over with, but George went into the bathroom, locked the door, and turned on the water. If she'd spoken up more quickly, she might have gotten out of the date altogether while he was still in shock.

To pass the time, Suzanne put on fresh make-up and the suit she'd arrived in. She set her hair to smooth it out, changed the style two times, and finally let it loose around her shoulders. At first selecting her highest heels so she could more nearly look George in the eye, she switched to low heels in case she offended him, or he offended her, and she had to walk back to the Hill.

Taking off the suit, she chose a black dress, a trifle short and low cut, to provide some distraction from the bad news. Oh, for heaven's sake, he was only George St. Julien, not some hot movie star or athlete she wanted to seduce. She should consider this a business dinner. She decided to take off the sexy black dress and put on the suit again, but struggled with the back zipper and caught it in the cloth. At that moment, George knocked and asked if she was ready to go.

"Not exactly. My zipper is stuck."

Nonchalantly, he entered her room as if he owned the place. Well, he did. His big warm fingers tugged the zipper free and up past the hooks of her black and lacy pushup bra. His hands lingered.

George murmured, "Ready?" and sniffed her neck. "Great perfume, terrific dress."

"I'm not wearing any perfume," she snapped.

This close, he smelled good, too, some kind of spicy cologne or aftershave, she didn't know which, and would hardly ask. Moving away, Suzanne kicked off her low shoes and put on her highest heels again. At least, she would be almost able to look him in the eye when she told him about the silver.

"Umm, nice soap or hairspray or whatever, then." George stepped back toward the door as if she had slapped him. "I meant to say you smelled nice."

"Thank you, but you shouldn't say things like that when we're having an ordinary, friendly business dinner, just boss and employee." There, now he knew exactly where they stood. This would not be a repeat of her problem with Paul.

With the heels, she barely reached George's shoulder, even slumped over as he usually was. Looking into his eyes—out of the question unless she stood on a stepladder. What an absurd idea. She would wait until after dinner and a few glasses of wine to break the news. She could do a "good news—bad news" routine.

"I've got some good news and some bad news, George. You have a lot of valuable antiques people will pay money to see, but the bad news is the family silver insured for $100,000 is worth about $10,000 because your mother was cheated on her deathbed by an unscrupulous dealer." Maybe he would laugh if she brought it off well, but she doubted it.

On the drive to the Roadhouse, they remained characteristically silent. She saved her energy for the evening to come. Once inside the eighteenth century building, Suzanne exclaimed over the ancient walls of handmade brick, the charming wrought iron fixtures, and the pewter plates. Her comments came out so loud in her nervousness, the owner, all aflutter, rushed over to seat them and restore the quiet ambiance of the place. He shook hands, called George by his first name, and asked where he had found such a lovely companion.

"She's working on my house, Bobby," George

replied rather tersely. "Maybe she could do something with the décor of this place, but she can't cook—something you have in common."

Bobby chortled and patted George on the shoulder as if the remark were a private joke between them, although George had not smiled when he made it. In a twinkling, Bobby went off to greet another customer.

"Wasn't that a little rude?" Suzanne asked, as insulted about the cooking comment as she was embarrassed for Bobby. She'd never cooked anything for George St. Julien—and now she never would, even if he had two broken arms and begged and pleaded.

"It's okay. I went to school with Bobby. He'd be the first to admit the food in this place is mediocre, but it's the only decent place in town to take a woman. Bobby is so very gay. He got his father to buy out Hippo Huval so he could do a little interior decorating with his boyfriend, Randy Royal."

"So Bobby and this Randy Royal are a couple? What do you know?" She stored that information away. "Well, the place is beautifully done. I think someone who has been to college should have a little more tolerance for people who are different."

"I'm sorry. I suffer from jealousy. Jeff Sonnier, Doc Sonny, is Bobby's father. I always wanted a father like that. Instead, I got mine, and Doc got Bobby."

"And are you jealous of Randy Royal, too?"

"No. I think he's a blood sucking leech." George raised his over-sized menu and hid behind it, conversation over.

He was right. The food turned out to be mediocre. The entire menu consisted of various fried seafood platters served with a tomato and shredded lettuce salad and a choice of French fries or baked potatoes. A glass of barely cool jug wine came with the meal. George ordered an additional carafe. They both decided on the shrimp. The entree came greasy and heavily breaded to the table.

Polishing off the wine, which Suzanne barely touched, George ended his meal with coffee. She ordered the bread pudding for dessert and bounced her spoon off the rubbery surface while delaying the inevitable. They had discussed nothing but the food and the weather for an hour. She summoned her courage to tell him that he was right about Randy Royal, when George let loose with another outburst. "I should have taken you into the city. This evening is a disaster. I knew it would be!"

His frustration made her pity rise to the surface. Another brief delay in getting the bad news would hardly matter.

"Look, we can salvage the evening. The night is young. Let's go dancing at Joe's Lounge!"

Suzanne couldn't tell if it was the light of the candle on the table or disbelief shining through George's lenses. "That's not a place you take a lady."

"Evelyn Patout goes there with her husband. Let's break with old-fashioned traditions. I'll take you. Come on!"

She barely gave George the time to pay the bill and tip the waitress, who looked like a perky high school cheerleader stuffed into eighteenth century garb. A new plan formed in her mind. She would show him a good time, get him a little drunk, and then tell him about the silver.

Suzanne fairly dragged George down the unpaved

section of Front Street. The bar sat close enough to the Roadhouse to leave the car parked on Main. Even before they passed through the red door of Joe's Lounge, they could hear the clink of bottles, the throb of the music, and the thump of heavy-footed dancing. Joe's came alive on Saturday night.

Crammed on an impossibly small platform bristling with mikes and fortified by amps, the musicians performed: an elderly man sawing at a fiddle; two middle-aged men, one banging a triangle, the other squeezing an accordion; and a bearded youth wailing out a song in the Cajun patois. All of them wore blue jeans and checked shirts. A banner swinging over their heads read "*Octave Dugas and His Boys,*" obviously, a family act.

Not a single table stood empty. They wove their way through the chairs and the cigarette smoke to the bar. Their drinks arrived served up by a secondary bartender since Mr. Hippo was engaged in tapping another keg. The set of dances ended, and a flood of thirsty patrons swamped the bar. Suzanne found herself next to Evelyn Patout who seemed to have come alive, too, once out of her guide costume and the Port Jefferson Museum.

She'd shoved her skinny shanks into tight, tight jeans. Her western shirt bore large red roses embroidered on each breast pocket. She teetered on heels higher than Suzanne's, though that hardly seemed possible. If she had been slightly overdressed for the Roadhouse, Suzanne was entirely out of place in Joe's Lounge. How she wished she had a large western shirt to cover what her push-up bra exposed. Evelyn did not appear to notice the wardrobe discrepancy.

"Say, you found yourself a date. Good girl! Ain't he a long one though? Would you look at the size of his thumbs? You know what they say!" Evelyn cracked Suzanne in the ribs with a sharp elbow while George cringed behind his drink.

"This here's my husband, Billy." She pulled on the hairy arm of a chunky man who wore his western shirtsleeves rolled up to his elbows and his jeans slung below his gut.

"We've met." George nodded and nursed his drink.

"Suzanne Hudson." She put out her hand, and Billy grabbed it as the band cranked up again.

"Come on, honey. *Laissez les bon temps rouler*! I do like a woman in a fancy dress."

"George!" Suzanne appealed.

Evelyn held up her arms in George's direction. "How about you and me, you tall drink of water."

"I don't dance. Have a good time," George said and finished the last of his first Jack Daniels on the rocks. He gave Suzanne a glance that said she was getting what she deserved for dragging him here.

"Well pardon me!" Evelyn claimed another man who looked like Billy's twin in a different shirt and with a larger belly.

Soon, Suzanne danced in a style she'd never danced before, the two-step and the Cotton-eyed Joe, slow dances with a funny beat and fast dances with complex steps, all to the tinky-tink accompaniment of a triangle. Overheated when she got back to the bar, she seized her diluted gin and tonic. George sipped his fourth Jack Daniels and half way dozed over the row of glasses. Billy Patout chugged an entire beer and pounded George on the back.

"How did an ole four-eyes like you get a girl like this, hey, Georgie? She's too much woman for you. I think my brother Rod would like to have her now I'm an old married man again. Hey, Rodney!"

Suzanne leaned away as the burly man with his arm around Evelyn came over to the bar. Billy offered a crude introduction. "This is my brother, Rod. Hippo says you got to come with a man, but nothing says you got to go home with the same one. Rodney shows a woman a good time. Don't you, Rod?"

Baring more tobacco-stained teeth than Suzanne cared to see in a human mouth at one time, Rodney grinned at her. He put a brawny hand on her wrist. Suzanne tried to shake him off. George, evidently, was not going to ride to her rescue, and she'd have to handle the unwanted attention herself. Mentally, she ran through a few self-defense techniques to use on strong but overweight men. Raising her hand sharply, she broke free and prepared to stomp on Rod's instep. She never got the chance.

"What do you say, Four-eyes? Rod will see your girl home sometime tomorrow," Billy prodded.

George woke up with the suddenness of an animal that had been poked once too often and unwound from the bar stool. He towered over Billy and Rod. Still hunched, he stood in the way a man does when he is guarding his vitals from attack.

"Don't call me that."

"What, Four-eyes?"

Evelyn heaved at Billy's arm trying to draw her husband away. Her high voice squeaked, "Now, Billy, now Billy, we was having such a nice time."

"You know what, Four-eyes? Your daddy hustled

you off to that fancy-dancy school before I could return the black eye you give me in grade school. And I got the strap, too, for fighting with Jacques St. Julien's kid. Daddy beat the shit out of me over you, Four-eyes. Son of the Capitaine and afraid to show his face in Joe's Lounge up 'til now, eh, candy-ass."

George did not reply. One of his long arms shot out at waist level and cut off Billy's air with a blow to the stomach.

"No, no, no! No fighting in Joe's Lounge! What for you want to break up my place?" Hippolyte Huval shimmied around the bar. "Your drinks are free, George. Now take your *jolie blonde* back up da hill. Your daddies would be mad over dis, yeah."

Rodney stepped up to George while Billy vomited on a table. George's arm swung up this time, and Rodney caught it square on the chin.

"Dere's more Patouts in dis room den you can take, Georgie. Come on now."

"Don't call me that, Hippo." George swayed and glowered over the fat man.

"Sure, George. Sure t'ing, Mr. St. Julien. Come now," implored Hippolyte, but he was too late.

Suzanne pointed frantically to a man, a slimmer, younger version of Billy and Rod, who had climbed up on the bar. He lowered a beer bottle toward George's skull, but George jerked back at the last second and caught the blow on the rim of his glasses. The bridge broke, and the two halves dangled. Blindly, George cleared the bar of his opponent and quite a bit of glassware, but at least he backed up as Suzanne dragged on one arm and Hippo dragged on the other. They rushed out the side door before any more Patouts could make their way over the fallen bodies and broken glass.

"Where's your car, *cher*?" Hippo turned a key in the exit door.

"Down on Main."

"Dis here's a fire door. I got to open it soon. Can you get him dere fast?"

"Sure. Thanks, Mr. Hippo. Come on, George. Want to run with me, George?"

Suzanne held out her hand. It took a minute for her to grasp that George could not see the help she offered. She led the way holding on to his arm, forcing him to a staggering jog down the alley running parallel to Front Street. Should have worn the low heels, should have worn the low heels, her shoes tapped out in the gravel. They reached the car, and she desperately searched George's pockets for the keys. He grinned stupidly at the body contact as if she werc feeling him up instead of trying to escape an angry mob. Keys finally in hand, Suzanne opened the door and sort of folded George into the passenger seat. She exceeded the speed limit all the way home.

George's height presented another problem when they got back to the Hill, but with him doubled over like an old man leaning on a short crutch, she did manage to get up the stairs. Suzanne let George fall face up on his bed. He grinned at her foolishly again.

"Well, I'm not undressing you, George St. Julien. You were very bad!"

"Bad," he echoed with some satisfaction. "Haven't had so much fun since I punched out that dumb shit in the second grade. Maybe it will all work out. Maybe."

He still grinned as Suzanne turned out the light and shut his door.

Chapter Seven

Suzanne's story

On Sunday morning, determined not to nursemaid George, Suzanne purposely fried bacon, knowing how nauseating that smell could be to a person with a hangover. Later though, when she heard him blundering blindly into the furniture in his room, she had pity on him and filled a cup with black coffee and a palm with aspirin. She went into his room without knocking, partly because her hands were full and partly because she doubted if George could find the door.

He stopped groping in the pine dresser where men's white briefs and balls of matched socks escaped over the edge.

"Coffee and aspirin, though you don't deserve them," she stated, setting the cup on the night table.

George blinked at her with his pale gray, bloodshot eyes. Without his dark-framed glasses, his face possessed a terribly vulnerable look despite an impressive dark stubble on his chin. The bridge of his nose had purpled and swollen, and he kept brushing his hair out of his eyes. For the first time, she noticed he'd abandoned the greasy hair cream, but had not quite mastered gel and hairspray. In fact, he must have had his hair styled in the city prior to their date. The cut looked fresh and far less dorky than his usual old-fashioned do. With too much on her mind last night to notice, she could hardly admire the remains of the styling now.

"Would you help me find my spare glasses?" he asked, his voice gravelly.

"Sure. Where are they?"

"In the top drawer somewhere."

She found them in a plastic case under a pile of neatly folded, white v-neck T-shirts. Athletic glasses in safety frames, they did nothing for George's looks. If anything, they were uglier than the black-rimmed ones he usually wore.

As he slipped them on, he said completely deadpan, "May I tell everyone you've been in my drawers?"

By the time she realized the always-serious George Washington St. Julien had been joking and reformed her appalled stare turned to a smile, he'd turned to the coffee and aspirin.

"I don't think that would be a good idea," Suzanne replied lamely.

George shrugged with his back toward her. "I think I'll take a cold bath," he mumbled. Taking the hint, she left.

****

The first Sunday in February turned out to be a lovely day, more spring than winter. Suzanne missed the flock of robins that had moved farther north when nature gave them this little nudge in the right direction. No one had brought in Saturday's mail or Sunday's newspaper. Savoring the day, she walked slowly down the long drive and back even more slowly as she sorted through the envelopes. Most were for George or

Occupant, naturally.

Her mother had written a long letter full of questions about the antiques. Mom hinted that just maybe, Dad could be persuaded to make a short trip to Louisiana when the azaleas bloomed. Dad did love a beautiful garden.

Dr. Dumont sent a timetable concerning her project and a scribbled note saying, "*C'est la vie*. Perhaps, Port Jefferson has other entertainment to offer." Tempting, very tempting to send her advisor an e-mail about the Patout boys and Joe's Lounge. Maybe she would do that this afternoon. She found nothing from Paul, thank God. When she returned to the kitchen, George sat eating dry toast and hunched over another cup of black brew.

"You make good coffee. Birdie's is always really strong because my father preferred it that way."

"Despite what you said last night, I make great bacon and eggs, too."

He turned a little green when she pointed to the bacon. "No, thanks. Not today."

"The mail." Suzanne placed his letters on the table.

He rummaged through the flyers. A business envelope addressed in dark lead pencil and bearing no return address fell out of the folds. "This is for you."

She drew her fingers back as if he handed her a red-hot poker. "Trash that, please."

Obediently, George put it in the waste can with the rest of the junk mail. They drank coffee and shared the Sunday paper in a very relaxed and domestic way. George's color improved as the double dose of aspirin took effect. Good a time as any to break bad news.

"George," she began, very seriously.

"Suzanne," he said with a hint of passion. This time she could tell he jested.

"This is serious, Mr. St. Julien," she snapped.

George put his hands over his ears.

"About your mother's silver. Most of it is, well, not as described."

"Not as described?" He gave her a blank stare.

"It's plated, not sterling, which considerably reduces its value, and some of it isn't even Victorian."

George took off his glasses and rubbed his eyes as if he did not want to look at the facts.

"I believe your mother was conned."

"No one ever conned my mother except my father when she married him!" He hit the table with his fist, and coffee sloshed from the cups onto the newspaper.

"George." Suzanne covered his fist with her hand, and his fingers relaxed. "Your mother was very ill, probably taking drug therapy, when all the switches occurred. It's very possible her judgment was impaired, or she might have been outright swindled. Perhaps, the dealer borrowed a piece and switched it without her knowledge."

"Randy Royal." His fist clenched again. "Always coming here when I was gone, always bothering her when the only person she should have been seeing was Doc Sonny."

Pale gray eyes could look fairly murderous, she thought. "George, George." Suzanne stroked his arm, and the glare in his eyes changed to a gleam.

"You still have Magnolia Hill. At first, I thought your mother had assembled all the antiques, but the documentation tells me most of it belonged to the Jeffersons and is original to the house. Even the gothic bedroom set was purchased by the first St. Juliens to live here. Your mother seems to have done the Eastlake parlor, your room and her own. Her major contribution came in creating the setting, the wallpapers and light fixtures, bringing it all together. Tourists love original furnishings. I'm going to write a fabulous history of the Hill that will bring them in droves."

"What about the silver? What about Randy Royal?"

"I'm not sure we can do anything without dragging your mother's reputation through the dirt, too. She isn't here to defend herself, and Royal could claim collusion. It won't help the tourist trade any if the work 'fake' is mentioned. I'll have to consult with Dr. Dumont about how to handle this. Meanwhile, you should confess that a 'mistake' has been made to your insurance company and lower your coverage."

"Goddamn. I always believed if things got rough enough, I could sell some of the silver. I wouldn't touch it while Mother was alive, and all those medical bills rolled in. Suzanne, it's all I can do to meet the mortgages, pay the heating and cooling, and put something toward the hospital debt. If Doc Sonny had taken what was due to him, I'd have gone under before she died."

Suzanne had never witnessed such personal despair before, not even in her own face when Barry Cashman left her for Beth Ann. Compared to this, all her problems seemed petty. And that's why she agreed so easily to the next thing George said.

"Could you delay telling anyone about this for a week or two, just until I get my act together?"

"Of course," she said and squeezed his hand. "Of

course." She had no idea then what an act that would be.

****

All week long, they shared the intimacy of two people keeping a secret. Once, she'd had a friend who had gotten pregnant. They kept the secret for a month until the girl made her decision and married the father. All during that month, the two of them would smile suddenly at each other and squeeze hands at odd moments to give reassurance everything would turn out right. She found herself doing this with George, and he responded with quick hugs.

To her relief, no more discrepancies turned up in the inventory, though she did come across some touching items while doing Virginia Lee's room. A little section of her files covered her collection of figurines. All of them were gifts from George, starting when he was six years old and continuing up until the year of his mother's death. The first figure listed—a pottery milkmaid, real discount store junk with sloppily painted features and "Made in China" stamped on the base. Virginia Lee duly noted the value as one dollar and the source as "Georgie."

The last figure in the collection, a contemporary Royal Doulton porcelain lady executing a graceful curtsy, Virginia valued at $250, a gift "from George." By the time Suzanne checked off each card, her eyes had misted over for the small boy giving his first gift and the young man spending $250 he could not afford on his dying mother. That evening when she had a nightcap with George in the Eastlake Room, Suzanne pressed his hand two times and sighed once, wishing she felt more than sympathy for this really nice guy.

George kissed her on the forehead outside her bedroom door when they went upstairs for the night.

No one would call George a talker. During their evenings together, he perused the newspaper or buried himself in some incredibly boring accounting magazine. She read a paperback romance she'd brought along for pleasure and sipped her drink. Now and again, she studied the portrait of Jacques St. Julien astride his white horse. She could make better sense of it now because an early Mardi Gras approached.

The little town came alive with excitement over the Courir. According to Birdie, the riders met every night at Joe's Lounge, planned their costumes and their route, arranged for the band, the chicken gumbo supper, and the *fais-do-do* where everyone danced until midnight. Suzanne could see an aura of that excitement and *joie de vivre* in the painting. What a shame that men who were good to their wives and mothers were seldom interesting. Why couldn't she fall in love with a sweet kind of fella instead of a rat like Barry Cashman? She had no answer to that.

****

George took her along the next Sunday when he went to get a chicken for the gumbo. He claimed he hated the Courir, a bunch of drunken rowdies, he said sounding like an old man. But the riders were sure to come to Magnolia Hill anyhow and would tear up the lawn with their horses if he had no chicken to throw. He overpaid an elderly black woman on St. Julien Street for an old rooster whose left eye had been pecked out by a younger rival. George fed the bird lavishly on cracked corn for its remaining two days of life.

As for Suzanne, she craved some excitement and a

little escape from heavy secrets and troubled finances. On Mardi Gras Day when every business in Port Jefferson put up its shutters and closed down, she watched from Virginia Lee's window for the approach of the Mardi Gras riders. When they came, they came grandly, charging down the shell drive on horses, black, bay, and pinto, their Capitaine riding a big palomino, leaving behind their slower entourage of wagons and a couple of tour buses. By the time the riders circled the house, the wagons had pulled up—one for the band, one for the beer and other beverages, and one for the captured chickens, donated sausage, and bags of rice and flour.

She went down to the kitchen door to join George. He wore a big flannel shirt, baggy jeans, and wrap-around sunglasses as if he were also in disguise. Clearly, he did not enjoy the event. The Dugas Boys pumped out the Mardi Gras song which they must have played dozens of times that day judging by the number of live chickens in the coops and the coolers full of frozen ones. The riders dismounted and began a burlesque dance.

Suzanne recognized Hippo Huval by his girth. He wore a maternity top and had a blond wig set in curlers atop his head. Big blue eyes, rosy cheeks, and big red lips adorned his mask. He linked arms and spun ponderously with one of the white-faced clowns having the squatty build of the Patout family. Cowboys and Indians in half masks cavorted together. Keeping order and looking fine in his purple cloak and gray Stetson hat, the Capitaine sat astride his palomino horse by the beer wagon and watched the festivities.

When the performance ended, Birdie handed over a

five-pound bag of rice one of the clowns heaved on top of the others in the supply wagon, and George reluctantly released the one-eyed rooster from its wire cage. Pandemonium broke out as the riders tried to catch that very canny bird. The rooster headed around the house, zigzagging and evading capture. Not wanting to miss a minute, Suzanne followed the chase.

Once around the building, the rooster fluttered up to the gallery railing and threatened his pursuers with raised hackles and a vicious beak as they tried to shinny up the pillars. The lightest of the Patouts standing on a burly brother's back nearly reached him. The bird took off, crashed onto the head of Hippo Huval, and after a brief entanglement with the curlers, launched himself into the thicket of magnolia clumps. The riders were on his tail when they stopped dead in their tracks. The rooster gave a triumphant crow from the top of a tree, and a white horse appeared, galloping up the hill from the bayou, its rider dressed all in black from boot toe to gauntlet to the tip of the plume on his hat. Under the hat, a piece of cloth tied pirate-style covered his hair. The upper half of his face hid behind a half mask trailing a swath of inky satin over the rest of his features. Through the holes in the mask, the eyes shone preternaturally blue. Across his broad chest, a golden bugle hung. The wind lifted the rider's cape, and the lining furled back over his wide shoulders like wings of red flame. He scattered the gang of chicken catchers as easily as a hurricane wind hurls clouds and rode straight for Suzanne. He reached down and heaved her across the saddle.

She shrieked in the spirit of the moment and asked breathlessly, "Are we going behind the barn for a kiss?"

The lips pressing against the black cloth did not smile. The dark rider wheeled the horse, cantered down the hill, and raced along the soft edge of the bayou. At first, Suzanne thought what a great story she'd have to tell Dr. Dumont and her friends back home, but when Magnolia Hill vanished behind its trees, and the saddle horn began to dig into her ribs, she suggested, "Don't you think we should go back now?"

He did not reply. Silently, he rode on.

"Okay. Enough is enough. Take off the mask, and let's go home."

No answer.

She began to struggle a little to see if she could slide off the saddle without killing herself. The rider stopped abruptly, pulled her up and around and tight against his hard chest. He kissed her so suddenly and thoroughly her lips bled slightly when she bit herself. Later, she would notice the bruises the bugle made on her breasts.

"Come on, man! You can do that some other time," a voice called from a copse of basswood. A huge black man pushed through the bushes. He wore a pirate's striped shirt spanning a very buff chest and a red bandanna with eyeholes cut in the fabric. One gold earring dangled from a long, brown lobe. The dark rider tossed Suzanne to him, and the pirate tied her hands loosely behind her back before she even considered fighting. As she gathered air for a scream, the accomplice gagged her lightly with a cotton scarf.

Her feet remained free. She could still kick—but this was a joke, a Mardi Gras farce concocted over beer in Joe's Lounge. Let's scare the newbie. They would probably take her downtown where the entire population of Port Jefferson gathered to await the riders' return and have a good laugh. So, she did not even consider striking out when they carried her to the boat.

Once aboard, she was simply too frightened to struggle. The boat, a shallow, narrow old Cajun pirogue, was not much better than a hollow log, worse in fact. Though the weather had been good lately, the bayou still ran high and rough with eddying, muddy water. She lay very still exactly as the pirate told her to do. The dark rider said nothing, though his very blue eyes glittered beneath the mask as he looked at her body.

The three started down river, the water moving them swiftly. The two men had trouble steering with their paddles in the strong current. Sooner than Suzanne thought possible, they reached the line of deserted warehouses along the Port Jefferson bank.

"Over there!" shouted the pirate, gesturing to one derelict building. The dark rider shifted his weight abruptly and dug in with the paddle. The pirogue turned broadside to the heavy flow and flipped. As the river sucked her under, Suzanne heard the pirate scream, "Gawd! I can't swim."

Chapter Eight

Linc's story

Linc and George St. Julien met freshman year at college, but knew *of* each other way before that. The Port Jefferson Capitaines and the St. Mark Eagles didn't play basketball in the same league, not by a long shot, but as star players, Linc St. Julien and George shared the headlines of the *Sentinel's* sports section often enough before they ever met in reality. After graduation, both signed on with the state university.

The big southern universities had finally figured out how great desegregation could be. Tall, black guys made up ninety percent of the recruited freshman basketball squad. They wanted guys like Linc St. Julien for sho', and those black b-ball players needed scholarships and were glad to get them, all tough boys from public schools who wanted out of whatever ghetto or backwater they came from—all except George, him being a privileged sort of kid and so very white.

The mistake made in the room assignment in the athletes' dorm was natural enough. Both came from Port Jefferson; both were named St. Julien; both were cursed with weird names their mothers thought up in revenge during long and uncomfortable pregnancies. So, they'd been christened George Washington and Abraham Lincoln, like it or not. The clerk assigning the dormitory rooms wasn't much of a sports fan and thought she had done a real favor, putting cousins or even twins together. Maybe, she just found the coincidence funny.

Fortunately, George St. Julien's parents, strange folks, did not see fit to get George settled at the university. They gave their son the keys to a new convertible, a pat on the back, a peck on the cheek, and sent him off alone with his belongings to the U.

Linc's mama spent two hours checking under the cots for dust and bedbugs, putting underwear in the dresser, and hugging and kissing on her only son with tears rolling down her cheeks, before she finally got out of the dormitory and on her way home. About fifteen minutes later, George walked in, carrying his genuine leather luggage. Two tall guys, one black, one white, staring at each other, saying nothing. Then, George threw one case on the free cot and started to unpack. About five minutes after that, Dean Emmet burst into the room apologizing to George all over the place.

"George St. Julien, grandson of my late good friend, the senator! If I had seen the dormitory assignments earlier, you would not have been placed with this, ah…this gentleman. I believe we have a private room available over in the new building. Shut that suitcase and come with me."

The dean was all over George like white on rice, tugging on his arm, his old bulldog jowls quivering and dripping saliva like a hound worrying a big knuckle bone. George stood there immovable.

Linc knew enough to stay out of the whole business. What did he care where the white dude slept? Up 'til that remark about the new dorm, this place didn't seem too shabby. Now, he saw it with new eyes. A second later, he saw the rich white kid in a new way, too.

George said, "If it's okay with the other gentleman, I'll stay here," quietly, just like that.

Linc kept his mouth shut and nodded, nearly breaking up when the dean recovered and backed out of the room while making some cryptic remark about what Huey Long had done to get votes. From that moment on, Linc knew George St. Julien was okay, but it took the other fellows on the squad a while longer to figure that out.

The first week or so of practice, the coach just studied each guy's styles, running the new recruits through drills, splitting them up this way and that. When he called out the first string of the junior varsity squad, George ended up the only white boy in the lineup. Coach placed him as a guard. Linc got center, his old high school position. He wondered how George felt losing the glory spot to a black man. If he was mad, it didn't show.

Two other dudes, both black, both centers on their hometown teams, played forward also. They couldn't keep themselves from roughing up George a little bit, tripping him up now and then, trash talking, calling him Georgie, the Friendly Ghost. Later on when they began to appreciate George for feeding them all those free balls, they confessed they wanted him to look bad so that a buddy of theirs, Lyle Woodrow, would be moved up to first squad. Well, Lyle bombed out on booze and drugs his sophomore year, but George stayed on right along through the championships junior and senior years. Part of his nickname stuck, too. Now, they called him Ghost, the only white guy on the all black starting team, the one who could slip in and steal a ball like he was invisible.

Being right out of high school, the guys might be forgiven for not seeing much in George at first. They played hard body ball in those public schools. None of the players knew the meaning of finesse until they got to State. Oh, George had done fine as a center for preppy St. Mark's. He had half a dozen inches on the rest of the boys, but here at State, the guys were all of a height, and George was no pusher. His real strength lay in being wherever a ball got handled sloppy. He'd sort of glide in and hand it off to the forward in the best position. Before the other team knew what happened, the ball headed the other way. He made the whole team look great.

That got George the respect he deserved because he was kinda hard to like at first. No riot in the locker room, he spent the weekends working on computer programs and advanced algorithms. He was some kind of math genius, at least compared to Linc St. Julien. Most of the team members majored in PE and spent a few hours each fall getting registered in the required courses taught by the easiest profs. One or two of the smart ones, besides George, took communications courses or business classes in case their basketball careers didn't work out. But, Linc St. Julien could not fail, no sir, not with George passing him balls to drive up the score, point after point.

Another thing about George no one could figure out was how someone with so much skill on the court never learned to dance, or how anybody on a winning basketball team couldn't make it with the ladies. About the end of sophomore year, Linc, out of the goodness of his heart, decided to help Ghost with his social skills. First, he tried to convince Ghost to learn how to dance. "Gotta dance to get those girls," he would say. He could tell George heard and took an interest because his ears turned red, the only part of his face not hidden by a math book.

"Why, I hear your daddy is the best dancer at the *fais-do-do*, a hit with all the ladies. I bet you have his talent hidden somewhere in that long, lean body of yours."

"I don't dance," George said, and he never did.

Linc had no idea then how it was between George and his daddy, but he began to figure it out. He could tell, though, George still had an interest in the girl part, so he fixed him up with his wild cousin, LaDonna.

LaDonna was real light-skinned and had dated white boys before. The talk around Port Jefferson said she took after her mother, Auntie Cerise, in more ways than one way, but Linc's mama wouldn't hear that kind of talk. She said it cast aspersions on her brother, Uncle Jack, a nice, caramel-colored guy. As a kid, Linc imagined Uncle Jack being cut up by little silver spurs in his side every time someone cast aspersions on his wife or daughter. Deep inside, he doubted he and LaDonna were blood relations. She was too easy to be kin to his mama. So, he didn't feel too bad about fixing her up with George.

They had some times with LaDonna being a real warm woman, and George, so grateful he'd let Linc and Doris use the convertible while he and LaDonna stayed in the room. When Linc left for the U, Doris, his high school sweetheart, did not take any chances on losing him. She enrolled at Southern close by, desegregated but still mostly black. She majored in Home Economics because she had faith in the power of Linc St. Julien. She wanted to be his wife and a mother by the time he made the majors, not a teacher or a practical nurse who had to earn a living.

A couple of times, Linc suggested they use the room while George and LaDonna took the convertible, but Doris said no. Definitely, she was the kind of girl a guy married, and well, if a man needed to find a little relief elsewhere now and again because of her being so strict, it was her own fault, Linc figured. Only a man of stone could watch George and LaDonna go at it and get none himself.

That didn't last though. The novelty of dating a six foot five white boy wore off over the summer for LaDonna, especially when he started talking marriage. Nothing scared LaDonna, not even Mrs. Jacques St. Julien. She might have accepted one of those pitiful proposals that went on all June, July, and August if she had been ready to settle down, but LaDonna had lots of corn to put up before she closed the kitchen. She went off to learn to be a dental assistant and left George alone at the start of junior year.

Still, he and Linc had an unforgettable season. George, not a man to mix up sex with the really important things in life, played as good as ever. The sports pages said Linc St. Julien was on fire. They both got a chance to start with the seniors and stayed on all the way to the national championships. Women crawled all over them, black women, white women. Then, Cherry Fontaine, who sort of specialized in winning athletes, discovered George. She'd been dating a senior who got benched early in the season with an injury. George took his place in more ways than one.

Cherry was a redhead, though that term didn't do her justice. Really, she had auburn hair, that rich red-brown color that usually comes out of a bottle. Maybe hers did, too, but the shade sure looked good on that long mop of curls hanging down below her shoulder blades in little twists and turns a man just naturally wanted to wrap himself in. Cherry did not go out for cheerleading, but she should have. She jiggled in all the right places when she cheered George on from the stands. Must have made her old boyfriend want to puke to watch it.

Cherry had no major. She switched about every semester. Maybe, she majored in finding a rich husband because she took courses sure to be full of men, a semester of computer science, then sixteen weeks of biology where the pre-meds studied. About the time the grades came out, she'd switch again. Cherry ended up in pre-law. She never got her degree, but she did get her a lawyer.

That man could have been Ghost. He had a habit of wanting to marry every girl he took to bed, all two of them. So, he hauled Miss Bounce-and-Jiggle home to meet Mother. A freakin' disaster. Virginia Lee served tea and cucumber sandwiches in the parlor, and the girl asked for a Pepsi. Even a black boy knows better than that. You eat what's served and say thank you in a fancy house like that, at home, too. Mrs. St. Julien tested Cherry on genealogy with the old "I'm descended from George Washington" bit, and Cherry said, "Really? That's so cool." At least, the bubblehead knew she failed the interview and announced their breakup while George still tried to figure out what had gone wrong.

Cherry went on to taking engineering classes and dating the ace pitcher of the baseball team. Just as well for her. That year George's daddy died riding home drunk after the Courir de Mardi Gras. He made the rest of the riders go to Mass, but for the first and last time, the Capitaine stayed on at Joe's Lounge and got stinking. Coming home, he tried to take a fence on a tired horse in the dark. Real bad judgment there. They found him, neck at a funny angle, all tangled up in his gold and purple cape. His white horse grazed right beside him, reins dangling, ground-tied the way western mounts are trained, a nice help if the man can crawl back into the saddle.

After the funeral, all the worms started coming out of the woodwork at Magnolia Hill. Seems old Jacques did most of his dealing on a handshake and a man's word. "You bring me fifty dollars cash each month, Rastus, and you can stay in that rat trap I own down in the Hollow as long as you live," he'd say, or something like that. Should have been as long as *he* lived.

When old black grannies and decrepit winos started showing up at the kitchen door on the Hill with soiled, wrinkled twenties in their hands, Miss Virginia, a true friend of the poor, started evicting. She wanted everything done proper, down on paper, and collected through her designated agent on Main Street. Those houses in the Hollow stood empty for a long time. During his last term, George needed a scholarship to return to college. You better believe he got it.

The U geared up for another hot season, only George roomed with someone else, which wasn't his fault. After his daddy died and Cherry took an interest in baseball, George began spending weekends at home after the season ended. But, plenty of girls wanted a piece of Linc St. Julien, and the room stood empty. Doris, being quick, saw the problem at once. With only one more year of school to go, she didn't plan on losing her man now. By May, Doris had gotten herself pregnant. Okay, Linc got her pregnant, his fault, too.

Now the only thing Linc's Mama didn't like about Doris was her religion. Doris came from a family Catholic through and through, her people being descended from St. Julien slaves like Linc's own daddy and never having seen the light. His Mama said no one ought to listen to that man in Rome, but to pray directly to Jesus like a good Baptist. Whichever way they thought, the answer came out the same. Doris said no abortion. Linc's Mama said listen to Jesus. Their wedding took place in June.

As newlyweds, they lived in Port Jefferson that summer. George stayed down in the Hollow a lot, trying to fix up his mother's rent places, but Port Jefferson isn't New York City. No one liked or trusted Virginia Lee. She got no takers on the property. George hung out at Linc's mama's house, spending plenty of time on the screen porch, eating yam pie, and drinking iced mint tea. Doris stayed trim and pretty during those first months, and the newlyweds had a perpetual summer honeymoon going on.

George liked their company, but he stayed in the Hollow for a purpose. Not to say he used people, but he used his brains. He had some of those rent houses filled by September. Papers had to be signed, and the rents went higher for the improved property, but he sealed the deal with a handshake. George asked Linc's Mama to act as his rental agent until he could graduate.

In the fall, Mr. and Mrs. Linc St. Julien got a little apartment of their own near the university, and George found a new roommate. Agents came waving big money around, tempting the big star forward to quit school and sign a contract with one of the NBA teams. But, Mama, the school teacher, said, "No way." That college diploma might mean everything some day. Her son would play out his senior year.

Doris picked basketball season to really pop out. She came to every game and sat in front looking like she had stole the ball and hid it under that stretchy pink top she sewed herself. The guys razzed Linc a little about Doris until they saw it threw his game off. Then, they let up, but the opposing teams caught on and said things that pissed him off so bad he couldn't see straight to shoot.

The Ghost, though, just kept feeding Linc the ball nice and regular until he got him settled down. Wasn't the best year, but the U made it to the regional championships, only not the Final Four this time around. That showed come draft pick time. Linc St. Julien didn't go as anybody's first pick, but he got a good enough offer to step up to the big leagues. He didn't blame the baby either for not getting a better placement. When little Tiffany came with her milk chocolate skin, big brown eyes, and velvet hair, her daddy wanted to make it as a star more than ever.

George "Ghost" St. Julien had some good offers, too. When Linc left for training, he wanted to say to his friend, "May all your troubles be little ones like Tiffany," but knew they wouldn't be. George turned down the contracts and went back to Port Jefferson to see his mother through the first of her leukemia treatments because she begged him to do it. He passed the CPA exams and set up his office in one of the family's rent buildings on Main Street. Virginia Lee decorated the place. He checked in with his rental agent about the problems she noted on houses in the Hollow and told her she had done a fine job, but he would be collecting the rents himself now. Without saying it, Odette St. Julien knew the people at the Hill could not afford her agent's fee anymore. Strange times when the rich become poor.

Old Jacques never had a sick day in his life and didn't believe in health insurance. Hell, he had wealth and good luck. And, he died early and easy. George carried the insurance the athletes were required to take, but that didn't cover his mama. She wasn't old enough for Medicare and way too proud for Medicaid. They would have had to sell the Hill and declare bankruptcy to get it, anyhow. Virginia Lee lingered on and on.

Being men, George and Linc didn't keep in touch much except for the phone call about the bombshell Doris dropped at Tiffany's first birthday party when she said, "And Mama's giving you a new baby brother or sister in about seven months." Doris found that a cute way of telling her husband. No way was Linc ready for another child. But when Crystal came along so tiny and delicate compared to Tiffy who, truth be told, had big bones like her daddy, he couldn't blame that child either.

Linc blamed himself that his career didn't go as well as it should. Now, Linc St. Julien was just one big man among a hundred big men. Lots of times he didn't start a game. Lots of times, he didn't get in a game. But when he went back to Port Jefferson and sat sipping a brew on the porch with George, he knew he had no troubles at all compared to his friend.

It seemed like George was turning gray, oh, not along the scalp line, but in his personality. Say "How about a little one-on-one." And he'd answer, "I'm not in your league anymore, Linc, old buddy," and have one too many beers. Linc's mama said George came to shoot baskets alone at the tattered hoop screwed to their garage, one ringer after another until little boys began to keep count. He'd give them a few pointers, and then go back alone to the Hill and his sick mother.

George took to slicking back his hair like his daddy used to with cream stuff. He even used the same cologne. Old Spice, maybe. Could be he thought this would remind his clients of the kinship or his renters of their lease, but it didn't help his looks any. Maybe George's old lady mother was trying to make her son over into a man like his daddy, but one she could control. Couldn't say anyone in the Hollow grieved when Virginia Lee died, though Odette St. Julien said everyone should pray for her soul.

By then, Linc came back to Port Jefferson for good. About the time Doris told him—this time there was nothing cute about it—that their number three daughter was on the way, he began feeling a little desperate. He made good money, but not great money, and keeping up the life style in a big city sure took its share. The signing bonus dribbled away, and his investments could only be called limited.

He asked George to find him some land in the country for his retirement. That much got bought and paid for. George served as his agent locally, but no one offered any big endorsements for a second-string player. Working hard on his game that year, Linc got it together. "Most Improved Player" they called Linc St. Julien. The next year, he started for the team, and Doris started on giving him a son, Little Linc. But, his knees didn't last. He blew out one, then the other—another career down the crapper.

That PE diploma his mama insisted on came in handy when the great basketball star had to go over to Port Jefferson High and beg for a job. He got on as a gym teacher and assistant basketball coach, glad to have the work. Not too much later, the high school made him head basketball coach. Lucky, and luckier to have George St. Julien as his friend, too. George saw to it that a brick house in the country got built with the last of the NBA contract money. He might have put in a word at the school board office, but he wouldn't tell if he did. Most of all, George never mentioned Linc's last big game except to say, "Tough break about the knees, but it's good to have you home again."

He owed George for that and for saying "if it's okay with the gentleman," freshman year. He owed the man for never razzing about Doris and her yen for motherhood. He owed his bro for all the basketballs he handed off to the star to dunk and dazzle the scouts in the stands. Linc owed George and wanted to do something for him. That's why he butted in when he got his mama's call, her all excited.

"Did you meet the nice girl working for George at the Hill?"

"No, Mama."

"Well, she's just right for him," his mama went on.

"And maybe George hasn't noticed that yet."

Linc stopped her right there. Mama's definition of a "nice girl" was any polite female who went to church regularly, not George's type at all. He liked those wild women.

"I'll check her out, Mama," he promised. "But I don't think…."

"I know what you think, Mr. Abraham Lincoln St. Julien. You think she's fat or ugly. Well, she isn't. She's nice looking, bright, and has a mind of her own, or I never would have met her. Now you just work on George. He might need a little help on this one, and he isn't getting any younger."

Linc gave up. "Yes, Mama."

****

Naturally, Doris thought fixing George up was a great idea. She thought everyone should be married and have four kids. She wanted to invite the both of them to Sunday dinner, but George needed to be sounded out first. He hadn't said a word about this girl as they watched the game the night before.

The two of them sat on the patio having a drink before dinner. The kids played on the gym set, and Doris fried up that special chicken of hers. Linc brought the subject around to women, and they talked about their old college days.

"I hear Cherry married a New Orleans lawyer, but sleeps with a pro football player. LaDonna doesn't have the energy to do it anymore since she had the twins, or so she tells my mama. Good thing you got away from them both, Ghost, my man."

"Yeah," George said like he didn't agree.

"Hear you got a good looking woman staying up at

the Hill right now. Anything happening?"

"Nope." George nursed his beer and looked away. Right then, Linc knew there was something in what his mama said.

"You never had any trouble finding women in the good old days, Ghost."

"Everybody loves a sports hero, Linc."

"You're the same fine dude you always was, man."

George belched for an answer.

"So when you're not a hero, you just have to put a little more effort in it. Do something romantic. And Gawd, get your hair fixed."

"My dad did just fine with his hair this way."

"You're not your daddy."

"Don't I know it? You should see the way Miss Suzanne Hudson ate up that portrait of my old man on his white horse. I hate horses."

"But you can ride, can't you? All you rich kids learn to ride."

"Yeah. I learned to ride on this nasty, little sonofabitch pony my dad picked out especially for me. My feet practically dragged on the ground. I went over that boneheaded bastard's head so many times I thought it was the only way to dismount."

"Take her riding if she's into mounted men."

"It's not just the horse. It's the cape, the hat, the eyes, the leer, the whole goddamn style of that kind of man. I haven't got it."

"So get it."

"It's not for sale, and I couldn't afford it even if it was."

"I don't know about that. Look, try the obvious stuff first. Have lunch together. Invite her out to dinner.

Try dancing. If that doesn't work, I have a plan."

Doris sent George home with some fried chicken and yam pie for his "friend." No surprise that the obvious didn't work because George had no confidence in himself anymore when it came to women. Seven years of nursing the ice queen had seen to that. He called saying his spontaneous arrival home for lunch with hot French bread hadn't worked out too well.

"Yeah, right. Nothing says romance like bread, George."

"She was upset over a letter in the mail."

"From a man?"

"I guess. I don't know."

"Great! She's on the rebound. You were always the best with the rebounds, George. Did you ask her out?"

"I was going to. I will."

"Look, it wouldn't hurt to tell her some of your problems without getting too wimpy. Women love to dish out sympathy."

"I don't think I can do that."

"Then, we'd better work on my plan. Mardi Gras is coming up. You go into the city to one of those big costume places and get yourself a cape, a plumed hat, the whole bit. I'll work on the white horse, one you won't be afraid to ride."

"This is ridiculous, Linc."

"If they want to be carried off on a white horse, then carry them off on a white horse. No wonder I was the one who always had to call the shots. You have no imagination, George."

"I'll feel like a fool."

"So long as you don't act like one. Now get on it!"

"Right, Coach!"

＊＊＊＊

George loosened up the next few days, especially after the brawl at Joe's Lounge. He didn't look like a man who kept in shape because he nearly always wore a suit that sort of hid his physique. He had that long kind of muscle, not the type that gets bulky. Linc and George, the two of them worked out with the weights and played ball as often as they drank beer at Linc's house. The strength of George's right arm must have come as a real shock to the Patout boys. How cool it would have been to see those rednecks pee in their pants, but blacks knew to stay out of Joe's Lounge. Still, getting drunk and flattening three Patouts probably did not improve George any in Suzanne Hudson's amber eyes. Passing out from a bad wound might, but passing out drunk had never been high on Doris' list of romantic ways to end an evening. Suzanne probably felt the same.

Plans moved ahead. George got the costume, a real beauty, all black with just a red cape lining. The costumer called it the Devil's Horseman model and altered it for George's length free of charge since he would be buying, not renting. The Ghost looked fantastic in that outfit except where the frame of his glasses showed above the black satin mask.

"Take off the specs, George."

"I won't be able to see."

"Whatever happened to those contacts you wore when we played ball, the ones with the blue tint that drove the women wild?"

"In my dresser, I guess. Mother said I didn't look like her son with those things in my eyes. I guess they were a little bizarre."

"Find them, or get another pair."

He tried to argue, but Doris barged into the garage just then to get Misty's bicycle. She gasped and put a hand to her throat, then relaxed. "Oh, George, if I hadn't seen those glasses I wouldn't have known it was you. You look so dashing. Getting ready to take Suzanne to Mardi Gras?"

Then, she turned on her husband. "Why don't we ever go to Mardi Gras anymore?"

Part Two of the plan was thought up right then—the part that turned out to be such a bad idea.

"Sure, baby. Why not? Can you make me a pirate costume?"

"Not like that. That's professional sewing," Doris said fingering George's cape like she could hardly keep her hands off him. "Would you just look at this heavy scarlet lining? I like the way they sewed on the braid to cover the seam when they lengthened the arms and legs. Very nice—like something you'd see at one of those fancy masked balls they have in New Orleans."

"No, no, honey, I don't need anything like that. I'll just put on some jeans and a tight striped shirt. You make me a mask out of a bandanna, and I'll wear one of my gold earrings from back in the days before I became a teacher. We can dress the whole family up the same way and take in the parades in Lafayette."

Doris liked the idea. Anything that included all the children softened her up.

"I only want to be back to see the Courir de Mardi Gras ride in, baby."

"That bunch of drunken cowboys!"

"This year is going to be special."

"Well, I can tell that," Doris replied, flirting her

eyes over George one last time as she wheeled the trike out for Misty.

By the time Doris left, George convinced himself to wear the blue contacts. Having a gold bugle slung across his chest would be a nice touch, too. Tiffy demanded five dollars for its rent and another dollar to get the bugle shined. She warned that any dents or scratches were taken very seriously by the conductor of her drum and bugle corps at Port Jefferson Elementary School. If the instrument came to any harm, she'd charge extra big time, Uncle George or no Uncle George.

"Yes, ma'am," everyone answered to that.

****

Linc found a white horse of sorts, one George could handle with no problem. The animal usually pulled Alcide Porrier's vegetable wagon, but during the winter off-season, Puffy went out to pasture for a month or so. His harness sores healed over, and his ribs almost became covered in fat again. The horse wasn't a problem, but striking a deal with Alcide Porrier came hard.

"Mr. Alcide, I'd like to borrow your horse for the Courir."

"Don't no black man ride wit' da Mardi Gras in Port Jefferson."

Being a basketball coach in a small town had its advantages. Mr. Alcide could have been ruder.

"For a white friend, and he wants a white horse. Only Puffy looks a little yellow to me around the mane and tail."

"Oh, we can bleach dat out, you got da money for da bleach."

"And he looks a little thin."

"Oh, we can feed him up wit' oats, you got da money for oats."

"Can he run, a little ways anyhow?"

"Ever seen a Cajun horse can't run?"

"Guess not. We'll need a saddle, a nice saddle."

"I can get a nice saddle if you got da money for a nice saddle."

"Fifty dollars the best I can do, man."

"Dat horse eat lotsa oats 'til den."

"Sixty and you be sure to get the yellow off him."

"Seventy-five, I shine da saddle, too."

"Done! Why you call him Puffy anyhow?"

"Oh, he puff up some when you put da saddle on. For five more dollar I make sure dat saddle's real tight."

Not wanting to spoil George's entrance if the saddle slipped, Linc paid out another five dollars. He picked up the tab for everything over the fifty dollars George contributed. That costume set Ghost back, but the shop wouldn't alter without purchase.

****

Part Two of the plan came absolutely free. What a great inspiration. Uncle Jack had a boat, a big, old-timey pirogue made from a hollowed-out cypress log that he'd lend. What could be more romantic than being abducted by a handsome stranger and paddled down the bayou to a secret destination?

This deserted cotton warehouse downtown had a broken lock. So, maybe every kid in the Port who wanted to sneak a drink, smoke pot, or make out, knew about the place, but for sure, Suzanne Hudson did not. An anonymous tip to the sheriff saying druggies were using the place would make the law walk through the building prior to Mardi Gras and get rid of any undesirables. Then, clean up a corner, stick a few candles in bottles for atmosphere, lay down some nice, soft blankets, stash some wine and chocolates, pack some clean clothes for the morning after, and put a new lock on the door—a perfect spot for a little Mardi Gras nookie.

George had to take things from there. He could pull off the mask and say, "Ha, ha, it's me." That would be like him. Or he could leave it on, untie Suzanne, and proceed to romance her from there. Or he could leave her tied up and…. Damn! The thought gave Linc the hots for Doris. The kids could go visit their grandmother this afternoon. What a crying shame and a pity George had no imagination. A good guy, but he might not be able to bring this off.

Mardi Gras day, the plan started off well. Puffy flatfooted along the river bank with his saddle still in place and George still in that saddle. Suzanne, slung over the white horse, had her cute little ass in the air, wiggling like she wasn't really scared at all, which she wasn't supposed to be.

Both George and the horse looked a little sweaty. After all, Puffy had been tied up out of sight below the ridge all morning, then asked to charge up a slope on short notice. George, to bring off the quick change, wore two sets of clothes most of the day so he only had the cape, mask, bandanna, gloves, and hat to slip on when ready to go. He put in the contacts and wore sunglasses to greet the riders of the Mardi Gras. Those blue, blue eyes sure looked wicked staring out from the black mask. He made an impressive move when he crushed Suzanne to his breast, as they said in those bodice-rippers Doris is always reading—and bruised her lips with his—okay, sometimes she read the good parts aloud to get things started in the bedroom—but George had no time to waste. Those crazy cowboys from the Courir might be following.

With Puffy tied a tree to keep him from wandering, Suzanne got hauled to the pirogue. She had a real solid heft for a girl, like maybe she worked out in a gym. She could have escaped if she'd put any effort into it, but tied real loosely, she didn't panic and went along with the joke.

George goofed when the water carried the pirogue past the warehouse and toward the bridge into full view of the town and everyone gathered on Main Street for the *fais-do-do* and gumbo supper. He tried to cut to shore too fast. Not all his fault, though. A pirogue is a bitch to steer. The last time Uncle Jack took anyone out in the boat, he made all the passengers wear life vests because, he said, the pirogue could get a little tippy. A little tippy, hell! Where were those life vests when the boat turned over?

"Gawd, I can't swim!"

Chapter Nine

George's story

Suzanne is dead, drowned in the bayou on Mardi Gras day. Linc went under and had to be saved. By the time he lay stretched on the shore and coughing up brown water, she'd vanished downstream. If her arms hadn't been bound, her mouth gagged, she might be alive, but no, they killed her trying to bring off a stupid, stupid romantic stunt. George St. Julien, CPA and murderer.

This whole crazy idea was Linc St. Julien's style, not at all the way George St. Julien would do things, but then he thought he never did have much imagination. Linc deserved to be called a showboat. Watching him do his stuff on the court, on the dance floor, with women—pure pleasure for one who always stood on the sidelines. A shy man needs a friend like that to make him take the chances he would never take alone. Linc is a generous man, too. He always left enough for good old George. During those years of taking care of his mother, George missed Linc's friendship the most, not the big games or the easy women.

Not to say he didn't miss being with women. When he first saw Suzanne Hudson at the airport, he thought she had warm brown eyes like LaDonna, but with little

147

gold specks in them, he noticed when he bent over to greet her, and a great, curvy build like Cherry Fontaine hidden away under that navy blue suit. George expected an academic geek wearing glasses even nerdier than the ones his mother picked out for him to wear, her hair all pulled back tight in a bun, not this young, sexy woman. He could tell right away she saw her new boss as nothing more than an employer. It took a winning game or a push from Linc for women to notice George St. Julien.

On the way back to Magnolia Hill, he put her straight to sleep with his company. George felt as gray as the clouds overhead, as uninteresting as the local crops in the fields. Sometimes, he expected to see gray hair on his head when he looked in a mirror. He'd been fading away ever since coming home to Port Jefferson to take care of his mother. Funny, they called him Ghost in college at a time when he was most alive. Now, the nickname fit.

George tried not to stare while Suzanne slept, but he liked the way her hair, the color of tupelo honey, curled softly around her cheek, the surprising candy pink of her half-open lips, the fullness of her breasts beneath the blue jacket. He felt a woody coming on and had to turn his thoughts back to ways to make Magnolia Hill pay for itself before he had to sell out. That always had a deflating effect. By the time they reached the Hill, he had himself tightly under control. Suzanne had gotten a little rest and was bursting full of questions.

They had formal coffee in Mother's uncomfortable parlor instead of in the kitchen with Birdie. He started to tell the George Washington's descendents story but Suzanne, being smarter than Cherry Fontaine, caught on right away. He would have enjoyed watching Virginia Lee and Suzanne Hudson going at it over tea and tiny sandwiches. George imagined Suzanne winning the conversation.

She passed your test, Mother, she passed, he couldn't help thinking.

Okay, he had another infatuation setting in. Linc said George was prone to them, that he didn't have to propose to every woman he dated. George thought he'd outgrown this failing with graduation, but his "dates" came few and far between afterwards, and he had no extra cash to pay for them. LaDonna knew they weren't right for each other and moved on. Cherry Fontaine—Mother said at least she least was white, but definitely trailer trash—had folded without a fight and found someone else. But, George raised his guard now. He did his best to nip this one in the bud by being as businesslike as possible. He would not make any stupid moves like the kid fresh out of St. Mark's all-male Academy.

He would have been safe if Linc had stayed out of it. George didn't know how his old teammate found out about Suzanne so quickly. He never mentioned her to him, but Port Jefferson is a small town, a place where people talk to their mamas every day.

Why did he let Linc talk him into the whole crazy scheme? First, Linc always led and fixed him up in college. Second, he always wanted to be like Linc St. Julien, the star player in the big leagues, the man adored by his mother, his wife, his children, and let's face it, lots of other women.

Why was it, George pondered, that women always wanted the bad boys, not a kind, intelligent guy who would treat them well and remain faithful? LaDonna and Cherry wanted the sports star, the big house, the presumed fortune. No chance he would ever be a star again. He neared losing the big house, and the fortune vanished a long time ago. Not much of a chance of being desired for himself. Chances. George decided to take this one, even with his brain and another good friend telling him, "No, no, no!"

The day he bought the costume and hung it up in his rented office space in Lafayette, he had a meeting with a long-term client, Robert LeBlanc, a cattleman from Chapelle, south of the city. Bob eyed the black plume, the red-lined cape, the whole shebang not yet concealed in the garment bag as they pored over his account in preparation for tax season.

"You wearing that for Mardi Gras? I just rent a tuxedo for the ball. Of course, I have to dress like a clown to ride on the floats in Chapelle, but I really, really don't do costumes unless I must. Besides, I thought you hated Mardi Gras."

Fine for Bob to say. His elopement with his second wife on Mardi Gras eve came pretty damn close to being a local legend, and George told him so.

"Oh, I see. You want to impress a woman. With that. I'd stick to a tuxedo. That's what I had on when Laura and I got hitched at Broussard's Barn. Of course, we'd both been drinking."

"There's more—a white horse, a pirogue ride." George laid out the whole scheme along with the spreadsheets they studied.

Much shorter than George, solid of build, and dark of hair and eye like most people having French ancestry, Bob shook his head. "Too elaborate. Lots can go wrong. Would be easier to get her drunk, and even then you have to face what you've done in the morning."

Sage advice he did not take. He felt he had to do more to impress Suzanne than wear a tuxedo. Those first fumbling attempts at spontaneity nearly ruined any chance he had with her. The lunch, a terrible idea, the dinner even worse, and that sideshow he put on at Joe's Lounge, a disaster.

He heard more about the fight around town on Monday than he could remember about it himself. Lonnie complimented him on showing some spine and putting the Patout boys in their place. He couldn't look his own secretary in the eye for most the day. But, the most troubling part, deep inside George enjoyed acting like an alpha male, like Linc, like his father. He had to go farther, be bolder if he wanted Suzanne to pay attention.

The only good coming out of that John Wayne episode—he won Suzanne's sympathy. She made it easier to tell about his trouble with Magnolia Hill than he thought possible. Suzanne liked to touch a person to give comfort. Her warm hands covered his. She touched his shoulders lightly. He hadn't felt a touch like that since Birdie said good-bye the day he left for St. Mark's Academy. His dad shook hands. His mother cried in her room. George went on to fantasize how Suzanne might touch a man in other ways. She had no idea what a brush of her fingers could do to him.

He wanted to be more than a person she could pity and pat on the hand. Linc's plan looked better every time she smiled his way. Mardi Gras is just a centuries-old excuse to do things a man would not ordinarily do, to be someone he is not while hiding behind a mask. The plan took his mind off the fake silver and what mayhem he wanted to commit on Randy Royal in real life. Randy could be dealt with after the Courir.

Mardi Gras day started out better than expected. Suzanne didn't seem to notice George sweated like a pig in August under the flannel shirt and baggy pants covering the Devil's Horseman costume and all but the toes of his boots. Pig sweat, didn't some experiment show women found the scent so attractive manufacturers used it as a base for cologne? Good, he needed all the help he could get.

Excited as a child waiting for the riders to come, Suzanne easily accepted his suggestion to watch their approach from his mother's room. She was like that about a lot of things, full of enthusiasm for robins and drawbridges and early flowers, ordinary, everyday things. He enjoyed that about her, but why went beyond male comprehension. Maybe, Randy Royal would have understood her better.

Still, her excitement about the Courir gave him the opportunity to slip out and check on Alcide Porrier's horse staked out of sight. Puffy cleaned up better than expected. With fifty dollars worth of oats and a good rest under his girth, he looked fairly spry. Another piece of good luck—the saddle, the very one once owned by his father, Jacques St. Julien, silver mounting and all. Old Alcide must have bought it when his mother sold off the horses and tack. Virginia Lee deemed silver saddles tasteless and probably sold it for a song. Its shiny rosettes sparkled now. Putting on his cape and plumed hat, George used them for a mirror, pleased with what he saw.

Finding a vicious rooster in Port Jefferson—no problem. Suzanne felt sorry for the one-eyed bird that would end up in a gumbo pot, but George had collected enough rents in backyards and around the Hollow to recognize a retired gamecock when he saw one. The granny who sold the cock figured the rooster's breeding days were over, but fed up on corn, he would give those riders one hell of a fight. He did, too.

They still hadn't caught the bird when the Devil's Horseman charged up the hill. Hippo and two of the Patout boys crossed themselves. The Devil's Horseman! Aiii-eeee! George threw back his head and laughed at the expression on their faces.

Not such a joke when he put his arms around Suzanne. He didn't want to hurt her or scare her, but could see she got into playing a part, too, joining in the game. They cantered away while the cowboys still said their Hail Marys.

They just about reached the boat when the saddle slipped an inch because of Suzanne's wiggling. George pulled her up and kissed her simply to be in character. Seemed like what his father would have done. The kiss grew harder along with another other part of his anatomy. He hurt her a little, but that's the way the Devil's Horseman would have kissed. Then, Linc said to hurry. For once, he wished Linc had let him take the lead. If he had been alone with Suzanne, they could have ended the farce right there or gone into the shady, private clump of basswood and made love on top of the satin cloak, the fantasy he really desired. But Linc gestured toward the boat and insisted on that damn rope and gag to "heighten the experience," he said.

Shit! That boat turned out to be the dumbest part of

the plan, free or not. When the pirogue capsized, he was the first with his head above the water. George hung on to the hull and scanned the river for Suzanne. Screaming his lungs out for help, Linc thrashed about five feet away in the slower water by the bank. George let him swallow one more mouthful of dirty brown water, then kicked the pirogue over to him and reached out a hand. Terrified, Linc just kept flailing and went under again. He pulled the master planner across the bow and kicked them to shore, all the while calling "Suzanne! Suzanne!"

Stripping off the cape, boots, and gloves, the mask and the sodden hat dragging at his neck by its cord, he threw the garments into the righted pirogue and began diving while Linc coughed up water on his own. The turgid bayou ran heavy with silt. He dove six times looking for her white blouse or fair hair, but no sign of Suzanne. George sat down in the mud next to where Linc still breathed hard and put his face in his hands.

"My God, Linc, we killed her. We drowned Suzanne."

Chapter Ten

Suzanne's story

Suzanne went into the water feet first, kicking off her shoes and surging upward, the loose bonds practically falling off her wrists. Surfacing briefly, she pulled the gag down around her neck, took a deep breath, and dove for the bottom, letting the current help her downstream. Nothing hurt except her pride.

She surfaced in the shadow of the bridge and looked back toward the boat where the masked man heaved the pirate aboard. Good. No one needed her senior lifesaving skills upstream. On one breath, she should have been able to go farther. Out of shape, definitely out of shape, even though she'd swum laps at the university pool whenever she could work the exercise into her schedule. Suzanne trod water in the little eddy beneath the bridge and watched the two maskers make it safely to shore. Judging by their postures, this attempted adventure had gotten a little hairy near the end, even for them.

She thought she heard her name being called, but with ears full of bayou water and a Cajun band pumping away nearby on Main Street, she couldn't quite tell. The tall man in black dove in, searching for her body. Well, they deserved the same kind of scare she got when they put her in that unstable craft with her hands tied. She took another deep breath and came up by the knotted rope dangling from the oak that she'd noticed on her walk back from the great-aunts' house. Crawling up on the gnarled roots of the tree, she huddled into its hollow bole. The day was mild, but the water chilly.

Shivering, Suzanne debated whether to go to the nearby house for help or boldly march over the bridge to join the party on Main Street and announce her miraculous resurrection. Her abductors would probably be there raising volunteers to dredge the river for her body, explaining their guts out about a joke gone wrong. What a great entrance—barefooted, a good pair of shoes lost kicking them off in the water in the best lifeguard tradition, and wearing a wet, white silk blouse now practically transparent and probably ruined. Her snug jeans, required dress for Mardi Gras in Port Jefferson she'd been told, clung even more tightly around her bottom.

The silver Navajo necklace, an expensive souvenir from her artsy-craftsy days, still dangled between her breasts. She'd toted it along to Port Jefferson, why? Because she thought the dashing, imaginary Georges St. Julien would have preferred it to pearls. The necklace with its turquoise pendant was the only bit of western wear in her wardrobe, so she'd trotted it out to display in this strangely cowboy oriented town. If it had fallen off, she would have demanded they dredge the bayou for *that*.

Suzanne tried the house first, thinking she might find a kind lady like Odette St. Julien who would dry her clothes and give her a hot cup of tea. No such luck, no one at home on Mardi Gras. She took another deep breath and started across the bridge. Her kidnappers had vanished, but their boat was drawn up on the bank. The loud band played on a platform erected on the lawn of the Farmer's Bank. People danced in the street, no undue commotion at all, no search parties being formed to look for her drowned corpse. Those two rats hadn't told anyone they'd killed her. In fact, all eyes suddenly turned in the opposite direction from the bayou.

Capitaine in the lead, the Courir riders bolted into town to the accompaniment of accordion and triangle and the squawk of doomed chickens. Hippo Huval's voice rose above the racket of wagon wheels rolling on the pitted macadam road.

"We seen a ghost, us! We seen a ghost!" he bellowed.

The Capitaine, a man named Jules Badeaux, put the cow horn to his lips and blew. Unmelodious but loud, it quieted the crowd. "No such t'ing, Hypolite. Dismount men. Get dose chickens to da cooks. Tap a keg and unmask!"

A small cheer went up, but almost everyone eyed Hypolite Huval, who took an enormous swig directly from the flowing tap and splashed more beer on his face and belly as a form of revival.

"We seen da ghost of Jacques St. Julien," Hippo swore. "Jacques, he come riding up da hill from da bayou, him. Had his same white horse and silver saddle, only his cape was black an' red, and his horn turned all gold."

"Shit, old man," interrupted Billy Patout, who shed his clown suit after delivering the chickens, and now appeared in his jeans and sweat-stained, black T-shirt with a skull logo stretched across his belly. "Jacques St.

Julien couldn't have been more than five-eight, and he's been dead ten years or more. That rider was plenty alive and at least six feet tall."

"You don't know no'ting 'bout Jacques, Billy. You just a kid. He looked six feet tall in da saddle."

"So why's he come back now after ten years? Tell me that, Mr. Hypolite."

"'Cause dis is Mardi Gras day, an' a blonde woman he want is living in his house. Dat's why."

"His wife died over a year. How come he don't know that if he's a ghost?"

"I suspect dey didn't go to da same place, Billy."

Their audience tittered. No one noticed Suzanne, dripping wet, on the edge of the crowd.

"Blue eyes. That rider had the weirdest blue eyes. I never seen eyes so bright. They bored right into me when he went by," the youngest Patout chimed in.

"Jacques always say he wished he had da blue eyes what da ladies likes so much. Maybe da Devil give him some."

"And a shiny new horn and a black cape. Shoot, Hippo, any minute now that rider is going to show up in town carrying Miss College Graduate on his saddle. I bet she was in on it."

"No, she wasn't!"

Suzanne hated to interrupt this really entertaining argument and draw attention to myself. She fluffed the blouse clinging to her pink bra away from her body, but the heavy necklace pushed the wet fabric back against her breasts again. A slight breeze ruffled across the crowd, and her nipples puckered up even harder. Billy Patout showed his appreciation by leering.

"What that ghost do to you, Suzanne, honey? Drop

you in the bayou?"

"Not exactly. Another man dressed like a pirate stood by with a pirogue. It capsized above the bridge."

"Well, you still look good to me, sugar. I like that sexy pink bra you got on." Coming up from behind her, Rodney Patout, put his large paws on Suzanne's shoulders and ground his solid belly against her back.

She turned to shake him off and saw George pushing into the crowd and gesturing to get the attention of the man with the Stetson hat and gold badge who was doing crowd control. So frantic, he didn't see her. She had to shout, "George, over here!"

He diverted from the straight line he was making toward the sheriff by shoving people out of his way. "Suzanne!" His big hands swept aside Rodney's clutch on her shoulders. Even less eloquent than usual, he said, "Suzanne, Suzanne", over and over again.

His hair had that slicked back wet look again. He'd changed his clothes and now wore a blue dress shirt open at the neck, khaki trousers and loafers, out of place among the jeans, T-shirts, and boots worn by the revelers, male and female. Sporting the black glasses taped at the bridge, George, inanely repeating her name, began to draw laughter from the riders.

"I'm fine, George. Look, I don't feel much like partying, and I'm still wet. Where's the car? I'd like to go home."

"I—uh—I came down on the band wagon," he murmured. "I was worried about you."

"Great. So how do we get home?"

"Just a second, missy." The man with the badge had answered George's summons. "Do I understand someone kidnapped you?"

"I think it was simply a Mardi Gras prank gone awry, officer."

"Sheriff Duval. You want to press charges against anyone?"

"Who? I have no idea who did it."

"It's a small town, Miss. You better believe I can find out."

"I don't want to ruin anyone's holiday. They were probably bringing me to the dance when the boat tipped over. The disguises, it's all part of the fun. What I could really use is a ride back to Magnolia Hill."

"Yeah, a real good joke, Sheriff," said the youngest Patout, the one who leapt out of the dark rider's path and crossed himself in midair.

"I tell you, me. Dat was da ghost of Jacques St. Julien come charging up da hill and blowing his horn." Listeners clumped around Hippo Huval to hear to his tale as George and Suzanne got in the police car. She didn't recall any horns blasting, only one prodding her in the chest.

"Purvis, you're on duty as deputy until I get back," Sheriff Duval called to one of the cowboy riders, "And don't drink nothing between now and then, you hear?"

"So what were you doing while all this was going on, George?" The officer put them both in the back seat of the patrol car behind the mesh screen as if they were prime suspects in a hoax. George swallowed, and the Adam's apple in his long neck bobbed. Being treated like a criminal unnerved him.

"I went to change my clothes. I had on a flannel shirt and got too hot. Birdie can tell you where I was while they chased the chicken."

"No need for a witness, George. Just asking.

Probably only Mardi Gras mischief. No harm done that I can see. If you have any more trouble up at the Hill, you call me. And you, Miss, are going to have a devil of a cold if you stay in those wet duds. I'll turn on my siren and get us to the Hill a little faster."

The shriek of the siren coming up the drive nearly caused Birdie to have heart failure, so she said. She thought the ambulance was arriving to collect Suzanne's remains, wherever they had been found along the bayou. The other birdie still stalked in the yard. The one-eyed rooster, forgotten when the rider appeared, scratched for bugs among the crushed shells in the drive. He flapped out of the way of the patrol car, saving his life a second time that day.

Birdie made Suzanne eat a bowl of steaming Mardi Gras gumbo laced with plenty of hot sauce before she bustled her off to bed in hopes of warding off an illness. Both she and the sheriff knew what they were talking about. By morning, Suzanne ran a fever.

Chapter Eleven

Suzanne's story

Dr. Jefferson Sonnier repacked his black bag while Suzanne lay propped on fluffy pillows in the four-poster and enjoyed the novelty of a physician who did house calls. In Philadelphia, they dragged their fevers to a specialist's waiting room. Doc Sonny, as he quickly told her to call him though she thought it childish, had a wonderful beside manner and an even better bedside appearance. Tall and lean, he possessed a head of iron gray hair sweeping back from a high and noble brow. His eyes, surrounded by just enough lines to give him an air of wisdom, were a serious blue-gray and set in a face marvelously long and craggy. She could picture him, captain's hat firmly in place, on the bow of a sailing ship setting off toward the horizon. For just a moment, she had the absurd notion he might be the dark rider. Then, her blurred vision snapped back into place as Doc Sonny dispensed the usual advice.

"Stay in bed and rest. Drink plenty of fluids. Alternate aspirin and Tylenol every four hours for the fever. More seriously now," Doc Sonny said as he swabbed her arm with alcohol and filled a syringe, "you could have picked up something more dangerous than a cold in that bayou. A lot of raw sewage drains into the water, and you have no immunity to local bugs. Not allergic to penicillin, are you? Good."

Suzanne winced as he eased the needle into her skin and wondered what this treatment would cost George, who clunked up and down the hall like an expectant father outside the door. He insisted on paying the medical bills.

The doctor expertly swabbed the spot again and covered the tiny dot of blood with a small patch. "That little swim shouldn't have brought on a fever so quickly unless you were already harboring a cold. Just in case, I'll give George a prescription for some antibiotics. Make sure you take them all, and we'll ward off whatever this is." His smile deepened the crags of his face and increased his air of benign authority.

"I've seen your face before—in a local history book, and I think, in one of the pictures at the museum. Are you any relation to Eli Jefferson?" she asked, ready to test her theory.

"On my mother's side. The Jeffersons are notoriously short of male heirs. No one white bears the surname now in this area, but it has lived on as a first name. I hope my daughter will see fit to use it if she has any offspring. You and Ginny have been the only outsiders to comment on the family resemblance, though."

Impressed by Dr. Sonnier's total acceptance of the fact that his gay son, Bobby, would not be the one providing the namesake, she was equally amazed that anyone would have called the stiff and proper Virginia Lee St. Julien "Ginny."

"Perhaps we both saw Eli Jefferson in you because Mrs. St. Julien and I shared an intense interest in the past more than in the mundane realities of the present," she commented.

Jefferson Sonnier considered her statement. "Ginny lived in the past. She held to a set of outmoded codes and standards, her source of protection and strength, I suppose, believing she was always right and the rest of the world in error. She had a Protestant background, yet she adhered to the indissolubility of the marriage vow far more than, say myself, with my Catholic heritage. She insisted on a formal mourning period for a drunken philanderer she ceased loving years before his death. She wouldn't consider re-marriage once her illness had been diagnosed because, and I quote, 'a wife must be able to fulfill the physical needs of her husband.' I suspect, Miss Hudson, the only thing you and Ginny have in common is George caring about both of you."

Right on cue, she heard George trip against the little gateleg table ornamenting the upstairs hallway. He replaced the vase he must have caught in midair with a thunk. Suzanne sighed as deeply as her congestion allowed. A fever and George's clumsy affection were more than she could handle right now.

"I didn't say you returned the feelings. Even propped in bed, you lack Ginny's ability to be a martyred saint requiring the unquestioning worship of her subjects. George is capable of worship. Be careful with him. That young man is inordinately upset over a little Mardi Gras prank. I'll send him back to work so you can get some sleep without all that thudding in the hall."

Doc Sonny closed the bedroom door behind him. Suzanne could hear him telling George firmly to let her rest. Then, the doctor doled out instructions about the prescriptions he wanted George to fill downtown this morning. She barely listened. Her eyelids grew heavy. The door clicked open. George mumbled something apologetically. He would be back at lunchtime with the medicine. She nodded weakly without opening her eyes. He went away. Suzanne heard Birdie's heavy tread on the stairs, and her voice as she asked the doctor to stop for coffee.

Then, she slept and experienced a wonderful dream. The well-maintained floor to ceiling window leading to the gallery slid upward with the smallest sigh of sound. Something warm brushed her forehead, then her fever sensitive lips. He kissed her very gently as if he knew about the small cuts caused by the masked man. Suzanne opened her eyes and stared into his strange, deep blue gaze. She put her arms around his neck where the black mask fastened. The satin felt stiff as it had been immersed in water, then dried. The dream, amazingly tactile, just kept getting better.

She drew his face toward hers. Putting his full lips against the hollow of her throat, he moved them downward into the V of the light, peach-colored gown she'd put on the night before instead of her usual oversized T-shirt. Had she hoped for this visit? He put one knee on the bed and rested more of his weight against her body. Suzanne closed her eyes the better to feel the length of him all the more. A small rivulet of sweat ran between her breasts, and her nipples pushed against the fabric of her gown where his hand rested. His fingers slid beneath the cloth and cupped her. She pressed him closer. If this was delirium, bring it on.

Then a noise like old hens fighting sounded at the bottom of the stairs, and her dark rider vanished. Suzanne opened her eyes as the commotion came closer.

"Now you give me that bowl, Esme! I made it. You'll spill it all over the place."

"I guess I'm not too old to carry a bowl up a flight of stairs, Letty, regardless of who made the soup."

Suzanne scooted the blankets up to her chin to cover any sign or scent of arousal. Dr. Sonnier, totally professional, had ignored the skimpiness of her nightwear, but she doubted if the great-aunts would let it go by without comment. Like ancient succoring angels, they descended on her sickbed.

"Look how flushed she is, Letty."

"And the window wide open." Letty closed it with a brisk downward motion that made the flabby wattles of fat hanging from her upper arms shake. She jerked Suzanne up by the shoulders and turned and poked her pillows before allowing her to fall back again, a relentless effort to make the young woman more comfortable.

"We brought you some nice, nourishing chicken rice soup." Esme tried to force a spoon past the patient's lips. "Letty made it," she said, giving delayed credit. "But Mama always said I had the most soothing hands around a sickbed."

"Eat it up, honey. It's still warm even if Willie's cab was slow getting it here. I simply can't believe they left you here all alone with the back door unlocked when you practically have pneumonia. I'll have to speak to George about his help. We could spare Sally for a few days until you feel better."

"Oh, no! I'm recovering rapidly. Honestly!" In her haste to show how well she felt, Suzanne sat up abruptly. The blankets slipped, and a spoonful of lukewarm chicken rice soup landed on one naked breast. The skinny straps of the nightgown had slipped or been drawn down to her waist. Letty raised her eyebrows. Esme tittered. Hastily, Suzanne slid beneath the covers and put her gown into place.

"You certainly look well enough," Letty remarked. "Quite healthy."

"I caught a cold from my dunk in the bayou, that's all. But thank you for coming." She hoped they would be mortified and leave. Certainly, she was embarrassed enough to draw the blankets over her head and hide.

"Nothing else happened yesterday?" Letty hinted.

"She means—she means—did he ravish you?" hissed Esme, leaning very close to Suzanne's ear.

"Who?" Suzanne asked, remembering her dream and feeling the heat of a blush spreading over her body even brighter than the fever flush.

"Jacques' ghost—the dark rider," Esme continued in the same hissing tone as an unlit gas pilot light.

"Rape. The word is rape, Esme. Did the man rape you, child?" Letty interrogated.

"No, of course not. It was only a Mardi Gras joke."

"Come now. I can see your lip is a little swollen. Did he rough you up a bit, girl? My Henry could be that way when he had a few drinks. Don't be afraid to tell me."

Before she could deny it, Esme added, "There is a bruise on your bosom. Perhaps you should see a doctor. You could be...well, you might be—"

She cut her off. "I have seen a doctor, and I'm not pregnant because I wasn't raped. His bugle caused the bruise when we were—dismounting." She hoped her fever would provide a plausible excuse for the waves of red washing across her face.

"Which doctor did you see?" The sisters, instantly and oddly distracted from the state of her chest, inquired.

"Dr. Sonnier."

The great-aunts exchanged a meaningful look.

"They say..." steamed Esme. "They say Virginia Lee wore sultry nightgowns like this. They say after she gave birth to Georgie, she couldn't wait to fit in one just like it again."

Esme laid her withered crone's hand on the slender strap showing on Suzanne's shoulder. "They say Dr. Sonnier gave her a shot so she wouldn't have to nurse her baby, so she could be in shape to do—you know—sooner."

"With him, with the doctor," added Letty.

"We never go to Dr. Sonnier. We go into the city, all the way in a cab if Georgie can't drive us."

"Who knows what Jeff Sonnier thinks when he touches a woman's body!" Letty ended.

"He gave me a very professional examination. Besides, George said Doc Sonny is an old friend of the family."

"Doc Sonny!" the sisters cackled. "He was an old friend of Virginia Lee's, that's right, but no friend to the St. Juliens."

Then, George came along and saved her from more of the same conversation. They all heard him coming awkwardly up the stairs. He cursed softly as he backed into the room carrying a small tray with a half-spilled glass of water and two pills on it.

"Aunt Letty, Aunt Esme. I thought I heard your voices from the kitchen. Why didn't you call me if you wanted to see Suzanne?"

The great-aunts looked ashamed of themselves. "We didn't want to put you to any trouble, Georgie," Esme answered with mock innocence.

"Well, let me drive you home. Suzanne is supposed to rest. I only came here on my lunch hour to bring these pills and check up on her. Birdie had some sort of family emergency after the patient went to sleep. She'll be back directly."

He set the tray on the nightstand and herded his elderly aunts toward the door. Suzanne mouthed a "thank you" to him when he turned back to her for a second. George smiled, rather sweetly, and reminding her to take her medicine, shut the door.

Suzanne swallowed the pills and ate the soup because Birdie wasn't around to ply her with food. She fell into a sleep so deep that whatever she dreamed this time evaporated when she opened her eyes.

This time, chaos in the kitchen awakened her. The setting of the sun left her room in darkness. According to the glowing hands of her travel clock, supper time had come and gone. She put on a thick robe and her slippers and made her way to the center of the disturbance, or—the scene of the crime.

The chandelier in the dining room illuminated the empty drawers and cabinets of the Renaissance revival sideboard. Every fish knife and asparagus tong had gone missing. The shelves sat bare of punch bowls and candelabrum. A fine black dust edged the drawers, coated the usually gleaming surface, and spilled down on the Oriental rug.

In the kitchen, Sheriff Duval loomed over a wailing Birdie. Unobtrusively taking notes, one of the deputies hunched in a corner. George hovered in the background.

"I been working here over thirty years. I never took nothing that wasn't give to me."

George intervened. "That's right, Sheriff. I had as much chance to steal that silver as Birdie. Why aren't you questioning me?"

"Why would a man steal his own silver? Besides, I already checked with the insurance company. They said your mother never upgraded the policy when the price of silver went sky high, so you are losing out. You'll get about $100,000 if the stuff isn't recovered, but you might have gotten more on the open market right now."

His deep-set dark eyes shrewd and considering Sheriff Duval looked closely at George. "You could be trying to collect the insurance and sell it both, but that stuff is traceable. We'll have alerts out to all the antique dealers in the state tomorrow. Miss Hudson, just the person I wanted to see. George was feeling protective, I guess, and wouldn't let me wake you, but Birdie took care of that. This has been quite a couple of days for you, now hasn't it?"

"Mrs. St. Julien's silver has been stolen?" Suzanne's mind felt as fuzzy as her dry mouth, but she could have answered the sheriff's question. Why would a man want to steal his own silver? Why? She knew.

"Correct. And you were in the house all day, right? Hear anything? See anything?"

"Not after lunch. I was sleeping."

"So soundly that stealing $100,000 worth of silver wouldn't wake you?"

"I'll answer that," George cut in. "She took a sleeping pill on doctor's orders."

Suzanne stared at George, amazed he would lie to keep her out of it. He noticed the expression on her face. "You did. Dr. Sonnier said young women couldn't be trusted to stay in bed even when they needed the rest. That's why I gave you two pills, an antibiotic and one to put you to sleep. I figured you would balk if I told you. The prescriptions are on file at the pharmacy. You can check, Sheriff."

"Guess that leaves you out of the questioning, Miss. I could use any notes you have about that silver, that being your job here, I'm told." Sheriff Duval eyed the inch of peach-colored lace her robe did not cover. He turned back to Birdie.

"So you were gone all afternoon because of a family emergency?"

"That's right, Sheriff Duval, sir."

"What was the nature of this emergency?"

"One of my boys crashed his car. Lionel, that's my husband, called right when I was serving coffee to Dr. Sonnier. He'll tell you. Doc Sonny waited in this kitchen here 'til Lionel come to take me to the hospital. My boy went into surgery for three hours, but he's gonna be all right."

"You left the invalid Miss Hudson alone in the house, and the back door wide open."

"Guess I did forget to lock the door since it stood open come noon, but this here is Port Jefferson. Hardly no one locks. And Doc Sonny said Miss Suzanne had nothing serious and didn't need no watching. I called Mr. George to tell him to check in on her at lunchtime."

"Did you take the key to the sideboard with you?"

"No. I never does. I keeps it on a nail up under the sink. Even Miss Suzanne don't know that, just Mr.

George, me, and Miss Virginia when she was living."

"Well, whoever took the loot knew. There isn't a mark on that cabinet or a fingerprint either. They opened her up, hauled it out, and wiped her clean while Sleeping Beauty here was knocked out. I'll want you down at the station tomorrow, Birdie Jones, to make a signed statement. A lie detector test might be in order, too."

Birdie's bulk trembled. The sheriff took note of it.

"Is that necessary? The lie detector test?" George asked.

"I think the insurance company will demand it, George. They may ask you to take one, too, but neither of you can be forced."

George's brow wrinkled, but he kept quiet.

"Step outside with me a minute, George. I want to have a talk with you."

The two men went out into the night, the note-taking deputy shadowing them through the kitchen door without closing it entirely. Suzanne went to put an arm around Birdie and watched George and Sheriff Duval through the crack left by the deputy.

Sheriff Duval did not bother to lower his voice. She suspected that the crack in the door had been left for her benefit.

"Judging by what she has on under that robe, your Miss Hudson might be an expensive piece of ass up from New Orleans, though she sounds Yankee enough to me. I'm going to be checking her credentials, you know. Now what goes on in a man's home is his own business, but that little caper yesterday set me to thinking. You know Jules Badeaux, the Capitaine, and he wasn't drinking. He says that rider stood way over six feet tall, real long in the leg. Now us Cajuns aren't known for our height. The only other man your size in Port Jefferson is black. So if you and Miss Hudson got yourself a little sex fantasy going, I say okay, fine, that's your business. But if you're planning to pay for it with your mama's silver, I'll be on your tail. Got me?"

George leaned over Sheriff Duval, looking directly down on the top of the lawman's Stetson, his neck so bent he resembled a shamefaced child. "Yes, sir," he answered.

Suzanne glanced at Birdie whose tears had dried. The housekeeper leaned close to the crack in the door and watched with the same amount of fascination she showed for the afternoon soap operas on the little portable television in the kitchen while she cleaned up the lunch dishes. Birdie rolled her eyes.

"Sex fantasies," Suzanne whispered. They shared a good giggle.

Chapter Twelve

Suzanne's story

As it turned out, the insurance company demanded a polygraph test of all three persons in the house. They had nothing to hide, right?

Birdie exited her test in tears, and George came out of the grim little room, serious and pale. The deputy, making sure they did not collude beforehand, led each person past Suzanne and directly into Sheriff Duval's office after their ordeal. The test administrator, brought in for the occasion and dressed as meticulously as an IBM salesman, beckoned her from the bench in the hallway. A little paunchy, a little balding, he looked to be around George's age but not as fit.

Her palms started sweating early. She felt guilty for no reason at all. The white-walled, windowless room with its single table and two chairs reeked of criminal intent. The light bulb overhead was not naked, but should have been. The man who hooked her up to the machine as professionally as Doc Sonny had done her exam was not a police officer, but an examiner sent out by Mutual Trust, Life, and Casualty. This came out in the chitchat as he attached the electrodes. "Call me Bill," he said.

Actually, the beginning of the test went no worse than a job interview. He ran over her name, address, age, and educational background. Suzanne began to relax when out of the blue, "Call me Bill" asked if she was having an affair with George St. Julien. That threw her for a moment, but she answered, "no", calmly and firmly, very pleased with herself until good old Bill started prodding about other affairs. How many? One, two? A dozen?

"Two," she answered truthfully.

How did they do it? The regular way? Oral sex? Whips and chains?

"Yes, yes, NO! It's none of your damned business!"

When he finally asked about the silver, Suzanne was so relieved to get away from the subject of sex that she would have confessed to anything. Aha, a tactic exposed. She gathered her emotions and clamped the lid down tight. She tensed only for a second when he asked her to estimate the value of the stolen items. Replying neutrally, she said she did not do antiques appraisals, had been hired to inventory and document the collection for historical purposes. Choosing her words carefully and telling no lies, she informed him that she'd heard the appraiser for the insurance company assigned a value of $100,000 some years ago.

Being out cold, Suzanne didn't have to lie about hearing and seeing nothing the afternoon of the crime. To a direct question on being involved with the theft, she gave a simple, quiet, "no." She rejoiced when he did not ask about that morning spent dreaming of a masked man, or if she had any suspicions on whom the culprit might be. The questions diminished down to the ordinary again, and then the ordeal ended.

Bill, detaching the electrodes, stroked her arm for a

second, gazed into her eyes, and asked if she'd like to do an evening in Lafayette with him before he blew this hick town and got back to Baton Rouge. So much for professionalism. She gave him the most emphatic "no" of the interview. He ripped off the last electrode and showed her to the door. Sheriff Duval would receive a copy of the test results.

Comparatively, the exit interview amounted to nothing. Sheriff Duval sat with his chair leaning against the wall, his Stetson pulled low over his eyes, and his feet in alligator boots propped on his desk. "I reckon none of ya'll are guilty, but I'll have to see about those test results first. Might be calling all ya'll back in. Something funny is going on up at the Hill, and I aim to find out what."

Leaving after that trite comment, Suzanne thought they might as well have acting out a scene from a Grade B western or a poorly written mystery and had to curb her smile as she exited the station. Her laughter bubbled up until she saw George and Birdie waiting for her in the gray sedan. In the back seat, Birdie wrung a wet handkerchief in her hands. George behind the wheel looked as if he prepared to drive in a funeral procession. The man was so transparent, so obvious at least when it came to her, Suzanne wondered how he survived the test. In fact, she half expected the examiner to throw open the station door as they drove away and shout, "I've found the guilty party, Sheriff. Arrest that man!"—another bad line from a poor script. But no one stopped them from leaving.

George's still sweaty palms slipped on the wheel of the car as he took the corners back to Magnolia Hill. Suzanne pitied this sweet man who had taken care of his sick mother and broke himself to save her estate. He simply was not cut out for intrigue or a life of crime. Still, some of the respect and liking she'd been feeling for George St. Julien had ebbed since he stole the silver.

****

Days passed. No one showed up at Magnolia Hill with a warrant for George's arrest. Suzanne stopped joining him in the den for a nightcap under the pretext of working diligently on her paper, which she did. Still, he rapped on her bedroom door three nights in a row and waylaid her in the hall to invite her for a drink. She refused to toast his clever solution to the problem of the fake silver. If the man wanted to steal his own silver, fine. Sheriff Duval would figure it out. Disguised by his drawl and his alligator boots, he did have a sharp brain under that Stetson, she suspected.

How the crime had been committed became all too clear to her as she worked over the facts in her mind. George knew Birdie left the house because of her family emergency. He gave her the sleeping pill and drove his aunts' home while the drug took effect. Returning, he unlocked the cabinet and hauled off the loot, hiding it somewhere or perhaps, simply dumping it, bobeches, grape shears, and all in the bayou. At least, he'd had the decency and enough wit to wipe off all of the fingerprints, most of which belonged to Birdie and her. With a scheme so plain and simple, she wondered why Sheriff Duval's squad car hadn't torn up the lane in a spray of shell and with red lights flashing to take George away.

A man connected with the case did arrive one Friday. A claims adjuster, he presented a check for $100,000 and a paper to be witnessed and notarized when he handed the money over to George. Summoned from her room, Suzanne signed as a witness, though Birdie could have done it just as well. She wondered if having her signature on legal papers made George feel safe from any accusations she might voice later.

George held steady throughout the signing, ironically taking place in the same room where the theft had been committed. They sat at the immense dining room table, George and Suzanne on one side, the adjustor and the notary on the other. At one point, she noticed Birdie's reflection in the sideboard mirror. She stood in the kitchen doorway and smiled as George seized the check.

As soon as the officials left after a series of solemn handshakes, George whooped in a way that shook the chandelier and bounded toward Suzanne, arms out, the slightly crumpled check still in one hand. She took a step back, so he grabbed Birdie instead and danced her around the table. "This pays off the second mortgage!" he hollered.

Suzanne looked on at what could have been a scene from a nineteenth century novel—master and servant rejoicing that the ole plantation had been saved. What did it matter if you took advantage of a few Yankees along the way? She felt used, more used than she had been by Barry Cashman, used by this clumsy conniver who had just knocked over an antique dining room chair. If George cashed that check, he'd commit fraud, and yet, she couldn't bring herself to turn him in.

She stalked off to her room while Birdie and George shared a glass of sweet wine in the kitchen, and answered a long, newsy message from her mother. Mom rattled on and on, saying again among other things, how great her daughter lived in a small, safe southern town for the moment. In Philadelphia, the Slasher continued to carve young women to pieces in their own bedrooms, such cheery news from back home. The Slasher was escalating, Mom said, having watched too many episodes of *Criminal Minds*.

At least, the weird notes from Paul had stopped coming. After opening a few, she blocked his e-mail and tossed any snail mail with his handwriting. He'd devised new addresses meant to sneak past her guard, and she had to block those, too. Now, she simply didn't open any mail she didn't recognize. Basically, Paul kept repeating the same theme: if she didn't return to him soon, he'd come for her and carry her bodily back to Philly—after he'd had his way with her. The messages went from simple warnings to elaborate, erotic threats involving ropes and her being spread-eagled across large feather beds, an oddly Victorian fantasy. No more Mr. Nice Guy. Suzanne no longer thought of him that way either. Mr. Sicko was more like it.

Should she call in a tip to the Philadelphia police about Paul's threats? Could he be the Slasher? Of course not. Paul, the nice, quiet guy in the next apartment, was still upset about being jilted. But, that's what the neighbors always said about sex maniacs after the criminal got caught. "I thought he was taking out the garbage in those big, plastic bags, not body parts. Who knew?" She pictured old Mrs. Minchin in 3-A saying exactly that. Perhaps tomorrow she should….

George knocked. She told him how very busy she was and that she did not care for any wine. Assembling the introduction to her paper, Suzanne revised the outline and began typing a businesslike report to Dr.

Dumont, mentioning the disappearance of the silver and stressing the uniqueness of the collection rather than its value. She asked if she should include the silver collection at all since it had been stolen. On the other hand, her notes were complete and the description of the items itself might be of value. She told Dr. Dumont that she planned to finish as soon as possible, perhaps by mid-April instead of May.

Then in a personal note, she found herself telling her advisor about the dark rider. She'd dismissed the incident as a prank in the letter to her mom and neglected to tell her about the dunking in the bayou or the erotic dream brought on by fever and drugs. Some things mothers should never be told. But she spilled it all to Dr. Dumont who would find the whole story exciting. Besides, thinking of the startling blue eyes and what might be under the black mask took her mind off the mess George had created with the silver.

After writing about that experience, she had trouble sleeping. Her letter to Dr. Dumont revived the thrill of the gallop to the base of the hill with the masked man and the crushing kiss just before the disastrous boat ride. Around two a.m., Suzanne crept down the stairs and made a sandwich and a cup of hot herbal tea. Having refused to go with George and Birdie for a celebration dinner in Opelousas, she was hungry, very hungry. Foraging in the freezer, she ate the chocolate chunk ice cream she found hidden behind a rump roast right out of the box. Around three a.m. back in her room, she put on the peach-colored gown, gazed out at the moon for a while, and left her window unlatched. Talk about wishful thinking.

****

The sound of George's sedan leaving woke Suzanne around 10:30 that Saturday morning. Alone in the house, she didn't bother to dress, just put on a robe and pottered downstairs to make some coffee. The carafe sat already full and hot with brew. Someone had set a place for her at the little oak table. She drank the slightly warm orange juice waiting there. A note from George on her plate said he would not be home until late in the evening, as if she needed to know where he went or had to keep track of him. She crumpled it up and tossed the paper into the waste can where it collided with a still sealed business envelope addressed in heavy lead pencil. Shivering, she picked the envelope out of the trash. Paul had written to her again. George, being protective, had opened the letter and not given it to her.

"I am coming to get you, and when I do I'll..." The same lurid stuff as before.

She mashed this note even tighter than the first and put it back in the trash where it belonged. Suddenly, juice and coffee seemed like enough breakfast. She put the biscuits George left wrapped in a napkin aside and tossed half a pan of congealed scrambled eggs out the back door. The one-eyed rooster came running. He wasn't a friendly sort but lurked nearby for handouts of any kind.

Dressing quickly, she worked diligently all day. The sooner she finished the job, the sooner she could go home, but maybe not to Philly. She might stay with her parents for a while. George did not come home by dusk. Since he'd made breakfast, she put together a simple dinner of salad and toasted garlic bread and heated a small frozen lasagna from the freezer. Suzanne ate alone when George did not arrive by seven.

Darkness closed in around the Hill so far from town, so far from anywhere. She left on a large number of lights until ten p.m., then thought about the utility bills and turned them out. Rain began to fall, gently at first, then hard enough to cover the sound of any footsteps in the mansion. She'd locked the doors of course. George had a key if not too drunk from celebrating to get it in the latch. Where was he anyhow? No use getting upset, acting like a child afraid of the dark, or more exactly, afraid of a few words printed on a piece of computer paper. Paul had been in Philadelphia four days ago when he mailed the letter. Probably, he was still there writing his nasty notes.

Foolish to wait up for George, she figured. At last, Suzanne shucked her jeans and shirt, then her bra and panties, and stood bare for a moment while she rummaged in the armoire for an old flannel nightgown. Somehow, she needed something warmer and more concealing than a T-shirt tonight. The peach-colored nightie hung on the hook inside the cabinet door next to the mirror bolted to the frame. She stroked the silky fabric for a second, and then shook out the flannel. With the gown half over her head, her arms still upraised, she caught a motion at the window in the mirror.

Unlatched from last night, the sash slid upward easily even in the dampness, the way it would for a strong man who gave it a good tug. She let the flannel gown drop into place, knowing he had seen all there was to see from the gallery. Black cloak, satin mask, burning sapphire blue eyes, he stepped into the room and crossed to her. He placed his gloved hands on her shoulders, took the worn, shabby material in both fists and tore it down the middle. The warm flannel pooled at her ankles.

She knew what would happen next with his blue eyes glittering over her, making her feel small and vulnerable in her nakedness, but it did not. He took the silk and lace gown from its hook and smoothed it over her body, down the thighs, across the breasts. He ripped the crocheted coverlet from the bed and wrapped it twice around her like a fantastic web of his own making. The mystery man stooped, picked her up effortlessly, and started downstairs. His black cape with its scarlet lining fanned out behind him in the draft of the stairwell. They went through the front door, across the flag terrace, his boots sounding on the stones, and out into the darkness.

Chapter Thirteen

Linc's story

Not good. No sir, not good at all. When Linc drove over to see his mama on Saturday afternoon, he found Ghost shooting baskets through that rusty old hoop on the garage. Crystal and Misty watched, and Linc was sure glad Tiffy wasn't there. Still steamed over bayou water getting in her bugle, she didn't feel too kindly toward the old Ghost at the moment. George did not need an angry kid in his face right now.

This situation reminded Linc of days past when Miss Virginia got on George about something, or when she lay up there dying at the Hill, making George pay for things his daddy done by keeping him next to her day and night. When George escaped for a little while, he came to Mama's house. Mama would give him a slice of yam pie, a glass of milk, and lots of sympathy. Then, he'd work it out shooting baskets or spilling his guts if ole Linc came around. Sometimes, Mama would call him to come over and talk to George. Today, she expected her son to pick up the kids, no call necessary. Sending the girls in to visit their granny, Linc sat down by the empty milk glass on the side steps.

"Ghost, my man, I thought you'd be out on the town with Miss Suzanne this weekend celebrating your good fortune. I heard Ernest Prevost's eyes just about bugged out of his head when you handed him that check at quarter to two on a Friday afternoon. Bet he had to work late erasing that lien against the Hill."

"Yeah." George went on shooting, bang-thud, bang-thud.

"Yeah. Yeah, is all?"

"Suzanne thinks I stole the silver. She hasn't said it out loud, but I know."

"Well then, she must have some feelings for you 'cause she ain't turned you in yet." That stopped George in his tracks.

"I didn't take it." George heaved the ball into Linc's chest. He caught it and took a few shots, bang-thud, bang-thud.

"You're about the most honest man in town, George. You wouldn't be doing accounts for the garbage man if people thought otherwise."

"Sheriff Duval seemed to have a few doubts."

"That's his job to hassle people." Linc passed the ball to George. Ghost needed something to do with his hands.

"How did the lie detector test go?"

"Not a pleasure. This guy, Bill, starts off with the usual name, rank, and serial number stuff. Then, he asks if I'm sleeping with Suzanne. I say no. He asks if I like girls. I say yes. He asks if I like boys, big ones, little ones. I say no, but he got under my skin with that. Then, he starts in on the silver. Did I steal it? No. Do I have debts? Big ones? Everyone in town knows that. Did I steal the silver? He came back to that half a dozen times, asking me different ways."

The ball hit the backboard hard, rebounded over the hoop and slammed to the concrete. George scooped it up. The *Port Sentinel* featured the case on the front page of its little rag every day, *"Heist Helps Historic Home."* The article started with a quote from Ernest Prevost declaring how it delighted him that Magnolia Hill was no longer in danger of becoming the property of the bank and ended with one from Sheriff Duval saying that work continued on solving the case despite the settlement with Mutual Trust. Making a big deal of it, papers all over the state followed the story.

"You must have done all right else Duval wouldn't have let you off."

"The trouble is, I know who did it, but I can't get Suzanne to talk to me."

"Bet the sheriff would listen to you. That would get her attention."

"No proof."

"Try it out on me."

"Randolph Royal spent a lot of time at the Hill while my mother was sick. He brought her things, took things away when I went to work. He cheated her, and I'm willing to bet he knew where the key to the sideboard hung. With Suzanne checking out all of the antiques, he must have gotten scared of being caught by me or the insurance company."

"One problem. Randy lives in Opelousas."

"But the light of his life lives here and eats lunch every day with his parents because he can't stomach the food at his own restaurant. Bobby goes home for a break, hears from his father, the good Doc Sonny, that Suzanne is in her room and sedated and Birdie is out with a family crisis. Bobby calls his friend. They clean out the cabinet to cover Randy's shady dealings with my mother. Randy moves the stuff along to the buyers of hot goods he already knows."

"I can see it. Suzanne should."

"She won't sit still and listen to me. Claims she's busy doing her project."

"Bet she wouldn't pull that stuff with the Devil's Horseman. He don't put up with crap from women."

George dropped the ball in mid-shot. "No way!"

"Way! She loved every minute of it right until the pirogue swamped. How did that costume dry out? You didn't burn it or anything?"

"You know what that thing cost me? No, I didn't burn it, but I paid an enormous dry-cleaning bill in Opelousas. I—uh—used it one other time." Ghost held the ball right up in front of his face, judging the distance to the hoop.

"You devil, you. You holding out on your ole buddy, Linc? What happened?"

"Nothing. We were interrupted."

"Look, I got this great idea."

George groaned, but Linc forgave him because they went back a long way. "My Uncle Jack has this duck camp about five miles north of your place in the swampy area where the bayou loops back on itself. It's real secluded like, but not too far to ride."

"Ride?"

"I saw Puffy kicking up his heels in Porrier's lot last week. He still looks real good. Vegetables won't be in for another month. I guess old Alcide doesn't need him and could use a little extra cash about now. We could get things fixed up for you and Suzanne by tonight."

The more he talked, the more George liked the idea, a romantic ride in the moonlight to a quaint cabin where no one would bother the couple until dawn. George and Suzanne could talk it all out, or do whatever else came to mind. Linc hustled George into the car before he could change his mind. Happy that George looked better, Mama waved from the porch.

The cabin was pretty rustic, the door not locked, nothing there to steal. Even if there had been, the thieves would never get it out in a truck. They had to walk in over this little spit of dry land Uncle Jack built up using sand and shell. The camp stood on stilts against the high water because sometimes the levee holding the river back gave in spots. Uncle Jack had hauled an old iron stove and a homemade table and chairs inside. When men went hunting out here, they brought sleeping bags and big coolers. Uncle Jack boxed off a little room to the side for a john. When a guy looked down through the hole, he could see the lake, but men don't care about junk like that.

Well, the place needed fixing up a little, but it was better than the warehouse with less chance of interruptions, nice and isolated. Unc Jack's camp would be a regular love nest by the time they got through redecorating Linc kept guaranteeing George.

It was, too, once they swept up and laid a nice fire in the stove and set out the hurricane lantern with one of the candles and matches Uncle kept in a waterproof box. Linc made a trip home for his very own deluxe air mattress and the gold sateen sheets Doris gave him for Father's Day a few years back. Those were lucky sheets he told George. Little Linc got conceived on those sheets. They covered that splintery table with the top sheet and put the fitted one on the pumped up air mattress. Linc sprayed around a little air freshener to sort of take the mildew smell out of the room and remembered to put a roll of paper in the john, women being particular about things like that. At night with the fire in the stove and the candlelight, the place could pass as a romantic hideaway. George and Suzanne would be gone by the full light of day, or else be so taken up with things of a sexual nature the surrounds wouldn't make a difference.

Linc left a cooler with two bottles of wine, cheese, and grapes, a big bar of chocolate, romantic kinds of things. He thought about oysters but didn't know if they'd keep. No sense getting the lovers sick. All told, he liked the total effect. Maybe he'd do the same with Doris one night if Mama would keep the kids.

After all the decorating, George went to get the horse, but when Linc stopped by Porrier's after stocking the cooler, George still hadn't closed the deal. He looked to Linc to chip in an extra ten bucks to get the silver saddle again and another twenty to shut up Alcide.

"You know, you boys, I heard what you been up to on Mardi Gras, yeah. But Alcide Porrier, he know a good joke when he hear one. Dem Patout boys, now, dey got no sense of humor. Wouldn't want dose Patout boys to find out, no. Dey never hear it from Alcide Porrier."

That Cajun bastard sat on his porch counting his bucks as George led Puffy away. Cost them another five to get the saddle put on right this time. They could have bought the horse for what those two rides cost.

"This was your idea," George reminded Linc.

Linc took the credit and shut up. After dark when it was about time to get going, George started backing out. They were sitting in Linc's truck waiting for the rain to let up while Puffy ate his oats in the rented horse trailer, another damn expense when the weather turned bad and George didn't want to let the animal with his dad's silver saddle stand in the rain.

"What if I screw this up again?"

"We all screw up sometimes. No big deal."

"Not Linc St. Julien."

"Well, the great Linc St. Julien has. Worse than you ever did."

Glad it was dark because Linc didn't want to see George's face when he told him. But a friend doesn't let another friend run himself down, so he let it all out. "Up there in the Big Time, I wasn't worth shit, George. My knees went bad on me. Doris was always pregnant, and I spent more money than I took in, mostly on women who weren't. I got kind of desperate toward the end and put this big bet on the other team. When it looked like we were going to pull it out of the fire in the last quarter, I smashed into my own man to keep him from making the shot. Racked up my knee so bad, I ended my career, but the bills got paid."

Linc kept staring out into the night. The weather turned uglier. For years, he had lived off of George's admiration. Now he was only a high school coach nobody remembered. He needed this man's friendship. George laughed, short and bitter.

"Well, Linc, I'd say we're two of a kind. That stolen silver was fake. I committed fraud when I handed the check to Ernest Prevost, and Suzanne knows it because she's the one who found out my mother had been swindled. I was trying to figure out how to deal with the situation, and the stuff disappears. Convenient, huh?"

"Man, you better be good in bed tonight. If I didn't know you better, I'd be thinking like she's thinking."

"Doris ever find out about your throwing the game?'

"Doris knew about the bills and the broads. I expect she figured out the rest, but she stuck by me."

"True love."

"Go get yourself some."

The rain let up. Linc drove up as close to the house as he could get. No lights burned around the back. They led Puffy around to the front facing the bayou and tied him to the pillar with the bullet holes in it. Nice detail, Linc thought. Where else would the Devil's Horseman hitch his mount? George let himself in and went up those stairs, quiet and swift in his court shoes to make his change.

Linc went back to the camp. By the time he got there, the rain let up a little. The water stood high around the spit, but he got in okay and lit the fire and a few extra candles. Halfway home and listening to music on the truck radio, he caught the storm warnings, more heavy rain coming, flash floods expected.

Linc drove on a ways with something gnawing on his mind, something about Uncle Jack's camp, some story Unc used to tell when they went out there duck hunting together when he was just a kid, some sort of horror story. No, not horror, but a disaster story about Uncle Jack getting caught out there once in heavy rains. Yeah, that was it. The levee gave, and the whole damn place washed clear off the pilings with him in it. Unc climbed on the roof and beat off moccasin snakes and nutria rats with their big orange teeth for two days until help came.

Suzanne and the Ghost would be at the camp by now and about to be interrupted again. Linc swung a U-turn on the rain slick road and very nearly ended up in the drainage ditch already filled to the top with water. The rain started coming again so fast his wipers couldn't keep the windshield clear. Afraid to miss a bend in the road, he crept along hauling that stupid horse trailer. When he arrived at where the dirt road turned off the hardtop back toward the lake, the little bridge over the swampy part had already washed out. The water rose fast coming at his truck engine. Linc backed onto the hardtop and got the hell out of there. Must be some other way to rescue Suzanne and Ghost.

Chapter Fourteen

Suzanne's story

The white horse waited by the pillar with the bullet holes. For a moment, the moon shone through a gap in the clouds, and the silver harness glittered like the dark rider's eyes. They mounted and passed in and out of light and shadow as the ragged clouds masked and unmasked the moon. The horse's hooves sucked against the wet earth.

"Who are you?" Suzanne whispered.

The rider covered her mouth with one gloved hand, then replaced his fingers with his lips. She asked again and received the same response. Each time she tried to speak, which was often, he answered with a kiss, an ever-deepening kiss. This time no bugle got in the way, and the horse seemed to pick its own path in the darkness. The sound of the hoofbeats changed as their mount thrummed across a small wooden bridge and came out of a cypress grove by the shore of a lake.

A stilted cabin stood out in the water at the end of a narrow path. Firelight glowed through the cracks in the walls. The dark rider carried her there, small waves lapping at his boots when the wind sprang up. The first step up to the hideaway sat under water, but inside, the cabin was dry and snug, shutting out the damp.

A pallet covered in gold satin lay near the antique

woodstove. He placed Suzanne there tenderly, hung his cloak and hat on a peg and threw his gauntlets aside. From a dark corner of the room, he brought her a glass of red wine. They drank and watched the flames in the open grate. The warmth of the wine, the fire, and his body spread through her from top to bottom. Not rape or abduction, but seduction.

At last, he unwrapped the lacy coverlet as if he opened a gift on Christmas morning and pushed down the thin straps of her peach-colored gown. Suzanne reached to unknot his mask, but he grasped both her wrists with one large hand, raised them above her head, and pushed her down against the satin. When he became preoccupied with her breasts, nuzzling, suckling, and lightly running his fingers along the soft sides, she began to unfasten the buttons of his shirt, one by one. This he allowed.

His skin shone very white against the sable of his shirt. Blue veins stood out across the muscles in his arms. A patch of dark hair, heart-shaped, covered his chest. She toyed with it and ran her fingers firmly over the nipples hidden there. He moaned and moved further down her body, dragging his tongue down her centerline, and supporting her hips with his big, cupped hands. He kissed the tender, sensitive skin of her inner thighs.

Suzanne could have lain there for hours reveling, but had to do her part. She rose slightly and ran her hands down his back to his buttocks, firm and lean. Reaching around his front, she fumbled with the stiff buttons on the archaic pants. He was long, so long all over. The boots presented a problem. He became impatient with them, sat up, heaved them off, flung them across the room, and then, he came to back to her. Suzanne reached out to cup him and stroke a truly urgent erection, but he took her hands away again and slid back and forth across the most sensitive spot on her body until her thighs ran slick with wetness.

The rain started again, drumming more loudly against the tin roof of the cabin than it had on the slates at Magnolia Hill. The wind whipped through the cracks and extinguished the candles. His face drew close. By the light of the fire, she gazed into his deep, blue eyes and gasped as he penetrated to the hilt. He paused to see if he'd hurt her. She dug her nails into his backside, spurred him on, and let him continue the whole night long.

****

Morning has to come, and everyone must open their eyes when it does. Suzanne woke not to the soft whisper of her name that she'd heard all night, not to the sound of gently falling rain or to the sweet trilling of birds, but to swearing. Her rider stood in the open doorway looking out at the flood. Water covered all but the top step of the tiny shack, stark in the daylight. The footpath had disappeared and beyond, water inundated the cypress trees half way up their trunks. The white horse was gone, but the black mask remained knotted in place. He'd pulled on the snug, black pants, and barebacked and bootless, he cursed their circumstances.

"God dammit, screwed up again! Fuck it!" He berated himself.

"Actually, you do it very well, George. Exceptionally well, I'd say."

"I'm not George. I'm the Devil's Horseman, dammit," he said hoarsely without turning toward

Suzanne.

She pushed off the coverlet and wrapped his ebony cloak about her. When he finally looked her way, she could see his eyes watering badly wetting the eyeholes in the mark.

"It is George, isn't it? Why don't you take out the contacts?"

"This time, I forgot to bring my glasses. I knew I should have gotten refitted for the soft contacts instead of using these old athletic ones, but I didn't want to spend the money. I forgot how much these could hurt when you wear them all night long. I forgot a lot of things." He frowned at the engorged lake.

"We'll be all right."

"Easy for you to say. You're not from around here. It could take days for the water to go down. If it rains again, we'll be swimming right along with the gators. This lake is full of them."

"We seem to do a lot of swimming together."

"Look, I just shoved a cottonmouth out of here with a chair leg when he decided to join us for breakfast. I'm glad you can joke about it."

"What's for breakfast, then—cottonmouth? I'm starving."

"Grapes, cheese, chocolate, and leftover wine. No water bottles. It's a good thing you weren't hungry last night because there is precious little of it."

"But I was hungry." She looked directly at the man in the mask. He flushed everywhere not covered by dark fabric. He had too much to own up to this morning.

"Are you going to tell me what this is all about?" Suzanne asked gently.

He sank down in the corner next to the ice chest containing the provisions. "Linc says if she wants romance, give her romance."

"The famous Lincoln St. Julien I've heard so much about?"

"The same."

"He's very imaginative."

"He always was a big hit with the ladies. Him and my dad, the original Devil's Horsemen."

"And you aren't?"

"No. I want to be, but I'm really not." George stared at his toes.

"George, come here." She patted the place next to her on the mattress. He stayed by the cooler but glanced up.

"Admit it, Suzanne. You pity and maybe like George St. Julien. At least, you did a few weeks ago. You came here with the Devil's Horseman."

She took her turn to blush. He was absolutely correct. If she had not held on to her delusion of a tall, dark stranger whisking her away on a white horse, she could have unmasked George at the start. Deep down, she recognized him from the first, even though she treated Sheriff Duval's suggestion that they were lovers as a joke. She didn't want to admit that her dark rider was George, plain, old George. Last night with those blue lenses so clearly defined in the firelight, she knew his identity for sure, but remained pleasantly surprised by the amount of muscle and stamina his gray business suits concealed.

"You're right. But, there is a great deal more to George St. Julien than meets the eye—or the hand—or the body."

He smiled a little at her truly pathetic joke. "If I told you right now…."

She held her breath, expecting something other than what came out.

"If I told you right now that I did not steal the silver, would you believe me?"

"Yes. I would believe George, but not the Devil's Horseman."

He unknotted the black satin covering his head and took off the mask. His hair, lank and sweat-soaked fell in his eyes. He pushed it back, groaned, and ran his hand over the dark stubble covering his chin. He became simply George St. Julien again, but a gorgeous, bare-chested George with a whole lot of potential.

He told his story then, featuring Randy Royal and Bobby Sonnier as the villains. This made some sense, only the timing of it bothered her—all the phone calls and driving that would have been necessary to commit such a spur of the moment crime. Suzanne pondered it over grapes and cheese. They finished the bottle of opened red wine, and George gallantly checked the bathroom for snakes before letting her use the facilities. She slipped back into the silky nightie and wrapped herself in the cape again. When she came out, George squatted on the edge of the mattress and stoked the fire with a meager supply of dry wood.

Feeling warm and cozy from the breakfast wine, she sat next to him. "George, I have an idea." He looked at her sidelong, hopeful, his bloodshot eyes gleaming. But no, they weren't going to have sex again right this minute.

"I've gone to Royal's shop before on the pretext of buying silver. I could go again and ask if he has something in the line of silver-plated ice cream spoons. I'm from out of state, just passing through again. He could sell to me safely. The spoons aren't the questionable pieces, but I'd recognize them if they came from your mother's collection. Then, we take the evidence to Sheriff Duval, and we've caught the culprit."

"And I have to repay $100,000 to Mutual Trust."

"You won't be any worse off than before the theft. I'll say I hadn't reported my discovery to you yet, or you could just keep quiet, take back the silver, and return the money."

"You'd lie for me?"

"I already have by keeping quiet this long."

"Would you marry a man deeply in debt?"

"I'm not sure. That would all depend on how well he made love with his mask off." She'd done it, truly done it, fallen in love with a nice guy—who was great in bed.

Isolated from the world, they had time for all the sex they wanted. The morning passed swiftly. Covered with only the black cape, they recuperating from trying out a new position fondly named "The Horseman's Bridle" when they heard the motorboat.

"Oh, shit," George said. "We're being rescued.

Chapter Fifteen

Suzanne's story

Suzanne finally got to meet the famous Linc St. Julien. Feeling "kind of responsible" for their predicament, he'd come to their rescue in his Uncle Jack's bass boat. She liked him immediately even if he did keep grinning and glancing at the stained gold satin sheet pulled half off the mattress. At least, he refrained from any wisecracks about George's half-buttoned pants or her ensemble of peach nightie and black satin cloak. She expected to endure locker room humor from the former jock and teammate, but Linc seemed so genuinely happy for George, she put aside preconceived notions about a man who would instigate stunts like these.

Linc smuggled them home with a minimum of fanfare. George and Suzanne sat together in the back of Linc's pickup along with the cooler, deflated air mattress, and the ball of badly stained satin sheets. He signaled them once to lie flat when a patrol car came up the road. She snuggled against George's chest in the bed of the truck and remained in that position until they came to the Hill.

Suzanne expected the interlude at the lake to change things entirely, but George became George again as soon as Linc disappeared from the scene. He went upstairs to put on jeans and a shirt while she, still clad in her best sexy nightgown, made coffee and sandwiches. George brought her robe from upstairs and very sensibly suggested they discuss the problem of the silver over lunch.

While she studied his body with a new appreciation and regretted the return of those black-framed glasses that made gazing into his plain gray eyes nearly impossible, George outlined the presentation of their suspicions to Sheriff Duval and his fiscal responsibilities to Mutual Trust. She ran her fingertips up and down his muscular arm until he moved out of reach, so she let him finish uninterrupted. Then, they argued.

"Let me try my plan first, George," Suzanne said, standing on tiptoes to rub his shoulders. He flicked her off.

"Tomorrow after I've thought out all of the financial implications, I'll share your ideas with Sheriff Duval." His tone implied "crazy ideas."

"No, George! Let me get the goods on Randy Royal first. Real evidence."

She liked the idea of trapping Royal single-handedly. All those Nancy Drew novels read in the sixth grade came to mind. She visualized the title on the spine of the book, *The Case of the Stolen Sterling,* starring that resourceful, honey-blonde antiques detective, Suzanne Hudson. George obliterated her fantasy.

"That is both dangerous and foolish. Let Duval do his job and search the shop."

Funny, he had not used the word "foolish" earlier that morning when they made love like the last two survivors of the Great Flood ready to repopulate the earth again. And she said so. George stomped out of the house and splashed down the lane. She watched him from the window, then went to change into something severe. Perhaps, the Nancy Drew novels had no sex in them because Nancy had to deal with stubborn, unimaginative idiots like George St. Julien.

When he returned carrying a damp Sunday paper and a mass of Saturday's forgotten mail, mostly flyers that went instantly into the trash, George tried to make up to her by putting a protective arm around her shoulders. This time, she shrugged *him* off. She went to work on her paper. George left for Linc's house, she supposed, but her mind continued to wonder how to confront Randy Royal in the morning. The various scenarios kept her company that night, too, because George did not come to her bed.

****

Miffed, Suzanne stayed aloof at breakfast. Whenever George reached across the little kitchen table, she managed to have her hands occupied with a knife and fork cutting into one of Birdie's superlative waffles or holding a scalding hot cup of coffee. Birdie had prepared a strangely lavish breakfast, which kept George at the table longer than usual. The housekeeper hummed "Strangers in the Night" as she waddled over to force more waffles on the couple, winked at George, and murmured scoobey-doobey-do in his ear. Suzanne wondered if Birdie had been talking to Linc's mama after services at the Pilgrim Baptist Church. At five to eight, Birdie made herself conspicuously absent by announcing she was taking out the garbage, an event usually done without fanfare. That gave George his

202

chance.

He stood behind Suzanne's chair and whispered, "I want you to stay out of this mess, Suzanne. I want you to be safe." George bent and kissed her cheek gently because she would not turn her head to accept a kiss on the lips.

"I'll call you this morning," he said and hustled off to the office. All the tenderness welling up with his kiss and his concern, she tamped down again, knowing he would be checking on her. Well, that's what cell phones were for—to be in contact anywhere a person happened to be—working on a paper at home or shopping for antiques in Opelousas.

Suzanne went about her job in the upstairs rooms and waited for his call. It came around ten on the Magnolia Hill land line. Perfectly cordial to George, she asked if he had seen Sheriff Duval. No, he said, the sheriff was late coming in this morning, having put in a long day Sunday checking the roads for accidents and helping out after the storm.

"Oh, when I see you later, you can tell me all about it," she replied innocently. "And, George, I may check out the attic today, so call me on my cell if you need to get in touch again. I don't want to drag dust and cobwebs through Birdie's clean house."

After he hung up, she called a number scribbled on a piece of paper the previous night. Then, she told Birdie she was going out to check the mail.

"Won't be here yet," she yelled over the roar of the vacuum cleaner she plied in the front parlor.

"I'll wait. I'm expecting some important papers for my project," Suzanne lied. By the time she reached the end of the drive, she could hear Willie's cab clattering up the hill.

"Business has sho' picked up since you been here, Miss Suzanne. Up this hill an' down this hill. I got me a new carburetor and a pillow for the back seat wit' the proceeds.

Considering she wore a dark skirt, she decided to avoid the chenille pillow covering the bare springs. The fuzzy fabric looked like a heavily shedding variety.

"To Opelousas, Willie. Royal Antiques." She flashed the address on Randy Royal's card at the driver and settled back to mentally rehearse her confrontation with the thief, a waste of practice as it turned out.

She asked Willie to wait for her, confident that it would only take a few minutes to wheedle a piece of stolen silver out of Mr. Royal with her clever ruse.

"Hello, it's me again," Suzanne warbled pleasantly, entering the shop. "Just on my way back home. I thought perhaps you found a few small treasures to sell me in the interval, Mr. Royal. You were quite right about there being nothing in Port Jefferson."

Randy Royal, sipping tea from a wonderfully translucent Limoges cup and paging through a copy of *Antiques* magazine at his sales counter, glared at her.

"You may drop the pretense, Miss Hudson, not Mrs. Hudson, formerly of Philadelphia, now of Magnolia Hill, Miss Know-It-All antiques expert. I have a few friends left in Port Jefferson, you know."

The memory of George and Bobby Sonnier exchanging words at the Roadhouse restaurant suddenly came back to her. The resourceful, blonde detective had just botched the job.

"Bobby told me all about the lovely girl staying with George St. Julien, what you wore, what you looked like. He thought we could all have lunch together one day and talk antiques. Bob is so naïve. He thought you were too fine for George. I set him straight on that. I told Bobby how you came here pretending to be someone else, snooping after the St. Julien silver. So you think you know something about Victorian teapots and candelabrum? I'm surprised you didn't bring the police right along and accuse me here in my own shop. I'm astounded you don't have a search warrant to tear the place apart. Maybe there's a punch bowl hidden in the rocking horse!"

Randy took a gulp of tea and replaced the cup against the saucer with a crack that made her eyes blink.

"You think I'm a thief. Well, I'm not. But I will tell you what I was—hagridden. Yes, hagridden by that old lady at the Hill who knew I wanted out of Port Jefferson more than anything on earth. She lured me with a cut of the profits when I sold off that silver. She told me what pieces to fake, what to sell off and when. And you know something else? She planned this robbery. I'm sure of it. Virginia Lee died before she could find someone crooked enough to carry it off for her. Why else would she sell the stuff secretly and replace it with fakes? She wanted her precious son to know nothing about it. Now here's the joke. You come along, and poof! The silver is gone on the eve of revelation."

Royal waved the Limoges cup, sprinkling the remaining droplets of Earl Grey in the air. Suzanne wished she had brought a recorder. Nancy Drew would have thought of that, but then, Suzanne Hudson, antiques detective, expected to purchase stolen merchandise, not elicit a confession. Not that what Royal said *was* a confession. If Virginia Lee commissioned him to do the sales and execute the replicas, they had a business deal, not a con job as George claimed, a business deal just shady enough to keep Royal quiet when the robbery occurred. After all, Virginia committed no crime in selling her own silver and replacing it with cheaper goods if she needed money and wanted to save face in the community. Only the possibility of insurance fraud made the deal dodgy.

"If you ask me, George is the thief. Like mother, like son, a streak of cruelty in the both of them." He thrust the cup at Suzanne and snatched it back.

"How could Bobby compete all those years with her son, tall, athletic, successful accountant? Bobby never had a chance with his own father. Either his medical practice or her up on the Hill took up all the doctor's time. You don't know how that hurt Bob." Royal leaned over his teacup as if he were about to cry into it.

Time to go. She did not want to hear anymore. Suzanne started for the door, a failed sleuth, but then turned.

"Where were you on the afternoon of the day of the theft, Mr. Royal?" she interrogated. Maybe she expected the full confession to come pouring out into the teacup. It did not.

"Right here. This is a one man show, Miss Hudson. If I am ill, a big, red CLOSED sign hangs in the window. That day, the store was open. I lunched across the way, called a good friend in Port Jefferson. The telephone records will bear me out."

"Your 'good friend' could have committed the

robbery for you."

"He dined with his parents and spent the rest of the afternoon at his place of business in full sight of several waitresses."

"So you have discussed this case with your 'friend' and worked out your alibis," she said, vaguely aware of having seen this episode acted out on a mediocre crime show.

"No alibis necessary, Miss Hudson, because we are not guilty." Randy Royal drew himself up with dignity. "Please leave my establishment." He must have seen the same show.

She had to write a check to pay Willie for the taxi ride. Only the tip came in the form of cash. The disappointment showed on the cabbie's round, brown face.

"Checks. You got to pay on all them checks come tax time."

"Sorry," she apologized. "Drop me off at the front of the lane, will you?"

She did get the mail on the way up the drive. Birdie remarked her shoes must be soppy as a sponge by now if she had been standing in the wet grass all this time. Since Birdie could see her perfectly dry footwear, Suzanne did not bother to explain. She had bigger problems. Paul's letter sat right on top of the mail. She shivered as if her feet really were wet. The crank notes seemed to be coming more frequently now that she'd blocked his e-mail addresses. They all said the same thing at the end. "I'm coming to get you."

****

Suzanne stayed close to George that evening. He came home late and remained preoccupied while eating the meal she reheated for him. Quiet herself, and unnerved by Paul's persistence, she remained unwilling to open the touchy subject of the stolen silver. George did that over the coffee and the slice of pecan pie he barely touched.

"Sheriff Duval never got in today."

"So you didn't present our theory to him?"

"No," he said, mashing the thick bakery crust into crumbs with his fork.

"Good—because we are wrong."

George gave her a grim look and speared a pecan, pushing it down into the gooey filling. He did not say a word.

"I went into Opelousas today and had a long talk with Randy Royal."

"I knew you'd try that. Look, Suzanne, I'm trying to keep you clear of this mess."

"That's not possible," she said, taking his fork and pushing the pie away. She held his hand to keep it still.

"Listen to me. Royal and his friend Bob both have alibis. In fact, Randy accused you. Like mother, like son, he said."

"What's that supposed to mean?"

"It means your mother was not being deceived. She commissioned Royal to sell off her silver quietly and replace it with replicas. Royal assumed you knew, that you and your mother plotted this robbery before she died."

"Do you believe that, Suzanne?"

From the intensity of his stare, she knew her answer meant more to him than the fact that she had defied him by going into town.

"The part about your mother, maybe. She was no

fool about antiques. I don't believe she intended to involve you. But we get involved when we care about someone."

"Mother. Mother would have been capable of it. She would never tell me, of course. She knew I wouldn't have the guts to carry out a scheme like this."

"I'd call it honesty or basic decency. Royal said you have a cruel streak. I haven't seen it. You still put out cracked corn for that one-eyed rooster."

George looked away. "I guess in Randy's eyes, I do. I gave in to the temptation to do to Bobby what the Patout boys did to me, especially after I convinced myself that Jeff Sonnier was my real father."

"That's a little fantastic, wouldn't you say?"

"Not when you are fourteen and begin to notice every time your father is drunk at a party or dancing with another woman, Jeff Sonnier takes your mother home—and stays for a while. What a perfectly matched couple—both tall, elegant, graceful. At least I was tall enough to build a delusion for a boy. As Jeff Sonnier's true son, it seemed okay to push Bobby around a little. Now it's just a habit he lets me get away with, I guess. A bad habit."

"Do you still believe the doctor is your father?"

"Of course not! Mother set me straight at the age of seventeen when I asked her outright. She said, 'Any son of Jefferson would have had more breeding than to ask. Your question is purely St. Julien.'"

"Somehow, I'm glad I never knew your mother."

"You could have handled her. Cherry was no match."

"Cherry?"

"An old friend." George colored slightly as if he

were overheated.

Suzanne could not resist a little innuendo. "Oh, yes. Odette St. Julien mentioned her and someone named LaDonna."

An expression so priceless crossed his face that she took a sip of her own coffee to keep from laughing and began to choke on it.

"Let's just say after the masquerade ended, I could tell you were no inexperienced virgin," she managed to say, still trying to clear her throat of hot liquid.

George did not miss the opportunity to change the subject. "Aren't you overdue for a checkup with Dr. Sonnier? Those lungs sound a little rough to me. All that riding in the rain was probably bad for you."

"Come upstairs," she teased. "I'll show you how awful I feel."

George carried her in those long, strong arms up the grand Victorian staircase. He undressed her and slipped her into a warm flannel gown, which she hardly needed after he finished stroking everything into place. Then, he turned down the covers on the four-poster bed and tucked her in beneath the blankets. When Suzanne reached up to unbutton his shirt and draw him down, George kissed her forehead.

"I think you should rest before your checkup."

He smiled and left the bedroom. Withholding sex for disobeying was so very petty.

Chapter Sixteen

Suzanne's story

George delivered Suzanne directly to Dr. Sonnier's office the next morning. He parked by the white picket fence and watched her walk around to the back office. She strolled slowly and glanced back a few times. George waved and leaned against his seat as if he intended to be there all morning, so she gave up and followed the brick path around the house, past the iris beds showing their first green spears.

Taking a seat in one of the rattan chairs on the rear porch, she settled in to enjoy the mild February morning. The azaleas showed plump pink buds, and early daffodils pushed up around an old, round brick cistern humping out of the grass near the copper rain spout. A tabby cat slinked from under the porch and leapt to the wooden lid of the cistern to loll in an early patch of sun. The lid teetered, and one crumbling brick slipped. The cat lifted a rear leg and began seriously licking its genitals. Too much early spring in the air had gone uncelebrated last night. Before her thoughts could go any further in that direction, the office door opened.

"Our first patient of the day. The doctor will be down in a minute, dear. I'm Helene Sonnier. I don't believe we've met."

The gray-haired woman in old-fashioned nurse's

whites held out a small-boned hand puffed out of proportion by layers of fat. On her left hand, a gold wedding band lay embedded in the flesh of her third finger. That her small frame could support so much weight and her white uniform could contain it amazed Suzanne.

"Suzanne Hudson. Dr. Sonnier wanted me to stop by for a checkup after my bout with some bug the other week."

"Of course. The girl from the Hill. I made a chart for you. Come in, and we'll get started before the waiting room fills up."

She led Suzanne through a portion of the house furnished with vinyl chairs and old magazines to the single examination room and kept up a pleasant professional chatter while she took the new patient's blood pressure, temperature, height and weight. Obviously a very nice person, but still Suzanne could not imagine Helene as the wife of the distinguished Dr. Sonnier. Perhaps, she was a distant relative instead of his next of kin.

"Are you and Dr. Sonnier related?" she asked casually.

"We've been married for twenty-eight years so you might say we're related, dear. We met during his medical school days. I was a student nurse and so short he could tuck me under his arm. He used to call me Tiny back then. Oh, we were quite the couple. My daddy owned a pharmacy in Lake Charles, and he was so pleased to have a doctor in the family he made Sonny's intern days a pleasure. We had this lovely apartment in Baton Rouge, and our daughter, Ellen, was born in the city. I would have liked to stay there forever, but nothing would do for Sonny but to come home to set up practice. When I saw this big old house from before The War, I could understand why he loved this town so. I wanted to fill every bedroom with children, but Sonny has very definite views on large families."

Mrs. Sonnier's multiple chins quivered. "Are you taking any medication, dear?"

"Only birth control pills." She took the package from her purse and let the nurse copy down the brand and dosage.

"Oh, the Pill. Well, Sonny will be glad to hear that. No woman should have more than two children according to Sonny. All of us should be on the Pill. Women in this town drag themselves down with childbearing, he says, and we must set an example for the community. Thanks to his restraint, we did. I didn't fail him there."

Poor, overstuffed woman, Suzanne could see how Mrs. Sonnier had failed her husband in other ways.

"He wanted me to work by his side, and I have for twenty-five years even when my feet were too tired take me to those dances he loved. But, I didn't try to keep him home because of me. I'd fix his tie and send him off to have some relaxation. A doctor needs that. Bobby, Ellen, and I would all sleep in the big bed until he came home from the ball. Sonny has so much energy."

The buzzer attached to the waiting room door shrilled twice in quick succession. Nurse Helene heaved to the feet that, once petite, now looked like bread dough rising out of her shoe tops. "Busy day," she sighed and left to listen to the woes of the two new patients.

In the interval, Suzanne mulled over Helene Sonnier's words and began to agree with Great-Aunt Esme about seeing a doctor in the city when Jefferson Sonnier appeared exuding his kindly bedside manner. She barely spoke to him as he checked her ears, eyes, nose, throat, and lungs.

"No harm done by that little dip in the bayou or anything else between now and then, Miss Hudson. I'm glad to see you are on the Pill. I usually take the time to counsel women of your age and attractiveness about birth control, but you have good sense and intelligence as well as physical attributes. I can understand why George hovers at your bedroom door. Just don't let him in if you forget to refill your prescription. Condoms are a good idea, too. Who knows where it's been, right?"

She recalled the day when the silver had gone missing, ashamed to remember that when half-feverish and half-drugged she thought Dr. Sonnier might be her handsome dark rider. The good doctor was just another man who cheated on his wife when she'd gained a little weight having his babies. Okay, Helene Sonnier had gained a lot of weight. Still, the doctor's wife had a sweet personality and showed complete, unsuspecting devotion to her husband. Suzanne felt like making good Doc Sonny squirm a little.

"If we married, I'm sure George would want lots of children. Such a pity his being an only child because his mother had a hysterectomy at such an early age. Was that because you botched his delivery?"

Dr. Sonny's bedside manner evaporated like the morning mist. "Actually, Ginny had a tubal ligation, not a hysterectomy, but that operation would have been unacceptable to her husband. Getting a woman pregnant again and again is a way men like Jacques St. Julien prove their virility."

Nearly snarling over past hatreds, Dr. Sonnier went on talking. "Ginny suffered terribly bearing her son. Jacques insisted on natural childbirth and a home delivery. I warned him that she wasn't going to bear easily, too narrow in the pelvis, but he denied her the comforts a hospital and a good anesthesiologist could have brought her. He said his own mother had given birth in that same bed with no more trouble than a bitch delivers puppies and his wife could do it, too. Ginny screamed for hours and hours before I was able to deliver her safely. George's vision problems might have been the result of that difficult birth. Ginny was one of my first obstetrical patients. When she asked to be sterilized, I carried it out."

Wow, so much for patient privacy, though Suzanne wasn't sure if dead patients counted. She had jerked open a door to the past and several large boxes of information fell out on top of her, but she still couldn't resist another turn of the knob. "And Virginia was eternally grateful to you."

By the tight look on his handsome, flushed face, she could tell she'd pushed too far and would be asked to leave an establishment for the second time in two days. Dr. Sonnier raised his voice and summoned the next patient.

"You may go, Miss Hudson. You seem perfectly healthy to me." He dismissed her entirely.

Back in the waiting room, Helene Sonnier had blown up a plastic glove to make a balloon for an irritable baby fussing in her mama's lap. She gave

Suzanne a cheery good-bye, hope to meet you again. Poor woman. As Suzanne stepped out on the porch a new theory about the crime came rushing to her. She would go immediately to George's office, brave his secretary, Lonnie Breaux, interrupt his work, and try out her new idea on him. Afterwards, maybe George would be up for an early lunch and a nooner. Feeling bubbly on this lovely spring day, she walked to his place of business.

Looking through the glass window of the office, she noticed Miss Breaux already had a pained expression on her face. Maybe she was perpetually sour, Suzanne thought as she passed into the reception area. As it turned out, Lonnie had cause to be irked. The high-pitched laughter of a woman spilled from George's inner sanctum. He laughed, too, a low rumble underscoring the female voice. George chuckled that way with Suzanne, but they hadn't had much opportunity or much reason to carry on like the twosome in the office.

"May I go in?" she asked Miss Breaux.

"Mr. St. Julien is with—a client at the moment. I'm sure he'll see you shortly. Take a seat."

"Oh, it can wait," Suzanne said, willing George to come out of his office so she could see what went on in there. At that moment, the inner door did open, and George asked Miss Breaux to bring coffee for Mrs. Angers. His new glasses must have been foggy because he did not appear to see his other visitor at first. Suzanne saw his client very well, however.

Mrs. Angers sat perched on George's desk, having shoved a calculator and several spreadsheets out of the way. She had red hair cropped fashionably at the sides and spiked into perky peaks on top of her head. The minimalist hairstyle brought more attention to her large, emerald green eyes and lashes thick with mascara. The woman wore a blouse of golden silk, boldly unbuttoned to show the top of a black lace bra and belted over black leggings displaying her long, long legs. Strappy high-heeled sandals encased her slim, pedicured feet with each toe painted a glowing coral. When the bimbo leaned forward to grab George's arm, Suzanne could see the sparkle of a pear-shaped diamond dangling on a chain in her deep cleavage just above a small butterfly tattoo.

"Rich divorcee or successful stripper?" she wondered. And George served as this woman's accountant?

"Miss Breaux, would you get us some coffee and pasties, I mean pastries, from the bakery, please. Take your time and get some for yourself, too," George ordered generously. Then, he noticed Suzanne.

"Suzanne! Great! It's been a day for surprises. Get a cup of coffee for Miss Hudson as well, Lonnie."

Plucking her sweater off the back of her chair as if she were tearing the heart out of a sacrificial victim who had interrupted her office routine, the secretary left on her errand. As soon as the door closed, Suzanne stalked over to George so she would not have to shout at him.

"Surprise? Was I supposed to walk back to the Hill after seeing the doctor? George, I need to speak to you—alone."

Too late, she noticed that Mrs. Angers had come up behind him. The four-inch heels on which she teetered allowed her to look down on Suzanne and cling to

George's arm for balance at the same time.

"Oh, Georgie, you devil, have you gotten this child into trouble? He was so wicked with college girls, don't I just know."

Suzanne expected George to blush and stammer, but he stood there content with being considered wicked. She felt hot, top to toe, for a variety of reasons as she watched the two interact.

George and the stripper looked fine together, about the same age, half a dozen years older than Suzanne—but that hardly gave them the right to call her a child. Mrs. Angers appeared to be very tall, at least in those high heels, and remarkably big-busted for a slim woman. Her red hair and very green eyes contrasted nicely with George's darkness. If she had been capable of objectivity, Suzanne would have said Mrs. Angers was just what George needed to put some fun in his life. Unobjectively, she felt she and George were having enough fun together without adding a third party.

"She can't be in trouble—yet," George roguishly denied to his "client."

Beginning to agree with Randy Royal about George's having a cruel streak, Suzanne scowled, and seeing her reaction, he sobered up.

"Actually, Miss Hudson is working up at the Hill. She was ill the other week. I drove her to the doctor for a checkup."

"And we have business to discuss," Suzanne added.

"Well then, George. I must go in search of a room for the night if I'm staying over to have dinner with you. I only intended to visit for an hour or so while I passed through. I never did send my condolences when

I heard your dear mother passed away. Ronald and I were having our own troubles at the time. I'm so self-centered, I'm afraid, but the divorce is behind me now. When I read about the robbery of all that silver from your lovely old mansion, I knew I wanted to stop by and cheer you up. Remember the old times when you'd come back to school from a weekend at home so low I practically had to crawl under you to give you a little pick-me-up. Remember?"

The divorcee ran one of her long, coral nails down George's cheek. Suzanne wondered if Mrs. Angers intended to give him a little pick-me-up right there in a public place in front of witnesses. Sure seemed so. Lonnie Breaux struggled to the door with four Styrofoam cups of coffee sitting on top of a flimsy bakery box threatening to collapse in the middle. Suzanne opened the door for the secretary and relieved Miss Breaux of two of the cups. She offered one to George while Lonnie shoved another toward Mrs. Angers.

"No, thanks. I really must go find a room."

"Look, Cherry," George began.

"Cherie. I changed it. Having a lawyer for a husband was so convenient for a while. Ronald felt 'Cherry Fontaine' sounded like a stripper's name."

"Or white trash," Miss Breaux added helpfully.

Suzanne nodded to show she agreed with both of them.

"Cherie Angers." She gave the name a strong French accent. "Has much more class than Cherry Fontaine ever did."

"*Basse classe*," said Miss Breaux under her breath.

"Cherry or Cherie, we have room for you at

Magnolia Hill tonight."

He took both of his old girlfriend's hands and smiled into her eyes. What a graceful gesture, one Suzanne had never seen George do, but perhaps, he channeled Jacques or the Devil's Horseman, her horseman.

"I'll call Birdie and make arrangements."

"And I'll be on my way. Until tonight, my dear Ghost."

Suzanne thought she might puke if George kissed Cherie's hand. Instead, he simply put an arm around his old girlfriend's waist to steady her as she crossed the cracked concrete of the pavement to her car. Cherie drove a two-year-old, racing green Jaguar without a scratch, ding or dent, parked at the curb. Somehow Suzanne had overlooked the out-of-place vehicle in her hurry to share a new theory of the theft with George.

She waited in his office while George completed an overly long good-bye, curbside, with Cherie. Jeez, he would see his old flame tonight. Catching up on bygone times could wait. She scalded her tongue taking an incautious gulp of coffee. Their conversation took so long she'd assumed her beverage would be cold by now.

George returned and spent a minute or two rearranging his desk before he felt like talking. When he did, he chose the topic of Cherie.

"She used to have long hair that hung down to here." He vaguely sketched two large breasts. "She's a real redhead."

But she's getting a little help from a bottle now, Suzanne thought.

"And she used to be rounder, you know." George

sculpted a well-stacked figure in the air. "But then, she's been through a lot. Her husband saw to it she didn't get a cent of alimony in an airtight pre-nuptial agreement. She got nothing but a few worthless gifts he gave her over the years."

"I really feel sorry for her, left with only a nearly new Jaguar, expensive clothes, and a diamond worth enough to feed a family of three for a year." Suzanne burnt herself again taking another gulp of coffee. "Look, I know who stole the silver."

"Again?" George snorted.

She could see his mind remained in another time when he reigned as the Ghost, a sports hero with a red-haired girlfriend and no financial worries, disgusting when they had a crime to solve.

"Okay, you don't want to listen. Then, drive me home. Tomorrow night, I'll invite a few guests to dinner. Maybe they will want to hear what I have to say."

"If you had decided to leave a little sooner, you could have ridden with Cherie," George said, annoyed, but then, so was she.

"I didn't want to ride with Cherry!" Suzanne shouted. "I want to ride with you."

"Don't be a child, Suzanne. I still have to work for a living, and you could have saved me some time."

"You had enough time to listen to poor Mrs. Angers' sob story," she shrilled at him. "And you—you are acting like an over-thirty has-been trying to relive his youth."

She stopped from saying "nanny-nanny-boo-boo" and sticking out her tongue. She really was behaving childishly over George, the real George. From his expression, Suzanne knew she'd wounded him. Sticks and stones *and* words can hurt you.

He did drive her back to the Hill at top speed and through the town's single red light. Suzanne felt sick remembering their more leisurely ride in the back of Linc's truck. She resolved to be more mature about Cherie Angers in the future, but the future came upon them before she knew it. Cherry Fontaine was unpacking in Suzanne's bedroom.

While Birdie explained the situation to George in the hallway, she got her information directly from the source. Mrs. Angers turned a brilliant artificially-whitened smile on Suzanne and talked as she unpacked a red lace thong from her bag.

"That gothic room is so gloomy and frankly, I knew I wouldn't get a wink of sleep in *her* room. You never met Mrs. St. Julien." Cherie lowered her voice. "A real b-i-t-c-h. I didn't think you'd mind sleeping in there for a few nights."

Suzanne wanted to ask when one night had become a few. Mostly though, she wanted Cherie out of her room, the one closest to George by both hall and balcony. "Act like a grownup," she told herself. Gritting her teeth into the kind of smile often seen on dead people's faces, Suzanne packed a few things in a carryall and moved into Virginia Lee's room.

The three of them shared an awkward dinner that night to say the least. Suzanne felt like the little daughter forced to sit through a meal while her daddy and a chum reminisced about the good old days. In this case however, the guest was a former lover who had added an extra layer of green eye shadow to her makeup and wore a clinging sheath of emerald, obviously her best color. Speaking of color, George had put in his absurdly deep blue contact lenses for the evening. They made his eyes sparkle as well as blink. Suzanne found she preferred his dowdy old glasses. He'd gotten new frames—exactly like the old ones, for heaven's sake!

None of the stories they told about "back when" ever finished in her presence. Each episode seemed to end with a wink and a leer.

"And then we came across that old motel with the little cabins in the back. The man didn't want to rent to Linc because of his being black, but you claimed he was your twin brother since you both had the same last name and age, so he let you have the key…." Wink. Leer. And George accused *her* of immaturity!

Birdie stayed late to serve the "something special" George asked of her. The menu consisted of smothered quail over wild rice with steamed asparagus. The asparagus was stringy, and the meat so scanty on the quail it was barely worth picking off those tiny bones, but her fellow diners did not seem to notice. Cherie drank the wine, fiddled with a quail leg, and laughed excessively. George consumed everything without seeming to taste the food.

Suzanne braced for more misery when the party adjourned to the red parlor for coffee and dessert. Birdie brought a tray holding china cups already poured because, of course, the silver service had been stolen. She also served chocolate cups filled with a mint liqueur on a clear glass plate. Suzanne managed to grab only one because the long-lost sweetheart gobbled them up. Clearly, she preferred booze and dessert to good, wholesome food.

Cherie had a friendly tussle with George over the last bit of chocolate. Naturally, he let her win. But then, Cherie told him to open his mouth and close his eyes. She popped the little delicacy between his lips, removed a drop of spilled liqueur from George's chin with her fingertip, and sucked her finger clean. By that time, George's eyes were open, wide open. He had this silly grin on his face that Suzanne wanted to wipe off with her cocktail napkin.

She sat across from the couple occupying the Belter settee and pleased herself by thinking how garish Mrs. Angers looked against the red velvet, how she contrasted poorly with the cool blonde dressed in white and pearls whose portrait dominated the parlor. As for self-evaluation, Suzanne felt the snug, black dress too fancy and sophisticated for the Roadhouse and Joe's Lounge wasn't quite enough this evening, even with her best pushup bra. She'd always been happy with her 36C's, but somehow, they no longer seemed adequate. Cherie Angers' breasts couldn't be real. They simply could not. George would find them hard as rocks if he touched them, certainly. That part worried her, too.

At least, the parlor locale improved the tone of the conversation. Suzanne drank her coffee, very bitter this evening, and listened to Cherie Angers hold forth on antiques, knowledge acquired when as the rich lawyer's wife, she furnished their place in the Garden District. Of course, Cherie still had some of the lovely things in her new apartment, but she no longer owned a grand old house like Magnolia Hill for her very own to love and care for. Oh, boohoo to you, Cherry.

What a pity the lovely silver service Cherie remembered so well from her first and last visit to the

Hill had gone. But then, how very fortunate the mortgage had been cleared and George could get on with his life, settle down, marry. Suzanne found this conversation only a slight improvement over what had gone on at dinner after all.

She excused herself early, went to Virginia Lee's room to work on her paper, and made little progress at the spindly-legged secretary. The twosome downstairs moved noisily from the parlor to George's den. Birdie had long gone home. Glasses clinking, they helped themselves to stronger beverages than wine, liqueur, and coffee.

Suzanne went into her former room to retrieve some notes, but could not concentrate afterwards. The image of Cherie's flimsy underwear tossed around the room, her provocative nightie, green and shiny and transparent, laid out on the bed, her heavy perfume stinking up the air, replayed in her mind like a bad song, hated but unforgettable. Sleep wouldn't come either. Tossing in Virginia Lee's bed, she heard Cherie and George come staggering up the stairs at midnight. Whispering and laughing filled the hall, but two separate doors closed.

She thought she could rest after that, but still awake at one a.m., she had to suffer through listening to more to-do, this time on the gallery. She tried not to think about George and his cape and the window she left unbolted hoping the Devil's Horseman might visit in the night. Putting the pillow over her head, Suzanne tried to stifle the sound of the giggles and the mock struggle on the balcony. Pulling the quilt over the pillow, she cried on and off until dawn.

****

Birdie woke everyone with her rendition of "Oh, What a Beautiful Morning!" Yeah, right. Suzanne looked into the mirror and saw awful—puffy eyes, dark circles, and pale cheeks. George, coming from his own room, appeared even worse, hung over and suffering. That shouldn't have pleased her, but it did. She wondered about Mrs. Angers condition, but being unemployed, the divorcée evidently planned to sleep in until noon. By the time George got home from work, Cherie would have pumped herself up to gorgeous again.

Suzanne worked on squeezing drops into her eyes to take out the redness and heard Birdie knocking politely to see if Miss Cherie wanted any breakfast. She hoped the divorcee gained five pounds from eating Birdie's biscuits because she certainly had. She attempted to keep her left eye open for the descent of the fluid while Birdie "took a peek" to see if Mrs. Angers was all right because she didn't answer. When Birdie screamed, the Visine squirted clear across her face. While still wiping her chin, Suzanne learned their guest had vanished. The window to her room stood wide open. Oops, her fault.

Chapter Seventeen

Suzanne's story

Frankly, Suzanne did not care if Mrs. Angers in an amorous, drunken passion had fallen off the gallery while trying to get to George's bedroom, but no broken body lay below on the verandah. Maybe George revealed during pillow talk after sex, that though he'd saved the old plantation, he had no money to support it. If Cherie wanted to be mistress of Magnolia Hill, she'd have to spend the rest of her life giving guided tours through the place. Suzanne imagined Cherie saying, "No, thanks," and deciding upon reconciliation with Ronald, leaving posthaste in the middle of the night to get away from the broke guy. Unfortunately, her green sports car still sat in the driveway.

George called Sheriff Duval. The sheriff took a glance at Mrs. Angers' room with its sexy clothing strewn about and its rumpled covers. Shaking his head, he went downstairs to the kitchen with George and Suzanne trailing behind like a police escort. While drinking Birdie's coffee and putting away a plate of biscuits, he gave them the lecture about how many hours a person had to be gone before being declared missing. He eyed George.

"George, looks to me like you did some drinking last night. Getting to be a habit with you. Lucky the

Patout boys didn't press charges the last time you went on a drunk. You get a little rough with Mrs. Angers and scare her off, huh?"

George flushed, whether from embarrassment or anger, Suzanne couldn't tell.

"If you had been on the receiving end of the kiss she gave me last night, you'd know I wasn't the one doing the assaulting, Sheriff."

"You tell him, George," she wanted to say so badly, but held it in.

"Okay. So, you had sex with the woman and then what?"

"No. Absolutely not. After that kiss, I went to my own room and locked the door. I don't remember anything since my head hit the pillow."

George glanced sidelong at Suzanne as if assessing her reaction. She wondered if she should tell the officer about the noise they'd made on the balcony. Sex comes in all kinds of shapes and flavors. Many don't require actual penetration. George could be using the Bill Clinton defense. Still, this lie lay between them, not George and the sheriff.

Birdie whimpered. "I just know something bad happened to Miss Cherie. When she stayed here last time, she wanted a big breakfast served in bed 'round ten."

Suzanne could see the sheriff thought black women were prone to hysterics. He cleared his throat and fiddled with his notepad.

"Come on now, Mrs. Angers might have wanted fresh air last night and opened her window. Maybe she's one of those gals who like to go for a long jog in the morning," Duval said.

"Not likely," sobbed Birdie. "Not her, she ain't the fresh air and jogging type. She'd tell me to crank up the AC and then go to some fancy gym in the city."

Pleased by Birdie's remarks making Cherie out to be a high-maintenance woman, Suzanne pointed out the unexpected guest brought only an overnight bag with her, and all the clothes they'd seen her wear lay in a heap on the bedroom floor awaiting maid service. No sign of the nightgown she'd seen the night before, a green transparent, slutty sort of garment no woman, even Cherie Angers, would wear outdoors.

"Miss Hudson, I appreciate your deductions. Honestly, I do. But, don't you think if Mrs. Angers went out for a walk, she'd be wearing any practical clothes she might have brought along."

"I've only known Mrs. Angers for a very short time, but she didn't seem like the kind of woman who would go anywhere without makeup, tons of it. Her case is sitting unopened in exactly the same place as last night."

"Amen to that," Birdie agreed.

Truthfully, Suzanne agreed with the sheriff. Cherie Angers was probably doing nude aerobics or suggestive yoga poses somewhere George could see her from his window if he'd put on his glasses first thing in the morning instead of stumbling to the bathroom half blind. She'd heard him bumping into furniture early that morning. Cherie knew how to hog attention and excelled at it.

"Ya'll call me if Mrs. Angers doesn't get in touch by tomorrow night. I'll tell my boys to keep a lookout for her in case she sprained an ankle along the road or got snake bit or something." Folding a biscuit into a napkin, the sheriff prepared to leave.

Very suddenly, Suzanne decided to take ill. She clutched her stomach and begged for Doc Sonny.

"I'm so upset about Mrs. Angers, I feel sick. Maybe I'm having a relapse. You know, Sheriff Duval, a serial killer of young women is on the loose in Philadelphia. Maybe, poor Cherie has become a victim of the same kind of man." She shivered, not faking it.

Begging the officer to remain until she felt recovered, Suzanne promised to reveal more about Mrs. Angers. Actually, she had nothing else to share about Cherie, other than a strong opinion that the woman was a slut. Revealing her latest theory about the stolen silver at a dinner party had gone out the window, upstaged by Cherie Angers' disappearance. There would be no Agatha Christie ending. She had to expose the villain in another way.

Feigning dizziness, she swooned into George's arms and faintly asked him to carry her upstairs to the room Cherie had vacated. While she fully enjoyed being pressed against the warmth of his broad chest, he whispered that she didn't feel very frail. He grunted when they got to the landing.

"You didn't complain about my weight the other night," Suzanne whispered.

"We were going downstairs the night of the storm, not up," he complained into her ear.

She would have punched him, but that seemed inconsistent with her illness. Besides, he might have dropped her.

"George, I know you were out on the balcony with Cherie last night. I heard you laughing and carrying on. Did you wear your costume? I thought that was our special thing," she hissed.

"I wasn't with Cherie. Why do you always think I'm lying?" George answered through gritted teeth.

He dumped her in the middle of the four-poster's mattress so hard she bounced. If the sheriff and Birdie hadn't been downstairs and Doc Sonny on the way, they might have worked out their problems right then and there between the sheets. Suzanne sighed and changed the sound to a sickly moan. They just didn't have the time.

****

Dr. Sonnier took his own sweet time arriving— Suzanne no longer being a favored patient—but he did come. Doc Sonny sat on a desk chair taking her blood pressure at bedside. She asked for Sheriff Duval. In a few moments, the stage would be set.

She tried to look as feeble as possible lying in the big canopied bed Cherie had left rumpled and unmade. The strong scent of hootchie mama perfume on the sheets gave Suzanne a headache and helped in achieving a pained expression. The linens also had a faintly musky smell as if they'd absorbed sexual juices. She wrinkled her nose. Damn, George really had lied about last night.

Still sipping coffee and brushing biscuit crumbs off the front of his uniform, Sheriff Duval arrived to lean in the doorway. Birdie pretended to dust antiques in the hall as close to the door as possible. George sprawled on the fainting couch at the foot of the bed, his long arms and legs dangling over its scrolled ends. Her proposed scenario would not get any better than this.

"I feel much better now, Dr. Sonnier. I wanted you here for another purpose."

"Then, I have patients who really need me. I have no time for this." The doctor dropped her arm, briskly unsnapped the cuff, and stood to go.

"You, Dr. Jefferson Sonnier, you are a thief," Suzanne accused and pointed what she wished were a longer, bonier finger at him. George toppled the couch getting up. Sheriff Duval stood at attention in the doorway. Birdie ceased her pretense of dusting. Jeff Sonnier laughed.

"Not a thief, Miss Hudson, because I've paid for the goods. In one way or another, I've paid for it all."

As if someone had pressed a button on Sheriff Duval's back, he began reciting the doctor's rights, especially emphasizing the part about the right to remain silent. Dr. Sonnier took the suggestion.

"Isn't it true, Dr. Sonnier, that you were having coffee with Birdie when she was called away on a family emergency? As a frequent visitor to this house during Virginia Lee's time, Birdie trusted you to let yourself out. You allowed the door to remain unlocked and returned after George had given me my sleeping pill. Using surgical gloves, you emptied the sideboard of its silver, having full knowledge of where the key was kept since you were Mrs. St. Julien's trusted lover of over twenty years!"

She paused to gauge her effect, but George ruined it all.

"Except I locked the doors when I left with my great-aunts."

"A woman's lover would have a key to her house."

Then, Sheriff Duval had to butt in. "Shucks, Miss Hudson, this is a small town. Everyone knew about Ginny and Sonny for years on end. We all figured since

Helene was Catholic she wouldn't give the doc a divorce, and old Jacques wouldn't let his wife go out of pride. I figured Sonny could have done it. He had the chance, being up here when the silver was took, but why in hell would he? He had years to take Ginny's silver. She would have given it to him. Why now, Jeff?"

"Why don't you ask Miss Hudson?" Jefferson Sonnier relaxed, reseated himself on the desk chair, and stretched out his legs. "She seems to know it all."

Suzanne conjured up a picture of Dr. Sonnier sitting hunched and concerned by the bedside of a dying woman. Virginia Lee asked one last thing of her lover.

"Sheriff Duval, the famous Magnolia Hill silver was fake, replicas and plate substituted by Mrs. St. Julien as she sold off the real things to pay her medical bills and keep this house in the family. Randy Royal can confirm this, though I am sure she kept no record of the sales. You see, she didn't inform the insurance company. You say the whole town knew about Sonny and Virginia Lee. Then, they must also know she was the kind of woman who would extract a promise from her lover to finish what she started. By arranging for the collection of the insurance money on the fake goods after her death, she freed her son of debt and saved the house, her only reward for a loveless marriage."

"That's right," Jefferson Sonnier said. His distinguished face remained unperturbed.

"No, no it ain't right!" Birdie burst in from the hall, knocking Sheriff Duval out of the doorway and filling the small bedroom with her bulk. "Take me, 'cause I'm more guilty than Doc Sonny. Take me." Asking to be cuffed by the sheriff, she thrust out her fat wrists.

"It was me who called Doc Sonny when Miss Suzanne found out about the silver. After Miss Virginia died, he wanted to just let things be, to see if Mr. Georgie could make it on his own or just outright give him a loan. I went along with that, but then, I seen danger ahead with Georgie being in trouble with the insurance company, and I calls and I says, 'Let's do it now. Let's give nice Miss Suzanne and Georgie a chance like you and Miss Virginia never had.' I was helping him load that fake stuff while Miss Suzanne slept that morning after he gave her a shot to keep her still a couple of hours when the call came about my boy. 'Go,' says Doc Sonny, 'You need an alibi anyhow. I'll hide the silver where it won't be found.' I went."

Defiant and belligerent, Birdie braced her hands on her wide hips. "Now Doc gets the blame of it. It ain't right 'cause I had the idea. Peoples think you so dumb they can sell good silver right out from under you, so dumb you can't listen at a dying woman's door. And you, Miss Suzanne, you ain't as nice as I thought you was. Look at this mess you done stirred up, ruint Doc Sonny, ruint me, hurt Miss Helene and Georgie when it all comes out. Why Georgie'd be as good off with that tramp who come here last night."

Birdie had powerful lungs and filled the air of the room with guilt that settled over Suzanne like a feather quilt, light yet smothering. She tried to shake it off, no longer interested in being the girl detective or the heroine of the story. She slid down the high side of the bed and went to George who stood there hunched over as if one of the Patouts had punched him in the gut. Putting her arms around him, she felt truly sick when he did not respond.

"Well, I'll be. I'll be," Sheriff Duval sputtered not knowing what cliché to be. "The polygraph man says he couldn't get a good reading on that black maid because she's so hysterical all the time, and here she is, the mastermind." He removed his handcuffs from his belt.

"Wait a minute." George looked up from the spot on the floor that had been occupying his attention. He did not glance at Suzanne. "I won't press charges against either of them. I knew the silver was faked when it was stolen, a detail Suzanne left out of her great exposé. That makes me liable to Mutual Trust. If Jeff returns the fake silver, I will reimburse the insurance company by getting another mortgage on the house. We're old clients, old family. I'm sure we can work this out."

Amazingly, George smiled. "Interest rates are the lowest they've been in twenty years. Financially, I will be better off than before, Birdie. Thank you."

"The silver is in my old brick cistern behind the house, Sheriff. I'm afraid it will take more effort to get it out than to put it in. That hole goes down deep and is full of water," Dr. Sonnier added.

"I can have my boys out there tomorrow, Jeff. I'd like to have a big write up in the *Sentinel* about how I cracked this crime, but I reckon I can live without it. I'll try to keep it quiet, but some is bound to come out, y'all know that." Sheriff Duval tipped his Stetson, which he never took off, to the group and started for the stairs.

Everyone behaved so nobly. They'd worked out a solution in a genteel southern way among themselves, and no one was going to thank the nosey, interfering Yankee from Philadelphia for raking up all this muck.

Suzanne felt truly nauseated now, but the least she could do was put her jealousy aside and be the one to say, "But what about the disappearance of Cherie Angers?"

Chapter Eighteen

Suzanne's story

"Give her overnight," Sheriff Duval said. "The woman's had marriage problems. No sign of struggle in the room. Could be a stunt to get her husband back or gain George's attention. Could be she threw herself in the bayou. I'll start asking around today. See if anyone's seen her. If she doesn't turn up, we'll make it formal tomorrow. Mornin', Miss Hudson, George, Doc. And you, Birdie, you, too." He tipped his hat directly at the maid and left.

With a weary step, Dr. Sonnier followed the sheriff. George shrugged Suzanne off and said he had to get to work. He phoned later to say he might go over to Linc's that night, not to wait up for him. She thought that was a good idea, knowing he'd talk things out with his friend, maybe get over being mad at her and realize she'd been trying to help. Birdie gave her the silent treatment. She went about her work as if she were the only person in the house.

Suzanne made her own lunch and walked out for the mail afterwards. Relieved, she found nothing from Paul for a change. She read a long, newsy letter from her mother, mostly about how bitterly cold it had been, would winter never end? Her brother, the lawyer, had won another case and might possibly be settling down

Lynn Shurr

with one woman at last. How was her only daughter doing? Had she met any nice men besides her employer? And Mom remained glad she did not live alone in Philadelphia anymore. The serial killer had struck again last week, a young woman exactly Suzanne's age stabbed to death in her bedroom. That made twelve victims in less than a year. Nothing like this had ever happened in her day. Sure, Mom.

Suzanne tried to work on her paper but felt too restless and wandered the house, double checking information on the furnishings. By the time she returned to her room, Birdie had made the bed and neatly repacked Cherie's clothes as if the woman would return at any minute and scold if the work had not been done. The window to the bedroom was latched again. Suzanne wondered if the linens had been changed. She'd prefer sleeping in this room rather than Virginia's, but not in sheets smelling of Cherie and George together.

She didn't own the man, hadn't even wanted him until that night in the cabin when dull, stable George turned out to be a devil in the sack. Ironically, George St. Julien was her ideal man—steady, nice, and a wonderful lover. Now, he despised her for meddling and wanted Cherie Angers. Magnolia Hill had no bodies under the beds but plenty of skeletons in the closet. She simply couldn't resist dragging them out and dusting them off like forgotten priceless antiques. Everyone had been unmasked now, thanks to the interference of Suzanne Hudson.

The telephone rang. Hoping George called, she got halfway down the stairs in an instant, but Birdie answered.

"Oh, no, oh Lawd, Lawd," she kept saying softly to the voice on the line. Hanging up, the housekeeper sat in the chair by the phone and wept.

"What is it?" Suzanne asked. "Is it George? Your son? What happened?"

"Doc Sonny's dead. Took his own life this afternoon. Odette St. Julien done heard it from the Sonnier's maid. Left a long letter saying to his wife how he was a liar, an adulterer, and a thief, and asking for her forgiveness. Left letters for his children and Mr. George. They say he went into Opelousas with his son after he finished his morning appointments. Come back an hour or so later and said he would be going up to his bedroom to rest before the afternoon patients, give himself a shot of something in the arm, and died."

Birdie didn't say it, but Suzanne knew what she thought. This was the city girl's fault, all her prying Yankee fault. Rip off the mask and some men crumbled, some stood tall, and some men showed an entirely different nature.

Paul was like that, a man in a mask, impeccably dressed and well-mannered, a methodical perfectionist but underneath filled with rage. What had his last letter said? "I'm coming to get you," just what they all said, another note to be disregarded and thrown in the trash. What if George had been telling the truth and hadn't gone to Cherie's room or tussled with her on the balcony? Had Paul come last night and found Cherie Angers in her bed? Had the kidnapped Cherie taken a knife meant for Suzanne and wielded by a serial killer from Philadelphia?

She knew which bed she would have to lie in that night. The one she had made for herself—and she'd be sleeping in it alone. Sure, she could call Sheriff Duval and share more of her fine crime solving skills with him. He would love that. He was probably going to be one of Jefferson Sonnier's pallbearers. Besides, she hadn't kept even one of Paul's letters. No evidence to show. No blood, no knife in the room, only a missing woman who had slept where Suzanne should have been, an old flame who thought at one a.m. her former boyfriend wanted to play wicked games. Cherie had laughed when Paul carried her away. Could she still laugh now?

Birdie, upset by Doc Sonny's suicide, went home early. George did not return, and the dark set in. Having creeped herself out with her theory about Paul, Suzanne stayed dressed in practical clothes—jeans and a shirt—and tucked a carving knife from the kitchen under her pillow. She put out the lights and drew the covers up to her chin. She lay there, so tense and afraid she quaked under the quilts. Near midnight, she heard a sound at the window. A dark figure filled the frame. The sash jerked so hard the ancient latch snapped open. Clutching her knife, she prayed.

"Oh, please, God, let it be George in his mask and cape. Let this all be for fun where no one dies and everyone lives happily ever after. Please!"

The person leaning over the bed was not George. Suzanne stared up at the face concealed by a black ski mask and tried to rip the butcher knife from under her pillow. His hand clamped on her wrist. He took the knife away easily, twisted her arm behind her back, and hauled his former girlfriend from the bed. Suzanne figured she deserved to suffer for the pain she'd given Paul, George, Birdie, and most of all, Doc Sonny.

Chapter Nineteen

Linc's story

Linc came home from school and found the Ghost working out with the weights, the sleeves of his white shirt rolled up and his tie undone like he'd come directly from the office.

"So how could you blow it with Suzanne in just two days, man! When I picked you up at the lake and dropped you off at the Hill, I thought I'd fixed everything up just fine, and here you are working it out with the weights."

"A lot can happen in two days," he told Linc.

"Such as…"

"Such as Cherry Fontaine showing up and disappearing. Such as finding out Birdie and Jeff Sonnier stole the silver."

"What you say!"

The Ghost was still filling in Brother Linc when the phone rang, and Doris came out to get her husband. His mama had called with the news about Jefferson Sonnier. Suicide, she said. He told the Ghost the call was nothing and let him finish what he had to say. All the while Linc wondered how he would tell George that Doc Sonny killed himself. Knowing how his friend felt about the man, thinking Doc should have been his father, not old philandering, hard-drinking Jacques,

Ghost would take it hard. Meanwhile, George kept talking about this good man who had kept a promise to a dead woman and tried to spare her son. All mixed up in this were Cherry Fontaine and Suzanne Hudson, the past and the future. Still working on his words, Linc noticed when Sheriff Duval drove up in his squad car.

Funny how a sight like that in these liberated times can still cause a black family to retreat, the children to seek their mama, the wife to move toward her husband. Having the law in your driveway never meant any good in the old neighborhood. The men in uniform rarely came to protect or to serve, only to question and to take people away, but the Man wasn't looking for Linc this time. Sheriff Duval wanted George.

"Miss Breaux told me you was out here. Guess you heard about Jeff Sonnier taking his own life this afternoon."

George dropped the bar he pressed into the rack. The sweat on his cheeks looked a little like tears as it ran down to his chin.

"Doc left several long letters and a will all signed and witnessed. You get whatever we find in that cistern tomorrow, but that's not what I come about, George."

Linc shook George's arm to make sure he listened. Not paying attention to the Law when it talks can lead to trouble.

"We checked out your old girlfriend, Mrs. Angers, with her ex-husband down in New Orleans and asked around town if anyone saw her since yesterday. They all said no, but Evelyn Patout over at the museum claimed a stranger came in yesterday morning who didn't want her tour or any historical information at all—a stocky blond fellow driving a light blue rent car.

First, I thought Mr. Angers had hired someone to tail his ex. Maybe he wanted to be sure she didn't sell off any of those antiques she took with her before their settlement. But, it turns out this blond guy only wanted directions to Magnolia Hill. Said he had a friend living up there named Suzanne Hudson, and did Miss Evelyn know her. Sure, Miss Evelyn says, and he'd better hurry up and get there because George St. Julien and that girl have been out on the town together, and Suzanne thinks she's too good for any other man in Port Jefferson. Leave it to a Patout, even one by marriage, to stir things up. Anyhow, this guy gets sort of red in the face and stomps out."

"Hippo down at Joe's Lounge says he ain't seen any strange red-headed women, just one fair-haired guy who come in late afternoon and wanted to know where he could rent a boat. Hippo told him Alcide Porrier would rent most anything he owned for the right price and gave the fellow directions. The man drove a light blue sedan. Some of the regulars at Joe's seen it parked along Front Street when they left around one a.m. Hippo says it wasn't there at three when he went home. George, I think your lady friend's been kidnapped."

"It should have been Suzanne," George said, looking like a weight had dropped on his foot.

"Would have helped Jeff Sonnier some if he'd took the Yankee gal last night," the sheriff agreed.

"No, I mean Cherie was sleeping in Suzanne's bed. Suzanne has been getting weird letters from some man back in Philadelphia. All they ever said was that he'd come to get her and then a lot of...well, descriptions of bondage. No threats against her life, but sick just the same. I pulled one out of the trash the other day when she seemed upset. After that, if I saw another in the mail, I threw it out. The guy sounded like some kind of psycho."

"If he is a psycho, he might make another try for Suzanne if we give him the chance. Probably, he didn't figure on two young women staying at your house. Since he wants to do things to her, he won't kill her right away. He could lead us right to Mrs. Angers. What say you don't get home tonight, George, in case he's watching the house?"

"Suzanne could be dead before you stopped him."

"And if we don't catch him, she could still end up dead."

Linc admired the sheriff's reasoning until he realized George was demanding to go along on the stakeout at the Hill. He started to say, "Look, George, we ain't playing Devil's Horseman here. Let the law handle it," when George volunteered his buddy to go along, too. The sheriff deputized them faster than Linc could back out. It looked like he and the Ghost were going to be spending more time together hunched in the magnolia thickets at the Hill waiting for another man to carry off Suzanne Hudson.

Chapter Twenty

George's story

The dew started to settle, but too much of a man to admit it, George felt cold in his shirtsleeves and cold around the heart, too. This is what came of wanting Suzanne to see him as desirable to another woman, not just some clown who had to dress up in costume to get her attention. He'd used Cherry as she had used him years ago, but kidnapping and murder made it an unequal trade.

He had plenty of time that moonlit night to lay blame. Finally, it came to rest, not on Suzanne, but on his mother for setting the whole chain into motion. Jefferson Sonnier's foot got caught in that chain, and it dragged him into the grave with her. By Virginia Lee St. Julien's code, appearance mattered—a marriage that appeared valid, silver plate that appeared to be sterling. Had she simply appeared to be a mother worried about her son's future when her real concern was saving Magnolia Hill as a monument to herself—even if it made her lover a thief and her son a liar?

The hum of a small outboard on the bayou drowned out the whine of the early crop of mosquitoes spawned by the flood and feasting on their arms and ankles. Tough to watch the man come up from the water, a shadow in the shadows, moving toward

Suzanne's room where the lights had gone out an hour ago, and not move a muscle. He passed the clump of trees where Linc and George hid, long-legged birds in the bush. Sheriff Duval and a regular deputy squatted behind the big azaleas near the entry.

The kidnapper, Paul, the name on the letters, went up the stairs to the upper gallery. He entered Suzanne's room by the window, giving it a mighty shove. George waited for her screams, for Sheriff Duval to surge from his hiding place. Nothing happened.

He wanted to move so badly his leg twitched and caught Linc in the shin. Linc gasped but sucked up most of the sound. The night stayed quiet, not a noise but a few plopping fish this close to the bayou. With Suzanne completely dressed, she and her kidnapper stepped out of the window and moved down the steps. The man wore a ski mask covering his face and the pale hair that would have shown in the moonlight. Why didn't she scream or run? George waited for the sheriff to strike. Damn him, the law did not make a move.

As the pair came closer, the rays of the moon glinted on the knife pressed into Suzanne's back. He remained quiet as he'd been told to do. The couple passed the trees to the river beyond. Not being able to see the abductor's face upset him internally. You can tell a man's intent by looking him in the eyes, which way he will toss a ball, when he is faking an injury. He wanted to knock the guy to the ground and tear off the mask, but, obeying orders, George waited until the noise of the small boat motor buzzed out of hearing.

Linc broke a branch of the magnolia in his hurry to get down. George was already out, running for the bayou when the sheriff radioed to his squad car in town to keep an eye on the blue sedan. He took the path along the river, a direct line into town, quicker than the roads. Linc pounded along behind him. Struggling with the mud left behind by the storm, he kept going down, once near the spot where Linc had waited with the pirogue. Linc pulled him up. Mud-soaked, glasses splattered, George finally reached Front Street. No light blue sedan in sight.

A squad car crept from its hiding place in the alley like a stray cat not sure of its welcome. George pounded on the deputies' window to let them in. They did, behind the grate they used to separate the sane and the law abiding from the crazies and the criminals. He swore at them to get going, but the officers explained that volunteer deputies were stationed along all the roads leading out of town. They would pick out the sedan and follow in an unmarked vehicle.

Forced to sit and listen to the radio's blare marking the progress of the light blue sedan, George fidgeted, bumping Linc with his elbows and knees as the culprit and his prey moved farther and farther away. The last voice to come over the air belonged to Billy Patout.

"Shoot," he said. "Didn't I just go and lose them somewhere on the old Baton Rouge road?"

Damn that Billy Patout. He did this just to get revenge for the brawl in Joe's Lounge, George believed. He banged on the grill separating him and Linc from the cops.

"I know where he took her. Let's get moving."

Chapter Twenty-One

Suzanne's story

The worst part was being in the trunk. Suzanne feared suffocation. Paul taped her mouth and tied her hands before locking her into the small, dark place, an insecure womb smelling of gas fumes, where she curled with her knees under her chin. She wanted to gulp air, but the tape across her mouth prevented that and also screaming for help from any late night denizens of Joe's Lounge. The trunk is not airtight, she reasoned. Breathe evenly. You will be all right. You will. You will. Doesn't want to kill you, only do obscene things to your body. Maybe, if he weren't the Philly Slasher, but what if he was? Not a comforting thought. You will be all right. She mentally repeated her not so calming mantra.

They drove on a country road, she could tell. Hell, the roads leaving Port Jefferson were all country roads. As the car banged across potholes, she counted the number of bruises the tire iron she lay on gave her. She tried to use the tool to work off the rope. No good. Suzanne wondered if Paul would use the tire iron later to bash in her skull. No, the Philadelphia Slasher favored knives and blood and dirty words painted in red on the walls.

She wanted air! More air! Sucking in what she

could through her nostrils, she began fretting about dulling her reflexes for escape with carbon monoxide and gas fumes. Should she try to kick out the taillights? Most of the cars in the parish had at least one bad light, and no one ever stopped them for it as far as she knew. Wouldn't a new vehicle have an inside trunk release. Yeah, but where in Hades would it be? She forced herself to be calm again and grope for it. Before she found the latch, the road surface changed to shell popping against the undercarriage of the car. The motor stopped. The trunk opened. Suzanne filled her lungs with the damp night air.

Paul jerked her out. Half pretending to be too dizzy to walk, Suzanne got her bearings quickly. They'd arrived at an old motel, the kind with little cottages in a double row running back into the darkness of the trees. The tourist huts of green stucco were roofed with red Mexican tile. The sign, so old it wasn't even neon, proclaimed this haven to be the Wonderland Motel. Or maybe, the current clientele preferred dimly lit advertising or no lights at all. The only cabin showing some life belonged to the manager who sat dozing by his window in front of a flickering TV while the Late Show rolled on. No one looked out to see a young woman, bound and gagged, emerging from a trunk.

They didn't enter the cabin where Paul parked. He steered her into the shadows by the pressure of the knife blade in the middle of her back. They moved toward the lodging farthest from the road. Holding his captive close all the while, Paul worked at a rusty padlock on the door with his knife tip. When the door swung open, Suzanne squeezed her eyes shut, afraid to see what might remain of Cherie Angers, or was her flashy rival already food for the gar and crawfish of Bayou Brun? And so, the smell reached her first—mouse droppings, mildew, urine, and the ripe stench of semen, but not the coppery scent of blood.

Suzanne opened her eyes as Paul shoved her forward into the room. Cherie lay bound hand and foot to the old iron bedstead. Somehow, she still looked seductive even with green eye shadow smeared across her face and her red hair pulled into wild, electric spikes as if someone, Paul, had held her by its roots. Despite the odor of decay, the single naked bulb illuminating the room, the sink in one corner with a faucet dripping rusty water in a steady rhythm, Cherie's linens were almost tidy, tucked in with hospital corners. A cheap, yellow motel blanket covered her breasts, and the straps of her slick, green nightgown had been aligned in perfect parallels over her shoulders. Cherie Angers' eyes were closed. Dead, Suzanne thought, arranged for burial.

Paul stripped the tape from his first victim's swollen red lips. The green eyes snapped open, and the mouth began to work. Suzanne should have known a tough cookie like Cherie Angers would be hard to kill.

"No need to be so rough, lover. Cherie has been waiting for you like a good little girl. I'm plumb wore out from last night and this afternoon," she drawled. Then, the former Cherry Fontaine noticed Suzanne.

"Now why did you have to bring her here, sugar? Didn't we have enough fun all by ourselves? Oh, I sure would like to see you without that mask, tiger."

Obligingly, Paul shed the woolen ski mask. His face burned red, his expression more petulant than psychotic. His nearly military crew cut stood up damp and darkened with sweat.

"Why, you're a real handsome man to be wearing a mask. I thought maybe there was something wrong with you, covering up like that, sort of the Phantom of the Opera, maybe. But I know for a fact the parts of you that matter work real well."

Suzanne couldn't believe this. Cherie Angers worked at seducing her kidnapper—possibly a murderer, a serial killer. The gas fumes must have gotten to her. Of course! She was distracting him, giving Suzanne a chance to escape. She edged toward the door, but with one swipe, Paul yanked her back and slammed her into a scratched and cracked plastic chair ending its days in a corner of the Wonderland Motel.

"Tell her, tell her all we did last night. She thinks I'm dull, not romantic enough for her. This guy George can give her a mansion and antiques and Mardi Gras balls and all that shit. Tell her what she missed last night when she was sleeping in his room. Tell her!"

"Oh lover, let's show her!" Cherie wiggled her shoulders just enough to displace the yellow blanket and make her nipples pout out under the sheer green nylon.

For a maniac killer, Paul seemed slightly shocked. "John was right," he marveled. "He said he met women all the time who wanted it rough, who wouldn't struggle when you tied them up. They liked to be threatened, he said."

As if demonstrating for Suzanne's benefit, he gripped Cherie's short hair with his blunt-tipped fingers and kissed her brutally on the mouth. Another chance for escape! She stood up and was betrayed by the creak of split plastic. Paul slammed Cherie's head back against the pillow and advanced holding the knife toward her.

"Fuck you, Suzanne. I wasted money on fancy dinners and a hell of a lot on postage. I come down here to prove I can be more exciting than some man with a mansion, and I find out you're not worth the trouble or the vacation leave time. Now that," he flicked the blade in Cherie's direction, "That is a real woman, and you don't deserve—"

The motel door burst open, splintering through the center where the termites had gnawed at it. George moved quickly on those long legs of his. He throttled her attacker with an arm across the throat and twisted Paul's knife arm behind his back to the point of snapping. Birdie's turkey carver dropped to the floor. Linc used the knife to free Cherie Angers from the bed and cut Suzanne's bonds. Two uniformed deputies with their pistols drawn stood wondering what to do in the doorway. George hadn't given them time to say "Drop you weapon" before he disarmed Paul. Sheriff Duval came in right behind them. The whole scene was very gangbusters—very exciting—very romantic.

As the deputies took charge of cuffing Paul and reading his rights, Suzanne hugged on to George, never wanting to let go despite his mysterious coating of bayou mud. He didn't so much as glance at Cherry Fontaine in her peek-a-boo green nightie, though all the other men in the room did, only at her dressed in plain jeans and a shirt. She didn't say a word—because George neglected to remove the tape from her mouth until he lowered his face for a kiss. Oh well, this was a good moment to do nothing but feel.

Cherie did not agree. She grew very vocal as the

youngest of the deputies draped the yellow blanket over her shoulders and asked if she wanted to see a doctor. Ignoring him, Cherie staggered from the bed and followed Sheriff Duval and Paul to the squad car.

"Now don't you hurt him. No harm done, none at all. Honey, I know a good lawyer. We'll have you out tomorrow. Now that I've found you, I'm not going to lose you, tiger. You hear!"

Chapter Twenty-Two

Suzanne's story

George had to be there to make sure things were done to his satisfaction, the executor said. George asked Suzanne to come, and she did, though she'd thought of a million excuses the night before to avoid watching the destruction of Helene Sonnier's garden this morning. The work crew drifted in between eight and nine and began tearing at the bricks of the cistern with crowbars. The old mortar crumbled easily along with the soft, handmade brick. Suzanne winced each time they tossed a block onto the heap by the porch and small chips of clay flew through the air. By the time the workmen finished the dismantling, the wicker chairs had a fine coating of red dust.

The pumps ran now, diverting the cistern water through the hoses laying along the side the Sonnier house and crushing the new iris shoots in the flowerbeds. The stream flowed out into the gutters of Main Street and followed the tilt of the land into the waters of Bayou Brun. Leakage around the pumps and hoses turned the pleasant back lawn into a morass grooved by the imprints of large work boots.

They reached a sludge layer at midmorning. Now, the workmen gouged into the hole with a piece of equipment that looked like an amusement park claw machine. It chewed out the prizes in huge bites. Metal struck metal. Suzanne shuddered. She'd begged everyone concerned to have the cistern emptied by hand, but the sheriff said this was no damned archaeological dig. His time was money, and the budget the parish forced him to operate on was ass wipe cheap. George could put up the funds for laborers if he wanted. George didn't have the money either. A laborer hosed down the load of mud by the side of the cistern. The replica silver appeared piece by piece.

She waded in and began carrying the bowls and candlesticks to a tarp placed out of the way of the heavy equipment and heavier feet. Sheriff Duval showed up, called, no doubt, when they uncovered the silver. He tipped his Stetson to Suzanne coated in grime, then stood by the fence silently witnessing the return of the stolen goods.

The screen door slammed. She looked up from a weighty piece she cleaned and could not quite remember having handled before. Helene Sonnier came onto the porch and began carefully wiping down the chairs and a small table with a clean white towel. She beckoned to George. He followed her with a serious and guilty look on his face into the house and returned with a perplexed expression and a tray of large sugar cookies, each dotted in the middle with a single raisin. Helene followed him with a sloshing twenty-four cup coffeemaker in her hands and a double package of Styrofoam cups wedged under her fleshy arm.

"Break time," she called cheerfully over the clang of machinery and the chug of pumps. She waved Suzanne in from her self-appointed task and begged George and Sheriff Duval to take a chair. George fidgeted as the workmen began lining up for coffee. Conscious of their dirty hands, they took only disposable cups. Suzanne seized a cookie and ate more to avoid conversation than to satisfy any hunger. The crumbs stuck in her throat. Her actions had killed this nice woman's husband.

George spoke up. "You know if half the crew took a break and the other half kept working, it would save the sheriff a lot of time and money."

The workmen at the end of the line glared resentfully, but when Sheriff Duval nodded, one returned to the dragline and another to the hose. George settled into the chair again and took a bite out of a cookie way down to the raisin in the center. Clearly, he did not know what to say to Mrs. Sonnier either. Helene carried the conversation for everyone.

"Beautiful morning, isn't it?"

Her guests looked out over the quagmire of her yard and nodded.

"You know, I had a call just this morning from that nice black lady, Odette St. Julien. She told me how sorry she was about Jeff and how she remembered her own grief when her husband passed away. She went back to substitute teaching to get in the stream of things again. She wondered if I might be able to spare some time to nurse at the free clinic when I feel up to it."

Helene brushed the crumbs of her first cookie from her lips and started in on another.

"I told her I would be in next week. And my daughter called to ask me if I would keep the house and equipment because she thought she might like to come back here to practice when she finishes her medical studies. Before, all she could say was how much she wanted to get away from Port Jefferson and her father's reputation."

Suddenly, Helene laughed deeply, tripling her chin. "You know, I always thought she meant his *medical* reputation up until now. *Everyone* loved Jeff. Oh, it will be good to have Ellen home and peace in the house. Now Bobby will feel free to live his own life with his friend, Randy. They want a place in New Orleans. Jeff never would advance them the money for it, but I'll soon have plenty to give away."

Sheriff Duval had been studying the black coffee in his cup. He looked up and directly at Suzanne while the widow rambled on cheerfully about her plans for the future. Could a professional nurse inject a sleeping man with poison without waking him, she had to wonder? She mouthed the word "murder" at the lawman. He shook his head slightly in a motion telling her to keep quiet and held the coffee cup to his lips.

The two laborers denied an early break queued up to the porch for coffee while the rest of the crew went back to work. The dragline operator leaned against a post and remarked, "Man, dat stuff ain't never gonna quit comin' out dat hole."

She glanced at the tarp. Her neat row of artifacts had jumbled into a heap of heavily tarnished silver objects, far more than there should have been.

"Excuse me," she said, distracted from her suspicions about Mrs. Sonnier. As she left the porch, Sheriff Duval came right behind her. He spoke to in a low voice as they crossed the lawn together.

"I know what you're thinking, missy. Well, let me tell you what you don't know. This ain't the first time Jeff Sonnier tried to take his life. Right after Virginia

Lee passed on, he swallowed some pills. Left those same kind of letters on the nightstand. Helene saved him. She worked real fast, made him throw up all that junk. Guess she figured things would be better between them with Ginny out of the way. Don't figure it was."

A merry laugh emitted by the widow reached across the yard. Helene pushed another cookie on George and took one herself.

"Still, not saving a man's life ain't the same as killing him neither. This time he used a needle. Much quicker, they tell me, and no pain. That's the way they're putting killers to death now 'stead of frying 'em. And the letters had to be new. They mention the stuff in the cistern, had the same thing in his will."

Suzanne only half listened as she knelt in the mud, but that last comment caught her attention. She rummaged in the pile, handling pieces more carelessly than she should have, allowing the metal to shift and collide as she searched for the copy to match with the original on top of the heap. There it lay neatly placed in her original row, the candlestick with the cement core. The core had fallen out, and its side been dented by the backhoe. However, its surface luster remained only slightly dimmed and spotted compared to its twin, the tarnished, blackened original with the heft of the real thing. She arranged items, two by two, copy with original: two teapots, two sugar scoops, two punchbowls.

"Sheriff Duval, some of this silver was in the cistern the first time Jefferson Sonnier tried to commit suicide, the silver he bought from Magnolia Hill through Randy Royal so Virginia Lee wouldn't know he'd purchased it."

"Still don't prove nothing, Nancy Drew." The sheriff spat into a puddle. "But now you got me wondering forever."

Suzanne came to a piece she could not match, so blackened she could barely make out the design elements. American Empire, yes, it looked like American Empire. A set of small candlesticks in the same state of preservation had an eighteenth century style about them.

"George!" she called.

He crossed to her in a few of his long strides. She watched Helene Sonnier who sat pouring more coffee for herself, enjoying the ruination of her husband's ancestral property as she hummed a little tune. George remarked in a whisper that Jeff's death seemed to have unhinged the woman.

"I think she became unhinged long before this."

Sheriff Duval gave Suzanne a warning glance.

"George, did your mother have any older pieces, pre-Victorian?" she asked.

"None that I know of. Why?"

The dragline came down on something in the hole with a thunk. Its bucket scraped across the surface of the obstacle like a fingernail over a chalkboard. Suzanne winced again. The operator pulled back the bucket and dug into the pit once more. This try, he clawed out a metal box. While the hose man cleaned off the latest find, he scooped out three more mounds of mud yielding nothing.

"Dat's all dey is folks. You want us to fill in dat hole wit' da bricks or jus' cover it over?"

"Fill it in and bring me a chisel and a hammer if you got one," Duval ordered.

A single strong blow took the rust-rotted lock off the strong box. It contained coins, mostly silver dating before 1860, and here and there, a bright bit of gold shining like new.

"George, this doesn't belong to Magnolia Hill. Or this, or this." Suzanne held up the oldest pieces exhumed from the well. "What we have here is someone's Civil War cache."

Sheriff Duval was happy to correct her. "No, Miss Suzanne, what you have there, according to the will, belongs to George."

Chapter Twenty-Three

Suzanne's story

George and Suzanne sat enjoying the balmy evening in late May on the verandah. The bayou whispered by at the foot of the hill, and the magnolias looked more dark and mysterious than ever on this nearly moonless night. Tree frogs and cicadas sang for them, though George assured her the torment of mosquitoes would soon make the lower gallery uninhabitable for the summer. Screens would ruin the lines of the house and be historically inaccurate, she commented absently. George just nodded in the light of the citronella candle.

Suzanne took a sip of cool wine, burrowed into the cushions of the wicker settee, and rested comfortably against his shoulder. Her paper was complete, her degree in the mail. The local print shop would start a run of the condensed and less scholarly version of the history of Magnolia Hill and its contents to be used as a tourists' guide very shortly. The original St. Julien silver, burnished by Birdie and lovingly restored by Randy Royal, sat safely locked in the sideboard again. All of the original pieces had lain in the cistern just under the replicas and above the forgotten cache of Civil War era coinage and plate never reclaimed by whoever had hidden it from the invading Yankees and failed to retrieve it.

The treasure belonged to George by right of Jefferson Sonnier's will. He owned the contents of the cistern. Doc's family hadn't objected. They wanted the whole tragedy to go away and cease being the major topic of gossip in Port Jefferson. The sale of the old coins had gone a long way toward reducing the debt on Magnolia Hill, and the best of the silver added to the glory and interest of its collection. Suzanne made a mental note to increase the insurance coverage and have a security system installed.

Poor man, poor man, she thought, not entirely free of guilt over Doc Sonny's death, though his letters to George, Bobby Sonnier, his wife and daughter attempted to absolve nearly everyone of blame. Using Randy Royal, the doctor had purchased each piece of silver as Virginia Lee put it on the market. Once, he had bought the little gilt mantel clock from her at an inflated price and returned it to her for a dollar. George's mother refused further help because it would have turned their magnificent love affair into an act of prostitution, quote Virginia Lee, southern gentlewoman. She devised her own plan, and he supported her in it, even to buying her silver through a go-between and later stealing the replicas for her sake. The tyranny of love, Jefferson Sonnier called it, and he could not live without his lovely tyrant. What a pair they were, Jefferson Sonnier and Virginia Lee St. Julien.

Suzanne told George her idea about Helene Sonnier as a possible murderess. He showed her his letter from the doctor. She thought it looked a little yellow and too creased to have been written recently. George said it seemed normal to him and besides, it mentioned that the contents of the cistern belonged to him. Ah, but the letter did not say anything about the theft of the fakes, she countered.

"I knew about the theft. He didn't have to tell me," George retorted, still defending the man.

The will had been altered to include the clause about the cistern on the day of Doc's death. Jeff had gone into Opelousas to see his lawyer, taking Bobby along as a witness. Father and son spent some time together. Bobby claimed his father had been especially loving and kind that day, even including Randy Royal in their luncheon. That stopped Suzanne from saying any more, but she could still envision Helene Sonnier's small, flesh-buried eyes watching the man die.

"You know Mrs. Sonnier who supposedly wouldn't condone divorce because of her religious convictions thinks her husband is burning in Hell right now because of his suicide," Suzanne said, giving in to George.

"My mother adored this house and would never have given it up to marry Jefferson and become the wife of a small town doctor, even if Helene had agreed to let him go. No, an affair with a man more elegant than my father suited her perfectly. She had the home she venerated, romance with Doc Sonny until the day she died, revenge against my womanizing father, and me to mop up after her. Wherever she and Doc are now, I am certain they are together."

George took a deep breath. Suzanne sighed and held him closer. She could just make out the shapes of the two white hens the one-eyed rooster had seduced and brought back to nest under the magnolias. The cock urged his ladies and a brood of motley chicks under the branches to roost for the night. The small flock was supposed to be shut up in the old stable with Puffy every evening, but somehow, the rooster always found a way to escape and take his family with him. Woe to the raccoon or weasel who tried to steal his chicks because Old One-Eye would be on them in a flash, spurring and pecking their startled faces.

As for Puffy, George had given him to Suzanne as a birthday gift, purchased for twice his worth in a grand romantic gesture, and to hell with worrying about money for a change. Alcide Porrier figured with all his rentals lately, and now the sale of the horse, he had enough money to put a down payment on a used pickup truck to haul his vegetables. The practical and disloyal steed had trotted back to his nice, dry barn as soon as the flood water rose over his fetlocks, leaving her and George plenty of time to get to know one another. The white horse would make up for deserting them by pulling their wedding carriage.

"What do you think Cherie and Paul are doing right now?" Suzanne asked, trying to divert the man she loved from all of the sadness in his life.

"Probably they're beating each other with whips in a motel in Doylestown."

She laughed. A lawyer from the firm of Ronald Angers had arrived to post bail for Paul Alvin Smith, Jr. Bail was denied pending a hearing and the receipt of DNA testing results, which the New Orleans attorney shouted was illegally taken evidence. Duval had cocked a cold parish sheriff's eye at him and said the evidence had been obtained from the sheets at the Wonderland Motel, and no attorney in his right mind would want to let a possible serial killer go running around loose, now would he? In the back of the courtroom, George whispered, "Take that, city boy," to her.

Cherie stayed at Magnolia Hill during the ordeal following her kidnapping. Suzanne no longer minded. Mrs. Angers had lost all interest in George. Cherie simply wanted her great big animal set free. They heard her say so every day during her daily phone call to the jail.

In a pathetic confession, Paul revealed his "joke." He'd had no intention of hurting Suzanne, he claimed. Paul swore he was about to tell his ex-girlfriend that she did not deserve him when George knocked down the door of the motel cottage where he had once taken Cherry Fontaine during their dating years. The only place to hide out on the old Baton Rouge Road was the Wonderland Motel, as the Patout boys should have known. Cherie swore Paul treated her like a perfect gentleman, and she had gone along with the farce to tease Suzanne.

In private, the divorcee pleaded with Suzanne to drop any charges against the man of her dreams. She also asked if Paul made good money. Suzanne said he did, but he'd prudently stashed it in an IRA and other long-term investments. Paul enjoyed talking about his portfolio. She suggested Cherie ask him about his stocks during one of her jail visits. He had a lovely two-carat diamond engagement ring available, too, she added. Cherie's face lit with joy.

Cherie's lawyer added his pressure to the plea. Mr. Angers, it seemed, wished to keep this post-marital scandal to a minimum. The one about Cherie doing an entire professional basketball team provided sufficient embarrassment. Her former husband most generously provided plane fare for the ex-Mrs. Angers when Paul was extradited to Pennsylvania to answer questions about the serial killings as a "person of interest." The DNA test and another gruesome murder committed while they held Paul vindicated him in the end.

Paul was no killer. Suzanne should have known. However, he did give valuable information during questioning. Another computer analyst, John Sydney Turner, had given Paul some very poor advice on dealing with wayward women. John Turner, as it happened, specialized in kinky pornographic programs as a sideline. He'd performed the murders, storing the details on jump drives as common and unobtrusive as a recipe file. That evidence set up John Sydney Turner for thirteen life terms in prison and a probable death sentence. The police freed Paul and thanked him for his testimony in a nice little deal. Now, he lived with Cherie in an antique-filled townhouse in Bryn Mawr. Suzanne heard through friends that the place had an interesting attic, full of strange equipment, but she did not inquire further.

"And what about Randy Royal and Bobby Sonnier?" she asked George.

"Content in their bougainvillaea-draped courtyard in the French Quarter, I guess."

They were. Dr. Sonnier blamed his failings as a father for his son's sexual preferences and left enough inheritance to Bobby for him and Randy to fulfill their dream of an antiques shop in New Orleans without Helene's help. Royal's of Royal Street, they called it. The sale of the Roadhouse brought them a nice profit, too, because of its meticulous restoration, not its recipes. The food improved immensely under the new management, and the historic tavern drew the tourist trade to Port Jefferson. Bobby and Randy often took the boy and his mother there for dinner when they came as a couple to visit Randy's son.

Helene Sonnier ate frequently at the Roadhouse. With her hair now a champagne blonde, she also went dancing at Joe's Lounge with one of Billy Patout's uncles, and the pounds came off. Evelyn Patout called her the Merry Widow, but the Lounge regulars said she was giving her dead husband the finger. Considering what happened the last time they'd gone there, Suzanne and George stayed away from the place.

George unbent enough to invite Bobby and Randy to their wedding. Helene would come as well, though she still gave Suzanne the chills. The whole town was invited in fact. Though Suzanne hated making their wedding a media event, the Hill needed the publicity if it was ever to be completely out of debt. She worked on the research to reproduce an antebellum ceremony. The historical society ladies along with George's great-aunts agreed to pitch in on making the dresses that would later to be used by the house guides. Birdie and Odette St. Julien organized the Ladies Guild of the Pilgrim Baptist Church to make the food, and her parents were enthusiastically footing the bill for the material and groceries. Her mother wanted the whole affair recorded to show her friends back home, and her dad was delighted that a big wedding in Port Jefferson cost a whole lot less than one held on the Main Line near Philly.

She had major problems with George and Linc. George absolutely refused to wear a Confederate uniform. She gave in on that one because of his size it would have to be custom-made. The very idea irritated

Linc, who pointed out that a black best man was not exactly historically accurate either. She suggested they bend history a little. Both men could wear frock coats. Linc and George exchanged looks over that idea and burst out laughing. They said they would provide their own costumes.

Suzanne tried to divine what George plotted behind those glasses with their heavy dark frames, behind those bland gray eyes. As usual, she ended up kissing her perfect man and found out nothing about his plans. She wondered if the Devil's Horseman would be showing up at her wedding. Whatever happened, George would supply the romance.

A word about the author...

Once a librarian, now a writer of romance, Lynn Shurr grew up in Pennsylvania Dutch country. She attended a state college and earned a B.A. in English Literature. Her first job out of school really was working as a cashier in a burger joint. Moving from one humble job to another, she traveled to North Carolina, then Germany, then California, where she buckled down and studied for an M.A. in Librarianship.

New degree in hand, she found her first reference job in the Heart of Cajun Country, Lafayette, Louisiana. For her, the old saying, "Once you've tasted bayou water, you will always stay here" came true. She raised three children not far from the Bayou Teche and lives there still with her astronomer husband.

When not writing, Lynn likes to paint, cheer for the New Orleans Saints and LSU Tigers, and take long road trips nearly anywhere. Her love of the bayou country, its history and customs, often shows in the background for her books.

You may contact Lynn at lynn.shurr@yahoo.com or www.lynnshurr.com or visit her blog— lynnshurr.blogspot.com.

~*~

Other Lynn Shurr titles
available from The Wild Rose Press, Inc.:

Goals for a Sinner	*A Wild Red Rose*
Kicks for a Sinner	*The Convent Rose*
Paradise for a Sinner	*A Trashy Affair*
Love Letter for a Sinner	
Wish for a Sinner	

www.ingramcontent.com/pod-product-compliance
Lightning Source LLC
Chambersburg PA
CBHW060530260626
47161CB00003B/830